The

Port of Gold

Devan Arntson
Illustrated by Geoffrey Bruick

What beneath the earth was whelved,
Fools and thieves now only delve
To seek the treasure cold
Behold the Port of Gold

Contents

The Port of Gold

Act I

1.

The Castaway from Nowhere.

The world was different for the young man. Before he ever knew of the treasure or the Curse. Before any of the great pirates went into hiding. Something changed for Levi. The boy lost at sea might not even recognize the man waiting to be hanged...

Waves collapsed onto the deck of the sailboat. Levi had one hand gripped on the rudder, with the other wrapped by line that held the sail. The treacherous rain beat down on the young man, drenching his clothes and filling his boots. A gust of wind took the sail and swung the boom about to the other side of the vessel, Levi's right arm with it. He screamed in pain as he tugged the sail back toward himself, trying to stay in control. He rode up and down with the waves. The small craft helpless to the forces around them. Where the black clouds met the roaring dark ocean, a golden light appeared. Not able to wipe his face of his long hair, Levi shook his head to wick away the drops of rain pooling around his eyes. He steered the rudder toward the light, which came and went with the breath of the waves. As the tempest wind slammed the sail forward, Levi began to make out an island around this light. It was like a shadow standing against the collage of grey sky. The aggressive gusts pushed him further toward his target, land only minutes in reach. The pressure turned and the wind blew back, Levi knocked out with the swing of the beam. The line constricted his arm, but kept him aboard the drifting vessel, as the billows of the storm tossed it about without mercy. Yet the surge of the waves pushed him towards the rocky shore.

Levi collapsed on the dock, hacking, and spitting. His shivering body drenched in saltwater. Rain continued to pelt his bare back, where his blouse had been torn.

"Come on up, lad," The old sailor grabbed him again by the arm, struggling to keep half-drowned boy alive. He carried him to the tavern called *The Rogue Star*, getting them both out of the rain. The building was two story and stood nearest to the docks of any building in town. On the main level, was the bar filled with wooden furniture and a single counter by the door. Upstairs held four rooms, which were almost always occupied by different travelers or men out of work. Most nights, when the weather wasn't so threatening, the tavern would be filled.

"Easy does it now," The old man sat Levi up on a bench by the fireplace on the back wall. He threw up a pool of saltwater and coughed to get air back in his lungs. The young man was lean and though he was hunched over now, he was tall when he stood. His face was clean shaven with bright brown eyes that complemented his dirty blonde hair. Most of his locks were tied back in a short ponytail, still dripping wet.

"Thanks," Levi muttered as the old man got a blanket and wrapped it around him. The pub was quiet and dark. Only the bartender, the old man, and a few washed up patrons were in the establishment. The weather outside thundered on, but the humble brick walls kept the storm at bay.

"What were you doing out in the water?" The old man pulled up a chair next to Levi to warm himself at the fire. His coat also drenched with rain.

"I don't know," He shook his head. "I don't really remember."

"Must've hit yer head pretty hard. You're lucky I found you washed along my shore, otherwise you probably would have died."

"Your shore?" Levi asked. The man was taken back not realizing the words he had picked.

"Lighthouse keeper," He admitted. The old man wore heavy wool clothes. His most predominant feature was his wide white beard that stood against his bronzed and worn skin. Levi simply grunted in response, still trying to get his energy back. He curled the blanket around him as he stared into the fire, still shivering in the bone. His shirt was torn in the back and hung loose now from his shoulders. The black pinstripe pants he wore had one rip at the knee, where the young man gashed his leg against the rocks along the beach. The cut continued to bleed down to his feet. Though Levi could no longer feel them, still sitting in water-filled boots.

"You stay here for the night, get some rest. In the morning, I'll be back," The old man pushed off from his seat, grunting as he stood. "We'll figure things out then."

Levi did not take his eyes off the bright fire as the lighthouse keeper walked away, putting his jacket and rain hat on as he left. The bartender left him alone, not wanting to disturb whatever was going through the young lad's mind. The few who were still drinking observed the whole thing. They each were drinking alone in different spots around the room, keeping to themselves.

"Mornin'," The innkeeper held out a plate of eggs to Levi, who realized he fell asleep on the creaky wooden bench. The kitchen was behind the counter of the bar, where the one man cooked and served everything in the tavern. He had his own room upstairs, running and living in the dark building alone.

"Thanks," Levi sat up, the damp blanket fell off of him and onto the floor like a mop.

"No worries, son. Just eat and we'll get ye cleaned up," The husky man scooped up the blanket and walked off. He wore a grey, faded shirt, and patched brown pants. He had a wide chin and a balding head. Levi sat, looking at the ash pile in the hearth as he ate his breakfast. He took his boots off and dumped out the excess water and hung them to dry at the fireplace, his blue feet exposed to the cold floorboards. From the windowpanes, Levi saw that last night's storm was calmed now as the early morning light was shining through. He looked around at how decorated the Rogue Star was. He hadn't noticed all the collected items in the haze of last night's events. Cargo nets were strung across the ceiling and held up crates. Mounted fish and a shark even were displayed on the walls. Old bits and pieces from ships that all ended up here littered the open room. Each article having its own tale, each its own fishing story or legend.

"Morning to you," The bartender greeted the old man from the night before as he walked in, stomping his boots at the door.

"Smith," He nodded as he went back to start the fire. Putting on fresh logs that were stacked nearby, he used flint and steel to ignite the fire. Then the old man took out a pipe from his coat and used a spare flame to light it. He huffed into the wooden pipe and then stood up. "Here, kid," The old man handed a bag to Levi. "Don't know if they'll fit right, but by the looks of it, you just needed something dry to wear."

"Thank you," The young man took the sack and went to the corner to change. He buttoned the dark blue sailor pants over his long johns and threw on the loose-fitting white shirt. Hanging up his old clothes, Levi went back to the hearth.

"Do you remember anything, yet?" The old man knelt down and stoked the fire.

"I just remember sailing, it got really dark. Nothing else," Levi scratched his head, his long curls still caked in the ocean salt.

"Hmph," The old man puzzled. "Name's Northrop, by the way. Forgot to mention that last night."

"Levi Benson. Pleasure to meet you," Levi held out his hand and shook his.

"Prepared a guest room at the lighthouse. You can stay there until we get you off of this rock or until you remember where's you came from."

"Where are we exactly?"

"Shorehaven. A little rock just north of the Crooked Island. If'n you know where that is."

"Glad I landed on English soil. I can't say I remember where I was going, but it doesn't sound like I'm close."

"Wouldn't think so. The very outskirts of the New World, we are. So, unless you were sailing over to Europe, I'd say you missed whatever piece of land you were aiming to hit."

"So," A booming voice entered the room. "There's our castaway!"

"Morning, Segar," Northrop nodded to greet the man walking in the door. Him and the innkeeper, named Smith, also exchanged welcomes. Levi looked over to see this new man. Segar was tall and muscular, middle aged or a little older. He was bald and had thick black eyebrows and a trimmed black beard. If not for his stature and weight, his boots alone could give off his commanding presence. He wore his old privateer's uniform, holding onto past days at sea, like a lot of the old timers in town.

"Not often we get new folks around here," He stroked his short beard as he sized Levi up. "Especially not by accident. Welcome to Shorehaven," He chuckled as he hit the kid on the shoulder. "I'm Segar, mayor of the island."

"Levi. Levi Benson," The young lad stood to shake his hand. Instincts told him to be extra formal when greeting his superiors.

"I trust you've been taken care of so far," Segar went over the counter, looking at the innkeeper. Smith was shorter, had a gut to him from eating too much of his own cooking.

"Yes, sir," Levi nodded.

"Good. I live in the big house just in town, best keep that in mind. We take care of our own. So, if you need anything, you know where to find me," With that, he stepped out of the building. His boots could still be heard hitting the cobble outside as he went past the tavern.

"We should be going, too. Get you settled in and show you around the town," Northrop turned to Levi, who was quick to gather all his articles that were hanging to dry. "Thanks, Smith," Northrop said as he went out the wooden door.

"Thank you," Levi waved as he hurried out to follow Northrop.

The sun hit a bit too bright as the two walked out of the dully lit tavern. Levi took in the palm trees and seagulls. The smell of the ocean salt fermented the colonial town, built with white walls and red brick roofs. Northrop's lighthouse was left of the docks when coming from town. A small cottage was built at the bottom of the tower. Most of the traffic the port saw was the islands own fisherman, but trading merchants were also common, often stopping here before heading over to Europe.

14

"Your room is upstairs," Northrop pointed to the steep spiral staircase that went up from the house to the top of the tower. "It isn't much, but there's a dresser and a stationary desk if you need it," The cottage was simple. The far-right corner from the door, near the stairs, had a stove. Along that wall was a small round table with two chairs, and a small cabinet for food. On the left was a small cot the man had just set up, a dresser, and a coat rack by the door. The house had no decoration to it, Northrop keeping his belongings minimal.

"Thank you."

"Oh, and we'll go down to your boat when you're done," The old man remembered as Levi ascended the stairs. The room was cozy, the roof of the house slanting in as the walls, with a dormer window on either side. One overlooking the town, and the other looking out over the water. The small bed was pushed against the far wall, opposite the door, with the dresser at the foot. The desk had a candle on it. After Levi set down the bag of clothes, he went back down the steps and met Northrop in the kitchen. He was tapping out the tobacco of his pipe into a ceramic dish.

They walked out of the house and crossed the pier to where the sailboat was sticking up from the rocks. The heavy stones were placed around the west of the island as a sort of retaining wall for the pier. A boardwalk ran parallel to the shore with two docks extending into the sea. Each jetty long enough and far enough apart to hold a frigate on both sides. The town then was built on a road going east from the docks, which went straight to Segar's house.

"Well, I was hoping we could get it fixed," Northrop said as they stared toward the ship on the rocky shore. "But after seeing this butchery in daylight..." He shook his head. "There's nothing we can do to save her."

The small sailboat Levi arrived in was split to fragments. The hull lay cracked open like a broken ribcage and the sails were torn beyond patchwork. The sea had eaten the dingy up and spit it out without remorse. Levi stepped across the rocks to climb to his ship.

"I'm not pulling you out of that wreck a second time!"

"Just getting my stuff," Levi grunted as he heaved a large trunk from the boards.

"At least you'll be set for some time now."

"Yeah, just thinking what I'm going do to get out of here," He hoisted his trunk onto the dock and had the old man take the other side as they walked back to the lighthouse.

"Finding work shouldn't be an issue. There're fishing crews and plenty to do. Could even be my apprentice now that I think about it. I *am* providing room and board after all… No, the issue is finding a ship around here willing to take you to wherever it is you have to go, once you remember where to go, that is. Most of us here are either content with staying in our little town or old sailors like me, who's days on the high sea are over. As for the flagships, they're too busy to pick up any stowaways."

"We'll figure something out," Levi sighed as they brought his trunk into the house. The wooden panels on the outside were painted white with black shakes for the roof. The tower itself was red brick and circular. The highest point in town, the lighthouse's lantern easily swept over the whole island.

"Piece of work, ain't she?" Northrop laughed as Levi struggled to pull the trunk up the spiral staircase. "Once you get settled in up there, we'll go around the town. I'm sure the folk are anxious to meet you."

Levi lugged the trunk into the spare room and opened it on the dresser to begin unpacking it. After sliding his pressed clothes into the drawers, he found a pen and ink set at the bottom of the case, along with a journal.

He sat down at his desk to jot down a quick entry. As he flipped through the pages, he noticed it was unused and void of any clues about his voyage. He dipped his pen in the inkwell and paused, hesitating until the right thought came to mind. As he looked up, he noticed a decoration on his desk that he did not see before. In a glass bottle, laid on its side was a ship. The galleon had several masts full of sails and each detail of the hull was intricately carved out. On the stand in a faded brass plaque, read, *El Puerto Oro.*

Levi spoke aloud as he wrote. "I've been shipwrecked on an island. I have lost all memory of who I am, except for my name and the obvious fact that I am, or at least was, a sailor. The town, called Shorehaven, has taken me in," He paused, hoping some memory would flood back to him, but nothing came.

The town had a main street that ran straight up from the pier. White buildings stood on each side of the cobble road. On the far end of the strip was Segar's mansion. It had a terrific view of the ocean, which Segar enjoyed looking out from his second story balcony. Halfway between his house and the docks was the marketplace. Stalls were set up in the open square and under the canopies of surrounding buildings. Alleys branched out from the main street, where most homes were built.

Fish was a staple in Shorehaven. Most people fished and would sell their catch to the fishmonger, who prepared them and sold them back to the islanders. This constant loop of currency worked through a whole internal system on the island between all the various goods and services. The townsfolk laughed about being England's forgotten island. No guards were stationed there, with no fort, save for the retaining wall by the sea which held one cannon. They bought and sold from merchant ships, which were the only transactions ever officially taxed by England. Segar set a humble sales tax to collect for himself and for public works, such as the light house. He paid Northrop to keep the place operational, who then began to give Levi a slice. Levi worked under the old man most days, learning the trade, and saving money for himself. Levi himself, hardly bought anything. It was Northrop who would give him money to buy food or supplies. The old man knew Levi would probably need a considerable amount of coin in order to pay the fare off the island.

2.

Descendancy of the Seas.

October 1714.

> *I've been on the island for a week now. The townsfolk have been more than kind to me. Segar introduced me to a man named Clay Clair. I've gone fishing with him several times now. He appreciates having someone on board who knows the ropes and can take orders. He says, "It keeps me worrying about the fish rather than my life."*
>
> *Northrop has shown me around the lighthouse, explaining how everything works. The old man hulls heavy canisters of oil up to the light to keep the wick burning. He showed me how to polish the lenses and grease the gears of the clock-like machine. The old man told me that it keeps him busy, giving him something to do in his retirement. He jokes that it is Segar's way to keep him out of town and out of sight.*

Levi dropped his pen as he heard a loud banging down the stairs. His door flew open as he looked down the spiral set of wooden steps.

"God!" He cried as he ran down to Northrop, who had fallen down, trying to carry up the routine can of whale oil. "You alright?"

"Yeah, yeah," Northrop grunted as he sat up. "I'm getting old, kid. Too dang old..."

"Here," Levi handed him a washcloth from the kitchen. "Looks like some of that oil spilled on you."

"Oh... thanks," The old man took it and wiped his tan forearm, which had black liquid running off.

"Is anything hurt?"

"No, I'm alright. Just go on," Northrop waved him away.

"Alright, I'm going into town. I'll pick up some more oil and food from the market. You just take it easy."

"Yeah," He grunted as he pulled himself up from the steel railing. He limped over to sit on his bed in the open room. "Ain't the first time those stairs have beaten me. Why don't you take care of the chores up there when you get back? I think I'm going sit for a while," He sighed and closed his eyes.

Levi took his coin purse and went out towards town. He had worked enough to buy himself more clothes that fit properly. Light tan breeches and a white blouse. His long hair was tied back in a ponytail, though it was still curly with some locks falling out. Bright brown irises lit up as he looked confidently around town.

The sign for the Rogue Star creaked as it moved softly in the wind. It hung straight out from the doorframe, which was in the very corner of the tavern so that the sign could be seen on the main street as well as the road perpendicular, along the docks. Rounding the corner passed the tavern, Levi walked the cobble stones to the market stalls.

"Good afternoon, Mister Benson!" The fishmonger with an eyepatch called out and waved to the young man. Levi's boots clicked as he walked on the stone over to the covered stall. Most of the vendors had different colored canvas stretched over their stand. The fishmonger's was a faded blue-green with yellow along the edge.

"Afternoon," Levi stopped by, seeing as no one was currently visiting the vendor.

"Anything I can do for you today? Got some nice fish here. Just pulled in this morning."

"Afraid not today, I have to get some oil for the lighthouse and then stop over at the *butcher* to get food for dinner," He grinned.

"Bastard's going put me out of business one of these days," The hardy man laughed and coughed. Hurley was his name. He worked the stand every day, except for Sunday morning church. "Take care now."

Levi went over to the general store, which supplied the whole town with various goods the ships would bring in. For the most part, the island was self-sufficient, but trading brought in some money for the locals. On his way, something blue caught his eye. Walking across the road, Levi went and examined what was just placed in the tailor's shop window. A bright blue jacket with brass buttons. Levi felt a memory come and go by looking at it. He remembered wearing fancy clothes like that wherever he came from. He remembered all the formalities. Getting dressed in layers of constricting attire. He left the window to go to his task.

"The old man send you out again?" The shop owner asked as Levi walked in the general store.

"Not exactly. Got himself hurt, so I figured I would go fetch the supplies for the day."

"He'll get it one of these days, working himself to death. He's what, seventy? Eighty?" The shop owner thought to himself. "I'm afraid, though, the ship still hasn't come in yet. Was scheduled to be here yesterday, but it must've been delayed again. So, whatever we have left will have to get by until it does show."

"Well, it didn't crash along our shore, I'll tell you that," Levi called out as he was picking out the lantern oil. The man behind the counter chuckled quietly. Soon after, the bell above the door caught Levi's attention. Segar had come in and spoke quickly to the merchant behind the counter.

"Christ," He muttered. Levi looked up at the two, trying to decipher what had happened.

"We'll talk about it at the tavern later," Segar spoke loud enough as to also include Levi. After Segar left, Levi checked out and handed the shopkeeper his silver pieces. Taking the road back across the square to the butcher, Levi was intercepted.

"Good day to you, Mister Benson," A young woman waved, almost cutting hi off from entering the shop.

"Well good day Miss Mertie," He chuckled at the attention she demanded from him.

"Buying goods for the old man, I see? So sweet of you," She smiled. Her dress blew with the gentle sea breeze. Her dark hair brushed across her pale, freckled face.

"Well, he's incapacitated at the moment. I suspect I'll be going out for him for a time as he recovers."

"Heavens, I hope nothing major has happened," Her flirtatious voice filled with genuine concern.

"I think he will be alright, he's tough as nails," Levi nodded gently.

"Very true. Well, I should let you go," She walked on.

"Take care, miss," The young man smiled softly.

"We've been here for weeks. When's England going to pay us?" Some sailors in the Rogue Star complained to Segar to no avail.

"I don't know. When I served as a gun, they paid me promptly," He nodded.

"That was a war ago, Segar. You old dogs got your rewards. We've been out of commission for months. My guess is they're out of money. Wars are costly. They hired us to fight but didn't think they wouldn't have enough to pay us," One blurted out. "Or that we'd be alive to collect."

"Aye, that could be," Segar concluded.

"And what of this shipment we were supposed to get?" A townsman with a heavy beard hollered out.

"That's what I wanted to address," Segar stood. Everyone knew to pipe down to let the mayor speak. "I know we missed last week's supply and I've been informed this week's shipment wouldn't be coming into port either."

"So, what do we do? You expect us to starve, live like rats then?" One stranded sailor complained.

"Our island has enough fish to feed everyone. I can't help that England hasn't paid you men," Segar addressed the group of privateers. They were originally hired to protect English ships on trade routes but were told to wait in port until they could be paid for their services. "Food, we'll have. But drink and goods, that'll be suspended until they can get here next."

"What happened to our ships?" A woman asked. Levi recognized her as Clay Clair's wife, who was sitting beside him at a corner table.

"They were intercepted. Thieves took off with the supplies, but the men and ships were supposedly left," Segar continued.

"Was it the Spanish? Those bastards always were targeting English trade!" Clay stood. The strong man had tattoos covering his body, more than any man in town. Though only the ones on his forearms were visible while we wore a plain shirt. The Clairs were modest in financial status, they lived in a small house on the east shore of the island, much like the other fishermen.

"I say it's the Curse. I feel its tide is rising again!" Another coughed out. Levi looked over to Northrop in confusion.

"Later, son," Northrop said under his breath.

"Quiet!" Segar hushed the crowd, growing rowdier. "I don't know who raided our ships. Could be Spain, could be some private merchants. Who knows? It is not the Curse; I'll tell you that. I didn't call this meeting to create an uproar, but to inform you. You may have to start fishing extra to keep up with demand. If you have not been paid and ran out of money, come talk to me. We'll have you work for stay. No one free loads here."

Most people cleared out of the tavern, as the evening was late. The ones who remained were the few renting the rooms upstairs. Levi and Northrop stayed, talking with the few sitting at the bar with them. The scene was quiet. Any conversation held could be heard across the stuffy room.

"Still think it's the Curse," One man said to himself as he stared down the bottle.

"What is the Curse?" Levi asked him, who was sitting at the counter with him and the old man.

"Only the most feared thing on this island," Smith leaned in, raising his rough eyebrow.

"It's bullocks," Another man said from the far corner.

"It's real and you know it!" Smith pointed at him, then went back to Levi. "The Curse is, uh, well it's more of an island, literally named *Isla Maldito*. The Cursed Island. Said to have a whole ship of Spanish gold buried somewhere in its sands. Captain Henry, no Hector, over filled the ship with gold. His cargo so heavy, caused the hull to break and his ship began to slowly sink. So, he buried it all on the island."

"So, what's the *Curse*?" Levi asked on.

24

"Well, as Hector was unloading the ship, it sank in the bay. His whole crew drowned except for Hector and his four other officers that were too busy burying the gold, but too paranoid to have his men help. Bad luck to have a ship go down without her cap'n, only evil can follow. Legend says Hector hid a map, written on a piece of the ship's sail, but anyone who has attempted to find the map and seek out the gold has died or *worse*."

"Aye," Northrop set down his drink. He wiped the ale from his beard before continuing. "The five officers who hid the gold, had to live on as the Curse set in. One after another, the Curse took them, each a more horrible end than the last. Until there was one left, one who sealed away their tomb with all the gold. They say the crew still haunts the waters, killing anyone who treads them, in hopes of taking revenge on their captain."

"And this is all real?" Levi looked up at the old man.

"As real as you see me now," Northrop nodded sternly.

"Easy does it now," A merchantman called. The pully system off the ship lowered crates onto the dock. The crew took the goods into the town, along with Levi and several other townsmen. Segar stood off the dock, speaking with the schooner's captain.

"This thieving has slowed down business. A lot of our crews have been forced to take the smaller, faster vessels to evade any possible threats. More ships have been hit, at least half dozen between here and Havana."

"What's being done about it?" Segar asked.

"Officially? Not a lot. Merchant ships are trying to hire on old privateers. So, there is some security, but hired guns go to the money. Lots are pier jumping to these new crews though. I don't know if these thieves are reselling the stock or using it for trade in their own towns, but they're getting a heck of a lot richer than we are. They have enough of our stock to start their own trade routes."

"They're starting their own towns?"

"So, I've heard. Suppose they need something to buy with all their silver."

"A whole crew of guns..." Segar thought in horror. "Sounds like a new kind of navy."

"Except with no side, no law as far as we know of."

"Maybe they'll start stealing from each other and kill themselves off," Segar chuckled as he adjusted his hat.

"That day will be much anticipated."

"You take care of yourself, Morillo. You find trouble, you know our port is always open."

"I may not have that luxury in the open water, but I appreciate it," The Spaniard crossed his arms, the two looking over the men unloading their cargo.

"And you've seen the Island?" Levi asked one of the sailors he was helping move crates with.

"Seen? No, sir. Bad omen to see the Island. It's clouded by fog. But been through those waters, aye," He replied.

"So, if the Curse doesn't kill you, the fog will have your ship run aground," Another sailor pitched in. "After the *Puerto Oro* was reported missing, wreckers went out to find it, most never returned themselves. Those who did, came back twisted, *accursed*."

"Hey!" Segar hollered. "Enough chatter!"

"Is it far from here?" Levi spoke quietly, keeping his head down, but no less continuing his investigation.

"Day, no more, but don't go asking where it is. The Island isn't charted on any map for a reason. The islanders here want to wish away its existence. So, by keeping it hidden, they keep the Curse away. Or so they'd like to think," He chuckled.

"You've seemed distracted lately. You know, it's hard to be efficient at work when your mind's vexed by something," Northrop found Levi atop the lighthouse that evening, leaning over the rail, looking out to sea. The waves that crashed on the shore sprayed the salt water into the air, reaching for them. "You've been fixed on the Curse?"

"The stories intrigue me," He didn't move his gaze.

"Don't let it get more than that, then. Knowing the stories. It's bad business, honest," Northrop struck a match and lit his pipe. The quick flame illuminating his tan face. "Segar's worried you're planning to go after it."

"I don't care what Segar thinks," Levi said without waiting to let his manners filter his words.

"Most of the time, I don't either, but I'm worried, too. You mustn't go looking for it. It's forbidden."

"Forbidden?"

"Town law. As part of our islands, Segar has jurisdiction there. No one is allowed to go."

"And what are the consequences of that crime?"

"Well," Northrop thought. Smoke leaving his mouth. "None have been set. Since everyone here complies with no problem."

"I'm not of the town, though, am I?" Levi changed his angle.

"You sure seem like ye are," Northrop said sincerely. "But every man must obey the laws of any town he's in. I expect you wouldn't be welcomed back if they knew you left to find it. We fear it because we've seen what the Curse has done. It twists men, drives them mad, if they even live to reach other shores. Besides, things have just been getting dangerous lately."

"How so?"

"There's been talk that some of the privateers are getting restless. With us and Spain no longer at war, England doesn't have a need to commission muscle. I reckon these men weren't ready to turn in their muskets. Sometimes men of war don't like to be told when they're done shooting. Some of these washed-up sailors have started to turn, descend from their codes of honor into something worse… In other towns, of course. But I fear it may come to us."

"The world's always been dangerous."

"Aye but know that we do what we can to keep each other safe. That's what we want, son. Keep you safe."

November 1714

Tonight, I spent some time talking to Northrop about the Island. He also seems very hesitant about my interest in it. Though if there's any opinion I respect on the island, it's his. He took me in, after all. He's shown me welcome like a grandfather would his own kin.

His age of experience has granted him wisdom. 'Feared is an old man in a profession where most die young,' as I've heard it said. The old salt had more to him than I originally thought. I found a navy uniform of his in the house. When I asked him about it, he just told me 'That was another life, lad.' I reckon his lack of words offset the surplus of experience he's had as a sailor.

Or fighter. Suppose he was an old privateer like Segar and the others, but that, I don't know for sure.

3.

The Cursed Corsairs.

"Sail ho!" The watchman called down to the deck of the Spanish frigate. "Alert the captain, incoming ship!"

"Captain!" A Spanish navy officer rushed into the quarters at the stern of the ship. "Ship quickly approaching," The captain got up from his desk and put on his tricorn hat as he stepped out onto the weather deck. He passed his crew members, all in uniform at their lines, as he went up to the helm.

"What do you see?" The captain called up to the watchman.

"Three points off the port bow!" He cried, not taking his eye off the spyglass.

"Well, who's ship is it?"

"Looks like one of ours!"

"One of- Look at the flag!"

"It's a Spanish ship, sir!" The watchman turned to look down at his captain. "But the flag is black."

"A black flag?" The captain turned to the others on the deck with him. "What country is that?"

"Sir, they're broad off the port bow! Five hundred meters, closing in!"

The captain went over to the railing and looked out. He took out a smaller spyglass from his coat. Looking at the ship head on, he saw panels on the side lifting open.

"Prepare for battle! Battle stations!" He turned and yelled to his men. They went below deck to get out their muskets and open their own gun ports. Teams loaded cannons and with pullies, drove them to the hull, the barrels just peering out of the ports. Just as the opposing ship had done. The captain hustled down the steps and went back to his quarters to grab his musket and put on the holster for his pistol. They were primed and loaded already.

"Ready yourselves!" He called out as he walked back on deck. His men in a stir. The two ships angled and began to drift passed each other. Their port sides now facing one another. The navy crew stared down the men on the opposing ship. As they waited for the ships to get in position, all the men stood, fingers twitching over their triggers. The still, hot air now buzzed with adrenaline. The ship under the black flag angled a cannon forward for a preemptive strike. The steel bomb flew through the air and soared straight through the front most sail, crashing into the ocean.

"*Disparad*! Fire your guns!" The Spanish captain yelled. The well-trained sailors took aim at the opposing crew and began to fire their muskets. The marauder crew was soon to return fire. Most bullets strayed, chipping away at the hull, or whizzing over the ship entirely. As the two brigs got closer, bullets began to make contact. Below the decks, cannons thundered and rocked the wooden structure, testing the integrity of the ship's construction. Each cannonball that hit directly, exploded, and wrecked gaping holes in the keel.

"Sink the bastard!" The Spanish artillery gunners called out. The black-flagged crew was clearly not as well equipped. They fired less cannons and only shot half as much from their rifles. Soon the keel, the bottom of their ship, was breached. The ship began to overturn. Water quickly filled the void that was keeping the structure afloat. The marauders stopped firing back and began to abandon ship.

"Cease fire! They're done for," The captain ordered, as most of the crew had stopped firing already. "Helmsman, steer us away from this wreck!" The ship resumed sailing toward their destination. The crew began working on damage control and patching any leaks sustained in battle, just enough to make it to port for official repairs. The captain returned to his desk and reviewed the paperwork his was ordered to deliver with his cargo.

"Mighty bold of them to attack a navy vessel," The ship's chief officer came in.

"It makes me uneasy," The captain sat back in his chair, nailed to the deck. "What are they trying to gain? They're not going after land, not trying to form their own country, they're just raiding ships. It's completely ballistic!"

"I don't know, sir. Power, maybe? I can't imagine they make enough to pay their crew."

"Could be promising commission off of their spoils," The captain tried for a moment to reason their motives, then shook his head.

"With ten pieces lost, how much would they have made?" The officer speculated.

"Ten ships full of food, that's what," The captain stood from his desk to look out the window. "'Mighty bold' is right. Did you see the name on their ship?"

"It was one of ours, sir. *San Jose.*"

"Bastards," He spat. "Was it even reported missing?"

"Not that I know of, sir."

"Blast," He took off his hat, scratched his head, and sat back down. "Get some rest chief, we'll be in port soon enough and deal with this all when I speak with the admiral."

The men slept hard that night, exhausted from the battle. Only a few watchmen took shifts patrolling the decks. The anchored vessel rocked gently on the quiet, black waves. Soft knocking came against the hull. One of the watchmen held his lantern over the taffrail to see what it was.

"Just water lapping against the ship," another said as he was sitting on a stool, half asleep. "You're spooking yourself."

"Could have sworn I saw something moving in the water," He continued to peer over the ledge.

"Well, as long as you don't go in the water, you'll be just fine," The other sailor closed his eyes as he leaned back against the mast.

"Aye, you're right," He turned to see the man now on the deck, with his throat cut open. Shaking, the watchman was met with a knife as well. From the anchor rode, marauders climbed onto the ship, silently taking out the watchmen with their daggers. When their ship had gone under, they swam to take hold of this one, clinging to their prey. This time, they waited until nightfall to finish the job.

The captain shot up as he saw a horde of men brooding in his quarters. One lurched at him with a knife, but the captain pulled his flintlock from his nightstand and fired. As he was fumbling to reload, the other raiders overpowered him and stabbed him repeatedly. The gunshot startled some of the Spaniards, who found themselves in the same situation, either meeting their end or instinctually wrestling men to the deck. Soon, those who were left alive woke and joined the brawl. Yet by now, there were more marauders than crew members and before long, everyone left on board was killed.

"Captain Hornigold?" One of the raiders went up to the deck. "What do we do with the bodies?"

"Throw them into the sea," A man in a long black coat ordered with a crooked grin. "Except their captain. We'll see he has a more fitting burial."

"Admiral Esteban, some men are here to see you," The highly decorated official turned from his window, overlooking the Havana Bay. Green trees could be seen below his balcony. Birds flew from the tops of buildings that stuck out from the canopy. Captain Morillo along with some of his crew stepped forward and bowed slightly to their superior.

"What can I do for you gentlemen?" The admiral asked genuinely, seeing the grave faces each man wore.

"Sir, on our way in we came across something disturbing that might be of interest to you," Morillo lowered his eyes.

"And what might that be?" Esteban raised his brow. He had on a long yellow coat and medals pinned to his chest. The admiral wore a grey wig underneath a tall bicorne hat.

"One of your captains, sir..." Morillo hesitated to answer initially. "We found him and his crew floating dead in the water."

"What do you mean by this?" The admiral trembled. "Show me," He ordered. They brought him down to their schooner and showed him what had been pulled aboard, now soaking the deck. "Who did this?" The admiral asked, quivering his lip.

"We found him near the bay, but we-" He looked over his shoulder. "We suspect the black flags."

"The 'black flags'? Those thieves have a title now. This is just disrespectful. Someone needs to put an end to this and it sure isn't our navy!" He hit his fist on a crate. The admiral turned and walked down the gangplank. "Bury him," He waved to his men on the dock, who ran up onto

Morillo's ship. The men grabbed the arms and legs of the dead captain, whose ship was taken. Tied to his hands and feet were strips of the Spanish flag from the main mast. His watered-down blood soaking the already red flag.

Levi walked to Clay's house in the morning when they would usually go fishing. It was a small wooden structure built on the coast not far from the lighthouse. Mrs. Clair was serving coffee and biscuits by the time the young man got there. Clay kissed his wife goodbye before meeting Levi, already at the boat which was pulled ashore. The two pushed the small vessel out to sea and rowed it around to the south of the island. The water was calm and blue. The inlets and skerries on that side of the island were a favorite of fisherman.

"What's with your tattoos?" Levi asked Clay as they rowed. His arms had different nautical symbols and animals dotted on them. His chest also marked, which could be seen from the low-cut collar on his shirt. Clay also had images on his on the span of his back.

"Kind of a coarse question to ask a man," He chuckled. "You keep a journal, aye?"

"Aye," Levi nodded.

"Like the well-educated lad ye are. See, and us sailors would find *that* odd."

"I *am* a sailor," Levi defended himself half-heartedly.

"The most sophisticated one I've ever met. A sailor's tattoos are his journal. They tell our stories because you know we can't write for crud," Clay laughed. "This one, here, I worked as a whaler when I first came over from London. And this one, when I was rum-running out of the caves. And, uh, maybe I won't tell you about that one," The two chuckled. When they got to the small bay they usually fished from, they threw nets into the water. Periodically they hauled them up to bring fish aboard. Other boats were with them out on the water, like usual.

"You're thinking something," Clay observed the young lad. Levi had been keeping quiet and staring off into the ocean as they worked.

"Have you ever been to the Island?"

"Been to a lot of islands, kid."

"The Cursed Island," Levi specified.

"You want to go, don't you?" Clay studied him.

"Aye," Levi chuckled. "Very much, so. It's intriguing."

"The Curse or a whole ship full of gold?"

"Either one."

"The Curse, I don't think is real. But there definitely was a ship that sunk in that bay. Whether it was filled with gold... I don't know that either. I'd doubt it, but everyone's too scared to go see for themselves. No one's ever left that island with gold. Don't know of anyone who's actually left that place."

"Why don't we go then?"

"The two of us?" The fisherman scoffed. "We'd need a bigger ship and a bigger crew. If there are large piles of gold laying around, we'd need a boat that could carry some of it back. Wouldn't want our treasure smelling like tarpon, would we?"

"I'm sure I can find someone in town with a ship."

"Hey," Clay got his attention, seeing as Levi was stirring with ideas. "This needs to be kept quiet. The Curse is a myth, but people are terrified of it. And blast, what people do when they get afraid. We've been welcoming to you so far, but soon as you start asking about the Cursed Island, expect that hospitality to go away."

"So, what do you suggest?"

"This is if we go. *If.* We need men who are not scared of this Curse. They can believe in it, but a good sailor keeps his head, they cannot be afraid. Secondly, probably more important, is we need good sailors. If we have a good crew, we can keep the numbers small, run a more discrete operation."

"Okay," Levi nodded, wheels turning in his mind.

"If, Levi. For now, just pretend you're not interested anymore. See if you can point out the people who don't fear the Curse, narrow down your candidates," They sat, waves rocking the boat ever so slightly. "A ship full of Spanish gold does sound nice."

The pub was full that night. Northrop and Levi were at the counter, laughing with Smith. There was a man in the corner, leading shanties with some of the other folk in the room. His voice was awkwardly high, but no one sang on pitch. He dressed well, finer than any other in the tavern. Brown breeches that matched his vest with a white frill shirt underneath. He had dark wavy hair, which bounced lightly as he danced. He looked young but was nearing thirty.

"Who's that?" Levi pointed to him.

"Gail Wickman," Northrop did not need to take his eyes off of his drink to know the voice that was singing. "Segar's nephew."

"Does he live in town? I haven't seen him before."

"No, he lives in his boat," Smith piped in. "Gail Wickman, captain of the *Gail Wickman*," He mocked with pompous stance, putting his hands on his hips, and strutting behind the counter bar.

"He named his ship after himself?" Levi chuckled as he drank from his glass pint.

"Aye, his father's fortune bought that little ship," Smith topped the young man's drink off. Filling the pint with ale.

"His father was a privateer with Segar, his brother-in-law," Northrop added. "Protecting English ships. Segar used his pay to establish Shorehaven, but Gail Wickman used all his father's gold for himself after he died from a sustained bullet wound."

"Master sailor, Norman Wickman was. Piss of the crop, his son. Segar isn't a huge fan of the boy either, but he is family. So, when he does wash up here, Segar takes care of him," Smith continued, wiping down the counter as he spoke. "His mother, Segar's sister, died when the boy was young. He's all the mayor has left of her."

"What does he do for a livin'?" Levi turned to get another look at the man.

"Nothing, he just sails around and drinks all the ports dry. He loves to gloat and impress the lasses, but he's just a pushover. Calls himself a sailor on the merit of being a drunkard with a ship. Although, seems to me, he sails it himself. Can't imagine he can pay a crew."

"I don't believe we've been introduced," Levi went up to Gail as the night was quieting down. "Levi Benson," He shook Gail's hand as he sat across from him.

"Captain Gail Wickman," He took a swig from his pint.

"Captain? A fairly impressive feat."

"Well, fate has a way of making men."

"I suppose," Levi didn't quite understand the saying. "What brings you into port?"

"Just making my usual rounds across the oceans, you know. Family of the mayor in town, I am."

"Must be pricy to keep a flagship going all year round."

"It's not quite exactly a flagship, but, aye, it does take some tender to keep everything afloat and the captain fed," He looked at his empty pint glass, then set it aside.

"I'm sure you have just a novel full stories and tales from the high seas," Levi was building up his ego.

"Well, I suppose I *have* been around enough to see some adventure."

"All without fear, I'm sure."

"Of course. A captain must be an example to his crew. Might I ask, Mr. Benson, why you're so interested?"

"Have you heard of Isla Maldito?" Levi looked over his shoulder, prompting Gail to cautiously do the same. "The Cursed Island?"

"I might have," Gail spoke uncertainly.

"A whole ship full of Spanish gold, just waiting for the taking," Levi felt inspired by his own words.

"How do you know no one has already taken it?"

"Because no man I've met is brave enough to go after it. Lot of danger that surrounds the island. But that much gold, I'd say it's worth any risk."

"The Cursed Island... And if *we're* cursed? Like the name suggests we might be?"

"Then we'll be known across the seas as the Cursed Corsairs, the crew who found the gold. Richest bastards in all hell," Levi smirked and sat back in his chair.

"That does sound enticing..." Gail scratched his head. His brown hair no longer kept after a night of merrily drinking. "I'll have to check with my crew..."

"No bother, I can supply the crew. I just need a ship and a captain," Levi leaned in.

4.

The Voyage of the Gail Wickman.

"Won't you tell me where you're going?" Mertie leaned on Levi. Both sitting on the large rocks overlooking the west side of the island. The west was forested, which extended to the north coast as well.

"Why?" Levi chuckled. "Surely it's not exciting."

"Well, surely it is, if you are keeping it from me," Mertie moved her hair behind her ear. "Bahamas," She guessed.

"No," Levi laughed.

"Kingston? Tell me you're going to Jamaica," She held his hand in excitement. Levi pressed his lips together and shook his head. "How long will you be away?" Mertie sighed.

"A week, maybe. I don't really know," Levi squinted as he tried to piece together the total length of his crusade.

"You probably have no idea where they're even shipping you to. You must tell your captain that isn't fair."

"Not fair?"

"Not for me," She laughed.

"Oh, lord," Levi chuckled. "And what if I told you *I* was the captain?"

"Then you're truly a fool if you don't even know where you're going," She smirked. Levi beside her, blushing red. "Tell me, how do you if you're going somewhere good?"

"I've seen this place already."

"You have? Yet you do not know where it is."

"I think I have. I had a few dreams of a beautiful green island. Lush forest and crystal waters, fair breeze for sailing," Levi gestured toward the ocean, romanticizing his journey.

"Wherever it is you go," Mertie leaned in and kissed the young man on the cheek. "Be safe."

In town, Clay was bringing his catch Hurley, the fishmonger. The man behind the market stall had a scraggly beard and rough skin. He had a patch over his right eye. People suspected that he took his own eye out with a fishhook, but when asked, Hurley gave a different story each time. Once he said it had been shot out of him, another time he told travelers that a stingray pierced it and rendered his eye useless. Despite his tall tales, everyone around knew he had retired to selling fish after spending most of his life catching it. It was even believed he caught the shark that was on display in the Rogue Star.

"Little bastards won't me leave alone," Hurley shoed a group of flies away with his hand, only for them to circle back to the fillets. The heat from the sun beamed onto the raw meat, stinking the air around them. The scent clung to Hurley almost permanently, though he hardly noticed the musk anymore.

"A good salesman would charge extra for them's, call it natural seasoning," Clay laughed at the flies as he collected his payment.

"Right, I'll let ye know how that goes over with the townsfolk," He shook his head. Hurley opened the barrel Clay delivered and grabbed a fish by the mouth. Slime oozed off of it and dripped on the rest of the catch. It thumped as it hit his cutting board. The fishmonger took out his knife and began cutting the meat away from the bone. Then Hurley and Clay spotted a young man approaching, wearing his usual white blouse and blue trousers. "Ay, Levi. Here's a deal. I'll only charge you double for the fish today, being that they have this special spice added by them flies."

"You would, too," Levi shook his head and went up to Clay. "We got a ship," He turned his head and whispered.

"Good news," Clay patted him on the back and stirred them away from the stand. "We be seeing you later, Hurley!"

"You got us a crew?" Levi asked as Clay handed him his share from the catch they sold. The two walked down towards the pier. Salt from the ocean freshened the air that hung over the market.

"Working on it," He cleared his throat. "I think some of these unemployed guns might be just desperate enough to join our voyage. I've gotten us some arms as well."

"Arms?" Levi stopped and asked.

"Swords, guns," Clay said quickly. "We don't know what we'll find there. Savages or other treasure hunters. Best we be prepared."

"Where did you come to find these?"

"Not hard. This town's built on privateers, old navy men. Lots of weapons between the all of us," Clay paused as they approached the docks. "So, which ship is it that we'll be taking? A schooner? Or maybe Segar's old boat?"

"It'll be that one," Levi pointed down the jetty. Gail loaded his ship with supplies he had purchased in town to restock. The caravel had two triangle sails that hung down from the vertical masts. It was a shorter vessel, but finely made. A cabin was built on the back, the wheel mounted on top.

"Gail Wickman?" Clay huffed.

"The only ship I could get. He hadn't even heard of the curse, so he's perfect."

"He hasn't heard of it because he's an imbecile. Just look at him. Fine coat and a vest. He's dressed more like a clerk than a sailor! He's not fit for a quest like this."

"Aye, he's spoiled on his money," Levi admitted. "But just look, he pilots his ship himself. He has to have some aptitude as a sailor," The young man pointed out, seeing no crew was helping Gail load his ship.

"Apti..." Clay shook off his confusion. "Look, I don't like it. He's too public, too weak."

"He's just going to get us there. He can wait on his ship while we get our hands dirty, for all I care. You said we need a ship and I got one," Levi began walking again to the docks. Clay waved as he went his own away. Levi stepped out on the wooden planks of the pier. Gail counting the boxes he had loaded already, trying to figure out if anything was missing.

"So, what say you?" Levi asked, startling Gail.

"Ah, your island of curses proposal," He gulped.

"You're not leaving an opportunity like this, are you?"

"No, no, of course not. It's just that a bigger, slightly more daring, quest came up and I really feel *that's* where I should go," He turned back to continue his arithmetic.

"This is more gold than you've ever conceived in your life. This treasure is a ship weighed down and sunk for how much gold it carried. Right? That's a lot of bloody gold," Levi gestured with his hands. "All you have to do is sail us there."

"I do have some debt and tabs to pay off."

"Exactly, just help us get the gold as a... warmup to your more daring adventure."

"Alright!" Gail caved. "When do we take off?"

"Tonight."

"Night?"

"The islanders can't stop us from going if they don't know we're leaving."

"I'm not liking how this voyage is starting out."

44

January 1715

We leave tonight for the island. Through persuasive means, we got ourselves a ship. Now Clay just needs to pull through on his end and find some crew. I've also saved up enough to swindle a deal on that blue jacket from the tailor. A fetching adventure needs a dashing captain, or so I've read in books. Though I aim not to be the fraud Mister Wickman appears to be. He is dignified, but I'm afraid Clay may be right as he may not be fit for the mission.

I've written down everything I know of the island and its Curse. The first thing we'll need to do is find the cave that holds Hector's map. The island, as I've heard is rocky and full of jungle life. As the stories go, all of it is toxic or venomous. I've had my bag packed for a while now, not knowing how long we will be gone.

If we find the map, then it should be smooth sailing from there. Spending time with Clay has made me more of a sceptic of the Curse and the possibilities of what it could do to us. Although, now that the time has come to actually sail for the island, I can't help but feel very anxious.

Levi and Northrop sat in the small dining room of the lighthouse and ate stew that evening. There was silence between the two men, only the creaking of the old wooden table and the clipping on spoons against the ceramic bowls. Northrop stared at the Levi, figuring out what the young man was up to. Without a word, Levi finished and stood to go up to his quarters. Northrop scoffed and lit a pipe as he slowly ate the rest of his meal.

Levi laid on his bed, waiting for the hour to depart. In his hands was the ship in the bottle from his desk. He studied it and held it close to his eyes, to make the ship appear as if it were real, studying the paint and carvings.

He stayed up, keeping watch out of his window until he saw a lantern flash by the docks. He put his notebook in his backpack and slung it over his shoulder. Softly opening his bedroom door, he then descended down the spiral set of stairs. Seeing the light was snuffed out, Levi sighed with relief and began to walk silently through the room.

"The last thing about the Curse you should know," Northrop muttered from his chair as Levi was sneaking out. The embers in his pipe were the only thing that shone. "The gold curses all who seek it. After the sea took the ship, the four officers with Captain Hector were cursed with a heart full of ink. Because no man with a beating heart would choose gold over men," The old man said sternly. Levi paused before pushing the door open to leave. He sighed again as he closed the front door, then walked around the house to the pier. Down at the docks, the *Gail Wickman* was being loaded up with the final supplies.

"There ye are," Clay was standing under the lantern. "Been waiting for you."

"Is everything ready?" Levi said quietly.

"Yessir, we got nine brave souls to help with the rigging and, if we're lucky, the digging," He pulled out a parchment that he had them sign as a contract to the mission.

"Good," The two walked further onto the dimly lit jetty. The volunteers were standing in a row. Exhausted, they waited for orders. They all varied in height and weight. One man towering over the rest.

"We have a Welham, Harper, Torie, Tanner, Lea, Flint, Cook, Crofton, and Jack. Mostly privateers, the washed-up swabs from the tavern," Clay read from the list.

"I'm sure Smithy will appreciate their absence."

As quietly as they could, the crew cast off the moorings and began drifting out to open water. All the light they had was the occasional sweep of the lighthouse. That beacon was the only thing to notice the ship leaving. Soon, the sails were raised, and the ship began to drive north. The caravel darted through the black ocean, Captain Gail controlling the helm. As they cleared sight of Shorehaven, they furled the sails and dropped the anchor into the ocean. The crew prepared their hammocks below deck as Gail, Clay, and Levi slept in the officer's quarters in the aft of the ship. They could afford to rest now that they left the town unseen.

As dawn quickly came upon them, they set off again. The men hoisted up the anchors and raised the sails to make haste for Isla Maldito. Gail had the helm, Clay navigating by intuition and memory of the old tales. Gail sang as the crew below pulled rigging and stood their posts. Levi was standing on the railing at the bow of the ship. The wind pushing against his face as he looked out over the open ocean.

"No help from Levi today?" Captain Morillo asked Northrop as the two men were hoisting cargo off a ship and onto the docks. Clouds covered the sky that day, but it was none the less hot.

"Seems not," He grunted. Northrop was as strong an ox for his lean figure, but he was getting old. He had gone to help unload the cargo ship in Levi's absence, which was a voluntary task of the people in Shorehaven.

"Heard he and some of the others went after the Isla Maldito," One of the deckhands pitched in. Northrop sighed, not wanting the truth to leak into the town.

"Fool, that lad," Morillo shook his head before lifting another box with one of his crew.

"Northrop!" Segar hollered as he walked onto the pier.

"Keep a watch on that boy, he's gonna find you more trouble than just *him*," Morillo said to the old man who got up to meet the mayor, standing on the port.

"How long have you known?" Segar demanded.

"Sir?" Northrop asked as he approached the mayor.

"That they were going to the island? How long have you known?" Segar raised his voice.

"Just yesterday, immediately before they left."

"Don't fool me, old man."

"Honest," He spoke plainly. Northrop was never intimidated by Segar's strict act.

"They've brought horror to us all. And that is *if* they come back," Segar leaned in.

"If," He nodded.

"You should have never taken him in. As soon as he started asking questions, he already stayed too long."

"The boy's marooned here. He has nowhere to go."

"Are you getting soft? He could swim off this rock for all I care. He brings a spot of that blasted curse back, it's on you!"

"It's on *him*," Northrop snapped back. "Levi has integrity. He knows it's on him. Don't let your anger seep into your judgement," Segar pushed off and stormed back to town.

"So, why is this island not on any map?" Gail asked at the helm. Clay was beside him, walking his drawing compass across the region's map, which was void of the infamous island.

"The islanders would prefer if Isla Maldito didn't exist. So, they do what they can to forget."

"Also, to avoid any from sailing to it," Welham called, one of the crew. He was a hardy man, mutton chops on his face, leaving him bald around the mouth and chin. He had short red hair and a heavy Irish accent. "First ship in a dozen years I reckon, we are."

"How do you know where we're heading?" Gail kept asking.

"The island be about twenty-five leagues from town," Clay continued. "Northmost of the chain we're on. We all know it, the islanders, but no one would tell you straight if ye asked. Everyone too scared..."

"Fog, sir," A sailor yelled from the crow's nest. He was slender and tall. Seemed an expert climber which granted him position as the watchman, being able to scale up the shroud and lines with no problem. "In the distance!"

"Aye, Torie," Clay acknowledged and took the helm from Gail. "Levi, fore lookout. We'll be getting in the thick of it; we need to keep watch for rocks."

"Aye, aye," Levi climbed down from the rigging and hustled over to the bow. His light hair tied back as usual. Soon, the caravel become swamped in fog. The thick, grey clouds filled the deck, not able to see the bow from the stern. Mist seeping up through the boards. Levi crawled out on the bowsprit to hang a large lantern to light up the clouds.

"Spot anything?" Clay called again.

"Negative," Levi shimmied back to the deck. "Wait, hold on. There's something in the water."

"Well, if it's a rock, you best tell me, lad!" Clay cried out. "I'm stirring blind," Levi studied the waves. Underneath the dark water, streaks of glowing green flowed. Like luminescent wisps of algae.

"I don't know what it is," Levi admitted. Another sailor went over to take a look. "There's something green in the current."

"Looks like a sea ghost swimming around our boat. There was a face just there!" Crofton let out. He was a usual to the tavern, so Levi recognized him, but never knew his name. He had short curls for hair, thinning enough to see down to the scalp. His wide chin laid the foundation of his dirty stubble. He spoke from the corner of his mouth, which pointed away from the gold ring in his left ear. He was lean and appeared older than the rest of the sailors aboard.

"As long as I can sail over it, it's of no concern," Clay kept their bearing, trying not to think of the possibility of ghosts. Appearing from the dense fog, dead fish floated on top of the waves, hitting the hull of the ship. Various scratching sounds came from under the keel.

"What are we rubbing against?" Clay hollered. Gail gripped the rail, afraid for his prized vessel.

"Nothing!" Levi looked frantically to see if they *were* actually grinding on anything. The scratches came unevenly as if from a host of small sources.

"Blimey! They really are sea ghosts," Crofton gasped, never taking his eyes off of the green fluid. "I saw a body float by, just there!" He pointed excitedly into the waves. Others on deck frantically scanned the water.

"I didn't see anything," Levi looked intently into the haze below. The green illuminated the fog around them, and lit the terrified faces of the sailors.

"Heavens above! There one is again. It's the drowned crew of the *Puerto Oro*!" The sailors looked at each other.

All the locals knew the legends, but not knowing if it was wise to believe in them, let alone speak the name.

"Stay in the boat and you'll be just fine," The Cook added. He was short and round, wearing a bandana over his head. "They ain't harming us now."

"What's the name of the ship?" Levi turned to Crofton.

"Sorry, bad luck to say its name. Dangit! I doomed us," Crofton began to sweat and shake nervously, running his hands through his thin hair. "The crew's already come. That be what's scratching on the keel!"

"Get a grip. What was the name?" Levi shook him gently by the shoulder.

"The *Puerto Oro*," Crofton admitted.

"Aye," Clay called from the helm. "The Port of Gold."

Once they got passed the fog, the water was calm and clear. In front of them stood a tall mass of land. The island had one mountain in the center, covered in jungle. By the bay, rocks protruded out of the waves, along with three wooden masts. As they lowered their sails and coasted the rest of the way in, they passed by the sunken ship. From the bright sun, the whole vessel under water could be seen from the surface.

It looked to be in one piece, but sea life was slowing eating away at it. Urchins and coral grew at its base, with fish and sharks making each nook their home. On the stern, the polished name was still visible. The bright hand-carved letters of *El Puerto Oro* seemed the most pristine after years of exposure. The *Gail Wickman* dropped anchor just offshore. Palm trees and bright sand welcomed the crew enough to brave going to land in the row boats.

"Other than that dingy fog, not a bad little island," Clay nodded to himself as he took in the scenery. Above the trees, bright colored birds soared from the mountain.

The jungle surrounding them teemed with life, bugs whistled and hummed to each other.

"Alright," Levi called out as the men were pulling the boats up on the sand. "Some of you, stay here and make a camp for us on the beach. Cook, see what food you can scrounge up. I'll take the others with me to hike up the mountain. We'll see what we see."

5.

The Island.

"I don't mean to intrude, Mister Benson," Gail hiked up behind Levi, seemingly not hearing him. "Sir!" Levi turned to deal with the persisting man.

"What is it, Wickman?" Levi snapped.

"It's exactly that. I will have you know; *I* am the captain of this ship and crew. I will be treated like it," He held his chin up. "You seem to think you're in charge simply for orchestrating the quest."

"Are we on your boat?" Levi got close to him. The young man held his blue jacket over his shoulder with the sleeves on his white shirt pushed up to his elbows.

"No," Gail muttered.

"Then you're not the captain," Levi turned, continuing up the trail. The others started to walk behind him, not having any respect for the roaming drunkard who called himself a captain.

"Right, you are captain of the expedition," Gail stood, composing himself, as Clay and the others passed by. "And I, the captain of the ship. I will return to my post and wait by my ship," He slowed realizing no one had paid him any mind. The man scratched his curly hair before turning back down the trail. Gail's leather shoes and long stocking, collecting unsolicited mud from the wild trail.

Levi drove up the mountain, cutting down bushes and branches. The black rock they climbed was built up to a pointed summit far above them in the heart of the island. Bugs whizzed and fluttered about. Birds chirped loudly, chasing each other, rustling the leaves as they flew by.

"So, what are we looking for exactly?" Welham called out from the rear of the group. "Just a pile of gold?"

"Supposedly," Clay began. "There's a cave with a map, that leads us to the gold. We're looking for a cave."

"It's impossible to see what's on the mountain with these trees in the way," Levi thought aloud. "Torie! See if you can climb one of these palms and get a better angle."

"Aye, sir," The man took off his boots, and using his feet, scrambled up the trunk of the palm. He reached up through the branched to pull himself on top. Nesting on top of the leaves was an orange and black tarantula. "Nice, bug. Stay, boy," He uneasily snapped a branch off the truck and flicked the spider off the tree.

"Christ!" Men jumped below. Welham pulled his pistol and shot the bug as it began to crawl toward him. A loud echo rang off the mountain side. Welham glared up at the young lad.

"Sorry," Torie shrugged. He sat on the top of the tree, with his feet hugging the trunk. He scanned the foothills below them, seeing the bay and their ship from his vantage point. He turned slowly and looked up and down the jagged black mountain, spotted by green clusters of foliage. On one of the rock walls, the mount borrowed in on itself creating a chasm. "I see a cave!" Torie called down.

"Do you see a way to get there?" Levi looked up through the canopy of leaves. Seeing a pair of legs dangling down.

"Yes sir, there's some rocks that snake up to it."

Torie slid down the tree and put on his boots. He led the line around the rock stacks that jut upwards from the earth. The rock looked as if it were stacked purposefully, as if the island was curating the trail they were on. With pen in hand, Levi sketched the trail they were taking; marking landmarks where the turned. His pages damp from the jungle mist. By now, the men were dripping with sweat from the humidity and panting from exhaustion.

"A rest, cap'n," One man begged. Levi was too determined to notice how worn he and his men were.

"Aye, rest here," Levi huffed. The downed logs they sat on were warm to the touch, compared to the cold, wet lumber on the ship they were used to. They sat and huffed to catch their strength, passing canteens of water to drink. The fermentation of coffee plants and fruits and the green of the earth filled the air. Fanned leaves around them collected drops of moisture that occasionally fell on the sitting men. Now they heard the sound of water trickling out of sight, the lost strains of rain coming out from beneath the mountain. "What's your name, sailor?" Levi asked a man sitting next to him.

"Leatherneck Jack," The man replied with a steadfast grin. He was a big man. Wide head with burly muscles on his body. Hardly had a neck to him, his shoulders were so broad and built.

"And how does one earn a name like that?" Torie asked. "A 'leatherneck?'"

"I was shipwrecked on an island. Indians tried to cut my head off. Unfortunately for them, I survived."

"Bull," Clay chuckled.

"Oh yeah?" Jack stood up, standing over the rest of the men. He turned and stared at each one before lifting his chin to reveal a scar that ran between the jawbones. He traced the wound with his thumb.

"Come on... And how did you escape?" Clay challenged.

"I beat him to the ground after he slashed at my throat. Then I went back to my wrecked ship and built me a raft. Rowed back to civilization," He folded his arms. "The bastard couldn't cut deep enough to kill me."

"Don't know if I quite believe you," Welham squinted at him, then started a low chuckle. "But if we run into any, uh, locals, we'll send you out first."

"There aren't any, are there?" Torie looked up at the group. "Locals?"

"No," Clay shook his head. "Not anymore. Heard the Spanish came and killed them all looking for the treasure."

They sat for a moment, taking in their fear, but eventually they collected their items and stood to walk again. On the move, they stepped up the rocky trail. Boulders and stacks grew around them, as the trail slowly became like a canyon. Even trees grew bigger inland, with their trunks like walls and roots that spread across the stony ground.

"This is the way," Torie called back. The canyon eventually fed them to a cavern. Stalagmites grew like teeth at the mouth of the cave. The frightening sight looked as though the mountain would try to eat them.

"Someone get me a torch," Levi ordered, without taking his eyes off the void.

"Here, sir," Welham handed him a torch, after lighting it with a match. Levi took it and held it up. Dew on the black rock ignited as well, reflecting the yellow flame. The cave snaked deeper into the belly of the mountain. Levi pressed forward as the others were still lighting their own torches. Their sweat became cold on the clothes as the men left the heat of the jungle for the dark, ruinous cave. Around several turns, opened a large cavern.

The room had several crates and a rusted lantern. Along the back wall, hung a sail. Painted on the canvas was a map of the island. The circular bay in the south and the mountain where they hiked. There was also a stretch to the north and a series of small islands of the east coast. The men held out their lights to examine the piece. Others looked around to find cots and old tools. The musty room looked to have been abandoned for years.

"By God, this much is true…" Clay admitted. As he stood with the rest, in awe of their discovery. Torie and Welham were looking at ways to take down the sail.

"Leave it," Levi quickly intervened. "I'll copy it down. But leave the sail. In fact, we'll each draw a copy, to ensure we don't miss any details," Welham stepped away from the sail and went to explore more on his own.

The men spent the evening in the cave. Most sat against the wall, waiting for their turn to draw the map, having only one pen and notebook. Levi and Clay sat on the cots, comparing their drawings, torn out of the journal, to the original. The map was telling a story and Levi was trying to read it. The map told where men struggled and drowned, where the survivors hid, and where they ultimately buried the treasure. "There's nothing on the map about the gold. Just ambiguous landmarks," Levi sighed.

"One of them has to be it," Clay coughed. He did not seem half as worried as Levi.

"No grave markers or the like."

"Grave markers?"

"It's said the men are buried with the gold."

"I don't see why he left a map in the first place, if he wasn't going to mark it with a big red X."

"So only they could find it again. But that's if they forgot where it was buried," Clay thought aloud. His tattooed arms behind his head as he leaned against the cave. "Yeah, I have no ideas."

When Gail finally emerged from the jungle, it was near dusk. At the beach, the found the rest of the men working on their hut. They fashioned rope to tie the timber together. The rope was made from small saplings, slicing down the middle into thin strips of fiber. They braided the strips into cords and knotting the ends. Some had blades to cut with, others took their shovels and used them as axes to cut down bigger trees. Wooden trunks made the floors and the three walls. Leaves and palm branches covered the roof to keep out any rain.

After they were done building, Cook lead the hunt for food. Some gathered the various yellow fruits and red berries the land provided. Others went to try their hand at killing an iguana they found on the beach. Crofton threw his dagger. It struck the lizard but didn't stick into its scales. The men laughed as it hissed and turned towards them. The iguana ran after them, the crew swinging at it with whatever they had in their hands to hunt with. Harper took out his sword and slashed at the animal. He was the youngest of the crew, only a few years older than Levi. A goatee filled his face and matched his dark eyes. His dark hair was tied back behind his head. He sliced several more times at the lizard until he finally struck it.

They cooked the iguana over a fire that night. Each man ripping off one piece at a time. Sparks flying up from the flames meshed with the light of the stars. Crofton stared into the water, looking for the green streaks he saw when they first came in.

"There's nothing in there," Cook said to Crofton.

"I'm telling you, I saw something," He defended. As the men each laid down in the hut to go to sleep, Crofton stayed awake. He kept watch from what he feared may come out of the bay. Stories said the drowned crew comes out of the water at night to kill anyone who dare camp on the island's shores. Crofton ran those stories over in his head until he passed out on the beach.

"By my beard, you're all still alive!" Gail exclaimed as he saw the line return out of the jungle the next day.

"You ain't got a beard," Crofton joked as he practiced throwing his knife into the wall of their shack.

"Did you find anything?" Gail asked.

"We found the map room, but nothing that leads us directly to the gold," Levi shook his head.

"Maybe there's more we have to find. A key or a puzzle piece or..." Gail trying to add some optimism to the quest.

"I don't know. Everyone took a copy of the map. So, maybe we'll find something."

"You don't actually have the map?"

"It was too big and frail to move. We couldn't risk moving it. These will have to do," Levi held up the copies in his hand. "Turn over a boat, we'll lay them out and study them. Maybe we'll find something if we all look."

The crew took a rowboat from shore and brought it over to their camp. Flipping it over, Levi placed the maps on the flat keel, using rocks to hold them down from the wind blowing off the sea.

"It's a moon!" Welham debated confidently.

"It's a C!" The sailors argued over all the maps. Each different from the next. Each symbol slightly altered from the original.

"Well, if you combine em, maybe they spell something," Crofton scratched his head.

"You idiot! These were all taken from the same map. Besides, you aren't fooling anyone. We all know you can't read!" The mob grumbled and bantered.

"This was a bad idea," Levi said under his breath. He scratched the hair growing on his face as he walked away from the group.

"What if — You just shut up — What if the gold is still in the boat?" The rowdy bunch all grew quiet as they stared at the man named Tanner, who gave the idea. Levi turned back to see men already jumping into the rowboats and paddling over to the shipwreck.

"I didn't say I wanted to dive to find it!" The sailors on the boat were attempting to throw Tanner into the water. He grabbed the seat and rail and anything he could hold to keep himself from going over. He grabbed the anchor and gripped it close to him.

"Mate, that just helps you dive," Jack said with a smirk. They picked Tanner up by the legs and flipped him overboard. The anchor pulled him under, deeper toward the seafloor. His screams came up as bubbles. Soon though, his panic cooled as the anchor halted, running out of line. He found himself suspended in the middle of the ancient wreckage. He let go of the iron piece and dove further down, his ears popping with pressure. Fish swam away as the curious diver intruded on their homes. His hands hit the corroded bars of the cargo hold. Shadows made it difficult to see what was inside the ship. The sun's light couldn't penetrate into the body from the angle it was in the sky. He pressed his face against the grate to see if he could spot anything. The cold metal scratched his face. His eye peering into the blackness. From his peripheral view, Tanner saw movement by the captain's quarters. He went to swim toward it, but he found his ankle was bound, gripped by a tentacle reaching from below the deck. As Tanner tried to pull it away, he looked up to see someone on the ship with him. A sailor, standing on the crooked deck as if a different gravity still bound him to it. The dead man began to walk toward Tanner, constricted, kicking more than ever to be freed.

The sailors on the rowboat were completely oblivious to the fate of their shipmate down below. Sitting and joking, eating fruit they brought on board. They saw bubbles popping on the surface but couldn't hear Tanner's cry for help. The diver began to drown, having screamed all the air out of his lungs. The undead sailor unsheathed his cutlass and pointed it at Tanner. His flesh was green and blue, algae growing on his skin and hair. He swung at the diver, who kicked his leg up, so the blade cut the writhing tentacle. He swam up with all of his force. The sunlight above, now fading to black. He reached for the anchor rode, but could not feel it, nor anything else. The cold water numbed him, as well as the lack of oxygen killed his senses.

"Christ!" Torie dove in, seeing that Tanner was now floating freely. He pulled him on board, looking down to the ship in horror, which now lay empty. "Bring us in," They rowed ashore and left Tanner to himself to cough up water he had taken in.

"Did you see anything?" Levi asked him. "Any gold?"

"Gold sir, no," Tanner hacked and spat more seawater out from his lungs. "Sea monsters, aye."

"Sea monsters?" Crofton nearly fell backwards.

"Like ye said, the undead crew."

"Enough!" Clay's voice hushed the rumble of men.

"I know what I saw," Tanner pleaded. "This isn't a good island. It's accursed."

"There are no undead on the island," he says again.

"What's the next move, captain?" Welham came up behind Levi, the crew waiting by their hut.

"Those who stayed here will come up with me to the cave. They can draw their maps, so we have more to go off of. Maybe I'll see something I didn't the first time," Levi addressed his crew. "Rest of you, maybe walk the beach. See if you can't overturn something, alright?"

"Me too, sir," Tanner pushed up from the sand.

"You sure you feel up to it?" Levi asked, looking concerned.

"Aye," He nodded. Tanner's chest still hurt, but he was eager to find the treasure like the rest of them. Levi led his group up the trail. Crofton, Tanner, Harper, and Gail following behind with two of the other sailors. Their names were Flint and Lea, but most addressed them as the brothers. Levi trimmed the walking trail further with his sword, cutting off leaves that were hanging low in their path. Grass and dirt below getting packed down from the lines of men retracing the ancient trail.

Along the beach, Welham and Cook trampled through the brush to find any clues or marks of the buried gold. The two walked the peninsula that arched around the bay. Torie had his map in hand as he went up the east shore. The island grew taller as he went further away from the bay. Cliffs and stacks lined the edge of the island. Great pillars of rock reaching out from the foaming waves below. He walked along the top of the cliff, scanning the shore, and occasionally looking over the edge to see if he could spot anomalies in the rock formations. Clay went on his own up the western shore. Foothills came down at the base of the mountain and sloped down to the long stretch of beach. As Clay walked the sand, he saw the mountain extended toward the north of the island before it leveled out again.

"Anything?" Welham called over to Torie as he returned to camp that afternoon. The man shook his head and sat down at the fire next to him. Cook was roasting some fish the men caught earlier. "We walked up and down this whole bay. Not a thing. No signs or *graves*. Starting to think this all may be a sham."

"You don't think there's any treasure?" Torie looked at him, worriedly. Behind them, the silver of the moon glistened off the soft waves.

"I think it's possible that there is no gold here. Just a map to take us as fools. Running in circles around the island, never finding a single piece," Welham sighed.

"Been long since we've had pay," Cook added. "I need there to be gold on this island."

"There is," Torie affirmed. "It's been buried for half a century, maybe more. We're not the first to set out to find it. If it's still here, it's well hidden. If it were recovered, I'm sure we would have heard about it."

"Besides, what better do we have to do?" Cook looked up from the fire at Welham. "Beats sitting in port all day."

The team on the mountain made a campfire in the cave as they studied the map. The dew inside was dripping down to the floor. Moisture also collected on the sail that hung freely from the wall. It stained the map and distorted the ink that was embedded it the old fabric. Levi sat where he did earlier, comparing his drawing to the original. The slightest blotch or mark threw the young man for a spin. What was a part of the original map and what was added with age wasn't clear. Levi tried to pull meaning out of each smudge, interpreting each iota on the sail. Nothing he gave meaning to confidently pointed to the buried treasure.

"Give it up, captain," Harper sighed as he approached Levi. "We can't find anything."

"It has to be here," Levi shook his head. "What are we missing?" He looked frantically at the map. Sounds of the night rang into the cave. Chirps from birds and bugs, sometimes not able to tell which was which. Wind filled the lungs of the caves, pushing water off the wall before it was ready to drip.

"Maybe there is no gold."

"Why would someone draw up a map otherwise?"

"Out of boredom? Marooned here and had nothing else to do. Rumors can be deceiving. We've found nothing to suggest there's actually gold here."

"There has to be," Levi looked down at the map in his hands.

6.

Under the Red X.

"Your stories are renowned. Here as much as in Spain," Admiral Juan Esteban slowly circled around the room, addressing the man standing in the center. "Rumored to soon be receiving a *Caballero hidalgo,* am I correct?"

"Yes sir," The man wore a serious face.

"Nobility due to a lifestyle of piracy. Knighted for being a killer. That makes your head spin, doesn't it? Although, since you have always contributed to the crown and never attacked a Spanish vessel, you are considered a necessary evil in the seas. A loose cannon pointed at the enemy."

"I am more than a pirate," The man lifted his chin, insulted.

"So, you say. The only reason you have not been hanged for brigandry is because you are so loyal to Spain. So, pirate or not, we graciously keep you around," Esteban nodded.

"I appreciate it, sir," The man said, huffing out his temper.

"Your kind is becoming more common here. Thieves are ruling the seas where Spain should be. These thieves taking what is rightfully ours."

"As long as there has been gold, there are those who seek it," The man said plainly.

"Which is why Spain needs her privateer. A protector."

"You want to hire me to protect your ships? Isn't that the reason you have a navy?"

"The navy defends our ports. I need someone on the offensive. These pirates are becoming more frequent and far too little is being done about it by our own navy. As Admiral of the Treasure Fleet, I am commissioning you to hunt down these thieves wherever they stalk Spanish waters. Make it safe for us to transport our gold. With the intent of course, you continue to pay your spoils back to the crown. I have your letter of marque already written."

"So, I am to do all your work and *you* get all the spoils."

"Of course, I know you do not work for free. Ten percent of the gold and silver can go right into your pocket. All goods commandeered come back to Havana. You have any piece from our fleet at your disposal. You are to captain the mission for the king of Spain. Truly a great honor if you accept."

"It is an honor indeed. For king and for country," The man agreed and saluted softly from his tricorn hat.

"Then I'll have you escorted to our port, Amaro."

Amaro Pargo had a black ponytail and a thin mustache on his scarred face. He wore a fine saber on his hip. His red leather waistcoat stood out among his own crew of tattered buccaneers. He was known across all of Spain for sailing between the Caribbean and the known world, pirating any vessel not under the Spanish flag. His devote loyalty to country and superior skills on the water made him a legend among Spaniards.

"The *San Francisco*, seventy guns," An officer escorted Amaro down the pier to find a ship of his choosing. "The *Santiago*, eighty guns," Amaro shook his head again. "*Nuestra Señora de la Concepción y las Ánimas*. Otherwise known as the *Spitfire*. Holds ninety-four guns."

"This one," He pointed to the red warship with white sails. It, like any other in the fleet, flew a huge white flag with a red X, signifying its Spanish origin.

"She has three decks of guns, as you can see, and can hold up to five hundred and fifty men. It is our largest gunship on this side of the ocean."

"It will be used to bring glory to Spain," Amaro walked up the gangplank. His black boots knocked with command, letting those on deck know he was in authority. "Tell my crew to load our gunpowder and weaponry onto this ship."

"Sir, this ship is highly equipped on its own," The officer protested. Amaro turned, towering over the officer. "Aye, sir. Right away," The uniformed officer caved.

Amaro took control of the *Nuestra Señora*. His own crew filled the ship, joining the other Spanish sailors assigned to that vessel. His men took a day to transfer their supplies to the new ship. The next day, men on the docks threw off the moorings, the sailors aboard quickly pulled the line on deck. They ran the line, laying it on top of itself in a figure eight. At the same time, men fed lines through the system of pullies to lower the sails. As the *Nuestra Señora* drifted away from the dock, the sailcloth filled with wind. The man at the helm, called a coxswain, stirred the wheel, painted white and decorated with a Turk's head knot on each peg. Cranking the wheel around, he stirred the rudder below deck and a small triangular sail on the rear-most mast. They began coasting along the north side of Cuba, east of Havana.

"Navigator," Amaro went to the men at the helm. The wind blew gently for them, pushing the ship with the clouds in the sky. "Bring our heading to forty-five degrees."

"Aren't we sailing along the coast?" The coxswain asked, not moving from his course.

"Do you question me?" Amaro walked closer to them, both the navigator and the man at the helm.

"It's just that'll be bringing us towards the Bahamas. That's English waters, captain."

"Spain has enough coastguardsmen as it is. I was not commissioned to be just another patrol ship. Now bring us to our bearing!" Amaro snapped.

"Admiral Esteban said that we were only to make our own waters safer," The coxswain refuted, still not moving the ships wheel to change their direction. "If we attacked near English land, it would provoke them. I believe the admiral's orders surpass yours," Some of the crew had stopped working to listen in. The crew of men Amaro took on were the first to shutter at the disobedience.

"Is that so?" Amaro said between his teeth.

"I am loyal to the admiral without-" Amaro grabbed the man by the neck and threw him to the deck. He yelped and scrambled to get up, but Amaro kicked him and dragged him by the collar. The captain threw the helmsman down the wooden stairs to the weather deck. The crew hushed at the sight. Only a soft breeze moved through the ship, the men all frozen in fear.

"Tie him to the mast!" Amaro ordered his men. Those who were sailing under him before were quick to respond. The sailors given to Amaro in Havana looked to each other in anxiety of what was to come. The captain removed his coat and took a whip from out of his cabin. "I will have discipline on my vessel. As your captain, you will do as I say. Is that understood?" Amaro addressed his crew. Sheepishly they nodded and mumbled. "I said is that understood?!"

"Aye," The crew agreed. The captain rolled up the sleeves of his black frill shirt.

"Is that understood, mister coxswain?" Amaro squatted down next to the man. He was put on his knees with his arms wrapping around the wooden beam and tied together.

"Yes, sir," The sailor trembled and nodded. Tears swelling up in his eyes. Amaro stood and walked back a few paces.

"Good, then we should have no issues here," The captain said. The man sighed with relief, thinking he was going to be let go. Then Amaro turned and cracked the whip against the sailors back. He screamed and bent his back in pain. With the swing of his arm, Amaro lashed the whip and cut deep into the sailors back. The snap of the leather rang out across the ship. The sailor panted as blood and tears fell from him, onto the deck. Amaro motioned to his men who promptly came over and cut the man's hands free. He collapsed on the deck, not moving.

"I believe I said forty-five degrees, mister coxswain," Amaro spat on the man, who could barely push himself off the boards. "Rest of you, back to your posts!"

"Prepare port side cannons!" A mangy captain ordered. His crew of fallen privateers jumped to their guns and loaded cannons with powder. The *Nuestra Señora* gained on the smaller vessel, coming up alongside of it. The great red ship with white trim towered over its prey in every respect.

"Fire the chase guns!" Amaro ordered. Cannons roared from the bow of the ship, blowing holes into the brig they were chasing. "Prepare to board. Starboard side, ready your cannons!" The pirate crew began firing their rifles as the *Nuestra Señora* drew near. "Hook onto that ship!"

Hooks and harpoons were thrown onto the deck, men pulling on their line from the other boat. Several cannons fired into the hull of the *Nuestra Señora*. Yet the sheer number of men flooding to the smaller vessel overwhelmed the crew. They shot their flintlocks and unsheathed their swords, but the Spanish force quickly overtook them.

"Mercy!" Their captain yelled. "We surrender," Amaro walked over to the man, judging this man's right to be a captain. His forces surrounding the smaller crew.

"A pirate asking for mercy?" The Spaniard questioned. "Am I to assume you gave mercy to anyone you stole from?"

"We only held up merchants and took from wrecks. Ye can ask any of me men," The captain with his hands in the air slowly began to lower his arms.

"Bind them up," Amaro called to his crew. They took line and tied those who were left alive to the masts. "Unload their cargo."

"Aye, cap'n," Amaro's crew took aboard their goods, including gold, spices, and close to a dozen slaves. Amaro went back to his ship with them.

"You want mercy, captain?" He called over to the pirate, whose hands were also bound. "I'm not a man known for mercy, but I'll let your men swim," The opposing crew looked around with anxiety. "Sink them."

As the *Nuestra Señora* pushed off, they fired their starboard cannons, battering the side of the ship. It quickly filled with water, which began to press down. The men tied to the masts hollered and squirmed, but soon found themselves being pulled to the abyss. The black flag was the last thing seen before the whole ship disappeared into the darkness.

"*Ándale.*"

The *Nuestra Señora* sailed through the seascape. With each encounter, they defeated the opposing crew with more brutality, sinking any plundered ships they came across. Any survivors left behind had to swim their way back to civilization. No crew dared try to take or stop the floating fortress. The men grew nastier and fought with rage under their new captain. Soon, Amaro found the men itching for battle. He was waiting until he found a pirate ship to cut loose, but his men were starting to demand they go after any ship not under the Spanish flag.

"He's turning my men piratical," Admiral Esteban sunk in his desk after hearing the reports of their activities. "That bastard took my ship and used it for his own gain."

"Actually, sir. You gave him the ship."

"¡Cállate!" He snapped. "I swear if that brigand makes a fool of me, I'll see the king himself puts him to death!"

"Perhaps he's just breaking in his crew."

"We hired him to take out these pirates, but he's plundering anyone for his own gain!"

"He could be fighting fire with fire. Perhaps he knows how to best them using their own methods."

"Draft up a bounty for him."

"Sir?"

"As soon as he even aims a gun at one of our own, we're hunting him down!" He went to look out the window, wanting to ease his trouble. "I'm going to find where these pirates are nesting and blow it to shreds."

"At the end of the day, sir, what matters is that they bring gold to Spain," The officer shrugged. "You said it yourself, Amaro is a necessary evil. If that evil brings us gold and silver, so be it. But, aye, we'll hang any man who turns on us."

The Port of Gold

7.

The Unwelcomed Return.

A flush of water met the men of the *Gail Wickman* as they landed back at Shorehaven. Each crew member splashed a bucket of boiled seawater to wash away the Curse, fearing it may have followed them back. The small vessel had nothing to unload except, its weary crew. They grumbled at their now soaking clothes, though it would soon dry up in the morning heat. From the mayor's mansion, Segar saw the ship return to port, securing its moorings to the dock. He stepped outside, startled to find a dead seagull at his door. With a huff of anger, Segar kicked it away with his heavy boots, then headed straight down the road to the pier.

"By your spirits, I'd say you didn't find it. That or you finally learned your lesson," Segar scolded Levi.

"We didn't find the gold, but I'm afraid I have not learned my lesson," Levi tried to walk past.

"Watch your tongue, boy!" Segar snapped, yanking Levi's shirt, then shoving him away. "Anyone falls sick or dies, it'll be your Godforsaken head."

Levi ripped away, fixing his blue coat as he walked off.

"Levi Benson! You dragged my husband..." Levi brushed off the woman who was attempting to scold him as well. "Clay Clair! You leave me again like that and you'll be sleeping in your boat for a month!"

The young man pushed open the door at the Rogue Star and sat down at the counter. With his hand, he wiped off the water that was on his face. He pulled his loose hair back and fixed the tie.

"Welcome back," Smith said over his shoulder, already pouring Levi a cold drink. "You know, liquor is a good cure for-"

"The Curse?" Levi interrupted. He slowed his breath after realizing he snapped at his friend.

"I was gonna say *sorrows*. You look tense, my boy."

"I'm sorry. We found a map but no treasure, and we almost lost a crewman," Levi took the pint in his hand.

"Aye, that is tough."

"And now I have Segar breathing down my neck and everyone else giving me looks," He pointed behind him to the rest of the tavern. The townsfolk quickly turning back to their business. Smith looked on him with empathy for a moment.

"That's cause we take the Curse seriously," The man went around the counter and sat next to Levi. "It's hard for us to see a newcomer, who we welcomed into our lives, not take our tradition seriously. We fear the Curse and the island because we've seen its wrath and horror. It isn't just monsters or storms, it brings. But madness, too. It's already growing. Making everyone, not just ye crew, tense and angry with each other. That much gold, accursed or not, drives men sick. Maybe Segar is mad because of your disobedience, but the old man and I, we just hate to see you hurt."

"Thanks, Smithy," Levi took a drink from the pint. Smith left him to return to work as others in the tavern wanted their drinks. The young man sat in silence while he finished his drink. Not one particular thought went through his mind. Just a haze of anger and frustration. As he drank, he tried to calm himself down but the tension he felt in his mind only grew. When Levi finished, he pushed out the door without saying a word to Smith. He was heading toward the pier when he noticed the lighthouse to his left. He had almost forgotten he had to go home to

Northrop. Going back to the ship, Levi grabbed his bag from the officer's quarters and walked the length of the pier over to the lighthouse.

"Saw you come into port," Northrop exhaled a puff of smoke from his pipe, sitting at the dining table.

"We didn't find it," Levi went to go upstairs.

"Maybe that's for the best," The old man thought.

"To sacrifice so much for nothing?" Levi turned from the steps. "To almost lose a life?"

"Aye. Better that than to have found the gold and actually lost someone," Northrop watched as Levi shook his head and climbed up to his room. Levi took the map out from his coat and studied it under the candle he lit. The events on the island ran through his mind. He saw the sail hung in that forgotten cave. He saw the *Puerto Oro*, lurking in the bay. Levi no longer saw what was in front of him, but rather the images in his mind. And as he thought over their voyage, he passed out.

January 1715

Not everyone is thrilled about our return. Clay's wife especially angry with us. She may be the only one I feel sorry for. None of the rest of us had family to worry about. Most, with Mrs. Clair, have avoided us altogether. So far, I'm still able to go into town to buy supplies and food, but their conviviality with me is running short.

I suppose I have Mertie. Lord only knows how she feels now after I left her to go to the Isla Maldito. I feel sorry for her, too. In my heart I hoped Northrop would be understanding, but I don't know how she ever could be.

I've been dreaming lately, since before we left for the Island. When I dream, I think they're memories about the voyage over here, though I'm not entirely sure. I see myself, sailing my boat through the storm. I see the island in the distance, with the light reaching out to me. I want to say it's the lighthouse, but this light comes from below, as if from the sea. The dark clouds make everything grey and black, everything except the beacon that would lead me to shore.

As I get closer to this island, I see a cave. Blacker than night, deeper and more void than the abyss. It's from this cave where the golden light shines from. Its jagged rocks are a crude welcome ashore, but then the last thing I remember was waking up on the rocks of Shorehaven. And the dream ends.

I remember now I'm from Charleston, I've seen that too in my sleep. The name echoes in my mind, I have no doubt that's where I'm from. I must've sailed quite a bit back home if my nautical knowledge was all I retained when I hit my head. After we get the gold, I intend to sail back. Hopefully find my family. Otherwise, Shorehaven is an agreeable enough island. Perhaps I'll stay and keep the lighthouse after old Northrop is gone. I'm getting ahead of myself. We still need to find the gold.

"Not a lot of stock to sell?" Levi asked Hurley in the market. The stall was nearly empty that afternoon. No barrels full of fish for Hurley to work through. The people who were out in town spoke quietly as they passed Levi. Only the sound of shoes hitting the stone road spoke to him.

"Been bad pickings lately," The grimy man scratched his face with his fillet knife before going back to his work. "Not too long after you's all left, the numbers been going down."

"Huh," Levi raised his brows. "Well, I'll just take the two then. Don't want to buy out your shop," Levi's smile quickly went away as the man gave him a crooked eye.

"You go fishing out with Clay again, you let me know what you pull in," he said as he wrapped the two large fillets in paper.

"Will do, sir," Levi turned to walk to the ship. Hurley glared at Levi as he went down the road. He turned and went back to work, chopping down with his knife and slicing a fillet off the fish's body. As Levi was leaving the markets, he felt eyes watching him. Scornful eyes, looking at the expatriate.

"Levi!" A familiar voice met his ears. The welcoming tone however was foreign compared to his recent encounters.

"Mertie," Levi turned to be met with a hug from the girl, wearing her usual modest-style dress.

"How I've missed you. I heard you had returned, but I haven't seen you around."

"I've been hiding from town. They're all pretty upset with me. I thought you would be, too..." The young man scratched his head, almost in shock that she wasn't part of the mob going after him.

"Heavens, no. I'm glad you're safe," She grabbed his hand and held it tightly. "They said you went to the Island, but you're with me now, so I know that's not true."

"No. What they're saying is true."

"Why would you go there? Such an evil place and..." Mertie let his hand slip from her grasp. "That island..."

"To see if the stories were true. To find that long forgotten treasure. Just think of the life we could have if I found only a fraction of the gold buried beneath that shore."

"Levi," She sighed, not allowing herself to be swept away in the young man's ambitions. "I am happy here with the things that I have. I am happy here with you. No treasure could ever give me more than that. That gold won't make you love me more."

"I have to find it. I-" Levi stopped to see her mournful expression. "Dear, this is what I want."

"I know," She took a step backwards.

"What's wrong?"

"I am in love with you," She pleaded. "All I want is for you to settle down here with me. But I see now that you don't want the same."

"That isn't fair," Levi swallowed.

"You want what's out there. In the world. If you're out there, you can't be here. You can't have it all. I won't be some sailors widow, waiting for her husband to come home," She wiped a tear from her eye. "Good day, Mister Benson."

Levi stood as the lady walked back into town. Looking up in frustration, he huffed and went down to the pier.

The *Gail Wickman* was raised for careening. Over the last several days, the crew scrubbed the underside of the ship. It was rolled up onto braces using logs at the far end of the dock. Segar saw to it the ship be cleaned, wanting to scrub the Curse off of the boat. Coral had grown wildly on the wooden boards, like yellow flowers protruding from the keel.

"Ever seen anything like this?" Cook asked, tired from their work.

"Not unless a ship sailed straight through a reef," Crofton replied, having done this on other ships he served.

"You sure we didn't?"

"I know what I saw. Sea ghosts, mate."

"Cook," Levi called as he approached the vessel. "Got some fillets here when you want to make dinner."

"Aye, sir," He called back.

Levi dropped the fillets in the galley and went up into the cabin. The maps spread out on the desk. Clay sitting inside, eating an apple as he lounged. Levi went to study the maps. Each copy different from the next. Some markings appeared in most of the maps, while others only appeared in a few. Most men could not even copy the shape of the island right.

"We have to go back and look at the original. We're not going to get anywhere with these. I don't even know if my map is right," Levi shuffled the papers in his temper. "What do these symbols even mean? A moon, a cross, and a *V*... Maybe they are letters. What's Spanish for ship?"

"Uh, *velero*. Right? I hardly speak English, lad." Clay had been sitting on the cushioned bench, both men ostracized from town.

"And grave?"

"*Tumba*," he said softly.

"And *C* for cave or whatever that is in Spanish," Levi concluded. "That's where we found the map. The rest of the symbols are landmarks. I'm sure of it."

"Is there a *T* on the map?" Clay walked over to the desk.

"Right there," Levi pointed. "On the north side. The little cross. That's where the gold is."

The two left the pier to tell the rest of the crew about the discovery and to prepare for a second voyage. The water below them brought in schools of dead fish, building up on the rocks with the ocean foam. On the *Gail Wickman*, some remaining members were lounging and drinking. The brothers went into the captain's quarters looking for more rum, as the returning sailors broke into the last of the barrels Gail had on stock.

"Dozen treasure maps, you would think one of them would have a hint of gold," Lea thought.

"Aye. Lot of men would pay mighty fine just to have one," Flint smirked. They stared at the stack of papers for a while. Then they looked at each other. "We each take one or two, then we can copy them's later," They folded up several of the maps and tucked them into the pockets on their coat and trousers. The two slipped away into the night, having it in mind to jump ships the next day.

"Aye, now we have more of a precise target to aim for," Levi told the crew of sailors that were found drinking at the Rogue Star.

"We thought you knew where the gold was the first time!" Welham objected.

"I never said that," Levi defended.

"Aye, we expected to get paid for this work. How am I to feed me-self now? We's been without pay for too long and we're sick of it!" Harper added.

"Well, to heck with the idea! I almost lost me life. Not to mention my leg still has an octopus imprint!" Tanner showed his scar. The others joined in, sharing their complaints.

"So, the gold isn't worth it for you? More bloody gold than the New World has ever known," Levi implored.

"What's the point of getting the gold if ye gonna die for it anyway?" Tanner kept complaining.

"What's the point of living with nothing? Lads, this gold will repay any risk taken for those daring enough."

"Forget it, cap'n. We're not sailing to no Cursed Island again." They grumbled. "Aye, we've had enough!"

"Hey!" A loud voiced silenced the whole pub. "You've done it this time, Levi!" A fisherman stormed in and threw down a net full of dead fish. They were corroded or bitten out of. The net stunk the whole room. Some of the men covering their mouths at the foul stench. "You brought the bloody Curse to us, you bastard! No one's been able to catch anything that ain't rotten!"

"You all washed us clean when we came in, didn't you?" The young man stood. The fisherman clocked Levi in the jaw, staggering him backwards. Levi threw himself up off the table and swung back at the man. Others quick to restrain them both, who continued to kick at the other.

"I oughta gut you, boy!" The fisherman spat, struggling to get back up to his feet. "You killed us all!"

"Come get it," Levi jeered, still fighting against the sailors that held him back.

"Oi!" Smith snapped. "Take your brawling outside! No need for that in here."

Levi straightened up, put on his coat and, with Clay and Gail, left the tavern. The fisherman glaring at them as they passed. The other sailors settled down and returned to their drinks. Tanner began to stumble about. He tried to talk, but no words came from his tongue.

"Out with it, lad," Torie joked, then gave him a closer look. "Oi, you look sick, mate."

"He's drunk like the rest of you. Put him outside in the open air," Smith called from behind the counter, shaking his head. Torie led his crewmate out the door. He collapsed, gasping for air, and gripping his throat. The sailor doubled over, trying to vomit. Then a pool of ink expelled from his mouth. The black fluid dribbling from his lips.

"Jesus Christ," Torie gasped. "Let's get you to the doctor!" He picked up Tanner from the ground and helped him into town to find the physician's office.

"Doctor!" Torie cried as he entered. A bell on the door frame rang excitedly.

"No! Get that cursed man out of here!" The nurse shoed them away, as she hugged the back wall.

"Leave em be," The doctor came in, putting on his apron. "What's the emergency?"

"He's spitting ink, sir. Choking on it, I reckon," Torie and the doctor put Tanner on the operation table as he started to tremble. His limbs began to shake more heavily. Tanner contorted and black pitch pooled out of his mouth. His eyes rolling back as his head rocked, slamming from the table to his own chest.

"Strap em down! Did he eat or drink anything funny?" The doctor ordered Torie and the nurse as he got out his toolset. "What is that?" He yelled. From the sailor's gut, a mass emerged and began on beat and move up into the rib cage. Tanner seizing and shaking uncontrollably.

"Get that out of him!" Torie insisted.

"I can't do that while he's living! Anything I could do would kill him!" Doctor unrolled his set of tools and looked between them and his patient frantically.

"He's gonna die anyway," The nurse shrieked. The mass slithered up to his throat, swelling his neck. From the sailor's mouth, now forced open, two tentacles appeared. Soon, other limbs followed as the purple-red octopus inside him was attempting to get free. It crawled and spat itself onto the sailor's chest. Torie drew his flintlock and shot the mollusk in fear. He stepped back, trembling, leaning against the wall for comfort. The office sat in silence and disbelief as the ringing of the gunshot dampened.

"Get him out of here," The doctor fell back to his stool, staring at the floor in shock. The nurse put her hand over her gaping mouth and went into the other room.

"What the heck, Torie?" The sailors at the docks stumbled at the sight of Tanner, dead in his arms. They were just putting the *Gail Wickman* back into the water when Tanner's body was brought to them.

"The Curse got him," Torie dropped to his knees on the deck, the cadaver in his arms. Tanner's chest was blown in and pieces of the fiend still remained suctioned to his body. Torie, who was beat from shock and exhaustion, no longer noticed any of this.

"That's it, we're leaving this port!" The sailors on the *Gail Wickman* threw down what they were doing and hoped off the ship to find another. Townsfolk who followed Torie back to the pier began to gather around.

"It's here!" They cried. "The Curse is here!" Levi jumped over the taffrail to see what was happening. Gail close behind taking the gangplank down to the pier.

"What happened to him?" Levi asked Torie, seeing the hole in Tanner's chest, bleeding onto the pier.

"There was an octopus inside him, sir. It was the abomination that killed em! An' I shot it…"

"Get off our dock, you bastards!" The townsfolk began to yell at the sailors, pushing them back to their ship.

"You killed em, ye hear!"

"You murdered him for going to that wicked place!"

Levi looked around into the eyes of the angry people and saw no one defending him or mourning his crewmate. No words rising above the shouting that was on his side.

"Enough!" Another booming voice came through. People quickly moved aside to allow Segar to walk up to the scene. "As mayor, it's my duty to protect this town. The Curse *has* followed you back from the island and I warned there would be hell to pay. Levi Benson, Clay Clair, Gail Wickman! You are banished from Shorehaven. You will be sent back to the island, so the Curse can deal with you how it sees fit."

"Uncle, you can't," Gail stepped forward in protest.

"Shut it!" Segar back handed the young man.

"And if we sail our asses somewhere else?" Welham shrugged. "What'll ye do?"

"A cursed man is one thing but running from a curse is a whole nastier lot," Crofton protested. "We can't run."

"Northrop will escort you to the island," Segar commanded without hesitation. "I'll put bounties on all of you. The authorities would chop you up as soon as you touched their pier. Besides, we all know your *captain* is bent to return," He pointed at Levi.

From inland, Flint and Lea hid in the shadows, watching all this take place. In the morning, they would board Morillo's cargo ship and sail away.

"You can't do this!" Harper drew his sword. Others pulled out their pistols from their belts. Crofton readied his knife to throw. Soon townsmen armed themselves with raised fists and whatever weapon they were carrying. Leatherneck Jack grabbed a pitchfork from one of the townsmen.

"Get on the ship," Levi ordered between his teeth. His crew looked at each other, puzzled by their captain backing down. "I said get on the ship!" They went up the gangway, sheathing their blades.

"Someone get the old man," Segar called to the mob.

"No bother," He stepped onto the pier in his retired navy uniform, glaring at Segar through the smoke of his pipe. His yellow peacoat stood out against his black boots and peaked hat. "I'm right here."

8.

Set Sail for the Curse.

"Brace yourselves!" The Spanish mariner crew hunkered down as an opposing ship rammed straight into them. The construction extending off the front of the enemy ship shattered against hull of the *Nuestra Señora*. Boards flew through the hot air. The jolt shook the sweat off of the men who were now colliding with blades. The ships drifted after the collision, racing each other on the rolling sea.

"Fire the port side cannons!" Amaro commanded. The guns thundered as the iron horrors tore apart the bow of the enemy ship. The bowsprit collapsing and taking the foresail with it. This brig had brown sails and a series of black flags. Flags marked with ugly skulls. Marauders who jumped after the collision, now climbed up the shroud onto Amaro's ship. Spaniards fired their guns into the hoard of attackers.

"Chain shots!" One of the crewmen cried out. The Spaniards ducked as cannons from the brown ship fired straight on. Chains linked two smaller cannonballs, causing them to spin with fury, sweeping a wider range. This type of shot was effective for taking out masts, or men. The sailors used the gunwale as cover between shots of their muskets. Amaro stood and fired with his pistol into the opposing crew. The brig yawed and rolled back toward the *Nuestra Señora*, running side by side. What was left of the forepeak slowly caught fire, its barrels of cargo with it.

"Fireship!" Amaro called out. "Brace all you!" Cases of cannonballs and barrels of gunpowder set off as the ships smashed into each other. An explosion jerked each ship to its side. Fire shot into the gun ports and up the hull of the galleon. The *Nuestra Señora* rocked with the impact, waves crashing in from where the ship was now dipping toward the sea. It rolled back to upright, the wooden hull, still ablaze.

"Douse the flames!" The captain called. Sailors took buckets and splashed the fire that crept across the wooden structure. As the *Nuestra Señora* leveled out, they could see their enemy ship sinking, diving nose-first into the deep blue. Soon, the fire died out, thanks to the sea more than the sailors. Amaro watched in frustration as the ship they intended to commandeer was completely swallowed by the ocean. Its crew jumped overboard and took hold of the *Nuestra Señora* and began to climb aboard.

"We're not out of this yet!" Amaro called. The Spaniards surrounded and aimed their guns at the oncoming men.

"Mercy!" The pirates waved their hands as they were clinging to the side of the vessel, exhausted from the battle and their swim. "We surrender..." As soon as they reached the deck, the men were thrown down to the boards. Their hands were tied behind their backs and they were lined up on their knees. One of Amaro's men walked behind them and pressed his pistol against the backs of their heads.

"Thought you had a chance, did you? A handful of men against the hundreds onboard," Amaro sat on a barrel in front of them. He looked almost untouched from the battle, still wearing his heavy red coat.

"Better chance than the water," One of them joked.

"Search them," Amaro stood up and waved for his men to rummage through the captive's coats and pockets. The men resisted and struggled as their belongings and clothes were being ransacked. Anything the Spaniards found was confiscated.

"Their weapons were already forfeit, but they had some coin and this," A sailor handed Amaro a bag of gold and a rolled piece of parchment.

"Trade ledger? Letter to *madre*?" Amaro mocked as he loosened the leather tie around the scroll and looked at the paper. "A map!" He looked up in shock. "What is this?"

"They're selling those poppies all over New Providence. That's a map to the *Puerto Oro*, the lost ship full of Spanish gold. Everyone's going after it. So, they say."

"What island is this?"

"That's the thing, cap," The sailor shrugged, his hands still behind him. "No one knows. Said to be cursed, that's the only detail we know of it. That's why no one ain't found it yet."

"You could perhaps be useful to us. Find them a cage until they're ready to recommit their service," Amaro turned to his deckhands.

"Aye, you don't have to pressgang us, cap'n. We had no loyalty with that bastard. We's happily join yer crew."

"Very well," Amaro nodded then took the map and pouches of gold into his cabin.

"By God, what did you do to my ship?" Esteban stopped in his tracks to meet Amaro on the pier. The hull was burned and broken. Boards roughly patched the hole that was rammed in. Sails were roughly repaired, and the paint was clawed away.

"Hunting pirates doesn't come without a few scratches. Be happy she's still afloat."

"I suppose," Esteban sighed. "At least you are serving your purpose. Or I hope that is what you've done."

"Do not take me as diabolical," Amaro stopped Esteban as they proceeded away from the pier. "My ship's in your port. If I were giving myself your due spoils, you would see it. Your men are unloading the cargo hold as we speak."

"Did not mean to offend," Esteban sighed. "She just an expensive ship..."

They walked up to the admiral's office from the bay. The crew was still hard laboring, unloading plunder and working on repairs. Esteban's mansion was close to the water. It was built up on a stone foundation that oversaw the docks. The house was nearly a fort, with walled courtyards and guards watching the property from all sides.

"I came across a peculiar map," Amaro said in the main office. He studied the map of Cuba and its surrounding waters, painted on the south wall. "Took it off of a swab from another ship. He said they were selling them near Nassau."

"Wouldn't surprise me if those rapscallions forged it themselves to turn a profit," The admiral chuckled as his servant poured him a hot drink. "That British town is a mere pig sty. Filthy black flags are said to be held up there."

"Aye," Amaro considered for a moment that the admiral could be right. "But this map leads to the *Puerto Oro*."

"What?" Esteban nearly spat out his first sip of tea.

"Apparently a crew found the island the ship's wrecked on and drew the maps. Unable to find the gold themselves, they gave up and but some of them sailed to Nassau and started selling the charts there. I suppose to gain some profit from the unfruitful expedition."

"Where was this crew from?"

"He didn't know. Apparently, this island doesn't even exist on most charts," Amaro tried to find an island on the painting that matched the shape on his map.

"There're countless islands in the West Indies, they just don't know where to look," The admiral got up and walked over to Amaro, his shoes clicking on the tile floor. *El Puerto Oro* last set off, heading east. The captain tried to take a short cut around Crooked Island, instead of taking the usual route along La Florida. He ran aground on some uncharted land north of there. Apparently, the locals named it 'Isla Maldito.' I have a new course for you, Señor."

"You want me to fetch you the gold?"

"Fetch Spain the gold it already owns. A ship full of gold and silver could come in handy, make yourself a mighty fine profit as well. If you're up for it."

"And what if some crew from Nassau already took it and made off?" Amaro asked.

"As I've said, they don't know where to look. Even if the crew that found the island goes back for it, they would never tell others where it is. They'd want to keep the gold for themselves. Get to it before they do and if you don't, you best recover every coin they took from that island."

"For you or for Spain?" Amaro sized up Esteban, who was not nearly as brawny as the corsair.

"For Spain," He turned and went back to his desk. "You'll have to take your own ship while the *Señora* is under repair. We'll send a fleet behind you, to ensure you stay on schedule and to help hull away whatever we pull off that rock."

At the pier, Amaro and his crew transferred weaponry and supplies to his frigate, *El Ave María y Las Ánimas*. The sails caught wind and set course, east from Havana to the Cursed Island.

The crew of the *Gail Wickman* were almost all tanned in the arms and face for being out in the sun most days. Their ship stood becalmed out in the open with no winds to push them. The men sat on deck, waiting for the breeze to pick up. Salt from the water masked the smell of what was being cooked below deck in the galley. Cook was frying some fish in a pan that the men had caught. Steam filled the hot room, Cook wiping the sweat off his face with his forearm. Jack was sitting below with him, waiting eagerly for the food to finish.

"I'd say we book it, there's no way they would know," Welham thought aloud. He sat at the bow on top of a crate.

"He said he would put out wanted signs for us. Put out a bounty for the ship," Torie replied from the railing.

"But how would he know if we went? Besides we're ahead of him already," Harper joined. "I'm with Welham. We run. Leave the ship and scatter."

The crew on deck debated as officers inside the cabin also discussed the matters at hand. Torie was still in the crow's nest, looking out over the flattened water.

"We lost Tanner. The brothers didn't return with us. What is that, nine now?" Clay thought.

"Ten," Northrop corrected, since he was added to the banished crew.

"Aye, that's enough to make the journey still. Less to feed," Levi nodded. "I see no issue."

"You're still wanting to go?" Gail looked up, shaking his head, and smiling in disbelief.

"Aye, yes," Levi shook off his confusion. "You don't?"

"I'm with you. We'll sail wherever you go," Gail sighed. "Just wanted to know your call."

"We sail for the island. We sail around to the north side, where the tomb is," Levi pointed at his map, getting to business. Other looked at him, reluctant about his ambition.

"Are we sure we want to navigate those waters more than we need?" Gail went along. "I'd say land on the south shore where we did last. We don't know what else is in those waters."

"Otherwise, we hike through the jungle. We don't know what's in *there*," Clay added. "That seems like a long way to traverse."

"Aye, but the stacks and skerries around the north and east of the island are too dangerous to sail around in the fog," Northrop mentioned.

"And how would you know?" Gail asked.

"Just look at the map," He pointed it on the desk.

"Alright," Levi scratched his facial hair, not tending to it since his first voyage. "We land at the south shore and go through the island. And hope the jungle is safe enough."

In the hammocks at night, the crew aboard the *Gail Wickman* sat up, conniving with each other under the dimly burning lanterns. Flickers of light briefly revealed their murky faces. All men present, serious with intent.

"They be sailing us to the island, no doubt," Cook started.

"The way I see it, it's all their fault. We's been a good crew, just taking what order's given. They're the ones who are lusting for the gold," Crofton sat, holding his knife.

"What are you saying?" Cook asked.

"They're the ones cursed, just how the island cursed the officers of the *Puerto Oro*. If we run, the curse won't follow us, cause it be after them," Harper, the youngest said.

"Aye," Jack agreed.

"Rowboats won't hold us all, will they?" Crofton asked.

"But it'll hold *them*," Welham added.

"What exactly are you plotting at?" Cook now leaned forward.

"You know," Welham said sternly. The sailors looked at each other. "We don't owe a spit of loyalty to those bastards, they dug us into this mess and didn't even pay us. They can't take us all. They have two abled men, the landlubber, and the old dog. I say we demand the ship. Giving them a rowboat is more than mercy for what they put us through."

"Aye, someone draft up a pact, a *round robin*. Let it be official. So, we know they aren't no cowards among us," They took out a parchment and signed their names if they could write it, most signed with an X, though. On the top was written, 'mutiny.' Torie lay still in his hammock, overhearing the uprising.

"Anchor aweigh, lads!" Gail called from atop the stern castle, up by the helm. The crew looked at each other, not moving their lines, but gathering on deck. "What's this then?"

"A mutiny," Levi stepped out of the cabin with Torie behind him.

"You snitch!" Harper took out his saber and lunged at the traitor. He dodged then unsheathed his own cutlass to defend himself. The attacker backed down, grinning as he kept his blade pointed at the officers. "Don't matter anyhow, it's happening."

"What about a vote?" Northrop reasoned.

"Vote's a stalemate. It be five on five since Torie's now with you!" Cook argued.

"Unless you give the dead a vote," Challenged Welham.

"What?" Levi staggered back at the repulsive thought.

"Tanner died cause of you. Cause of this crew! He died for your filthy treasure," He pointed at Levi. "So, either you take our ballets or our bullets."

"Oh no, you men aren't going anywhere!" Gail called over, walking down the stairs to face them.

"Nay, *you* are," Welham mocked. The officers all stood with Gail, on the weather deck where the crew was arming themselves. "We'll be giving you an option, yeah."

"And what'll that be?" Levi demanded.

"You can row yourselves to the island," He pointed to the rowboat with his flintlock, then turned it to aim at Gail. "Or you can save yourselves the energy and have a burial at sea."

"The island's in sight, lad. Take the boat," Northrop cautioned. The mountain could be seen peeking through the clouds on the horizon. "No one has to draw blood."

Gail quivered in anxiety, his finger tapping his holster. Clay saw this and slowly moved toward Gail, putting out his hand to try and ease him. Yet Gail drew, fired, and hit Welham. The gunshot echoing across the open water. The sailor tried to shoot back, but his gun misfired.

"You idiot," Levi stepped past Gail, who was in shock to see the man bleeding out on the deck. Welham clenched his arm, where the bullet borrowed straight through. The officers all pulled their weapons, standing off with the crew, armed with a mix of swords and pistols. They looked to each other for who would take the first swing.

"Counteroffer..." Gail got their attention, still shaking. "You take the rowboats and you can have all the rum."

"You're out of rum," Cook called back.

"I restocked before we were thrown out of town. We're chock full of rum," The crew looked at each other.

"Row!" Welham called out, who patched the hole through his bicep and could not row himself. "Row!" The crew tied all the barrels of rum between the two dinghies and rowed with oars in unison. The ocean waves pushed them around as they made their voyage back to Shorehaven, drenching them with each rush. As they worked, the men began to chant:

Row! Row! Row! Row!

Row this chariot through the seas
O' we row!
Let our sails catch the breeze
O' we row!

Coming hard upon a storm
O' we row!
We'll come back all dead or worn
O' we row!

Storm-tossed and half full of rum
O' we row!
Never thought that I'd die this young
O' we row!

Row! Row! Row! Row!

"Oi, open one of em!" Crofton called out as the seas died down later on. "Might as well drink while we have breath!" Harper, sitting on the barrel, popped the cork out of the bung hole and peered inside.

"No! He hornswoggled us!"

"What?" The men stopped rowing and looked up.

"It's empty," Harper pointed.

"Ahoy! This one be full," Cook shouted. Others scrambling to check if luck graced them to have rum in their barrel. Waves rolled through their bundled raft. Each boat or barrel would lift and fall with the rippling water.

The five remaining men worked the deck of the *Gail Wickman*, hauling the lines and keeping the rigging in order. Gail had the helm, being that no one trusted his strength to be useful anyplace else. Isla Maldito was quickly approaching, no fog kept it this time, the island was eerily welcoming. The *Puerto Oro* still sat lifeless on the bottom of the bay, holding back whatever it had in store.

"Take us into the shallows," Clay called from the deck. "We have to swim ashore if we can't put her on the beach."

The caravel glided up onto the sand, the men furled the sails and dropped the anchor onto the shore. The bay was almost a perfect circle, like the island was cradling them. Palm trees that lined the sand made a wall between the crew and the outer ocean. Making it impossible to see if another ship was coming or if one was already there. After tying up the sails and securing their tools, Levi led the line to their camp on the far side of the beach. Drawing near, they saw the roof was collapsed and one of the walls were pulled down.

"Sink me!" Clay scoffed at the sight. They ran to see the wreckage. All of them, trying to think of ways their hut could have been broken by natural causes, but without words, they all knew it had been manually ransacked.

"We're not alone here," Northrop scanned the bay. The others looking into the trees and up the mountain.

9.

Prisoners of the Plunder.

"Blast, that's a lot of men," Levi said to the others as they hid in the brush, spying over another ship anchored off the shore. The *Ave María* with her army of men took up the western beach. Their camp had been set up before the *Gail Wickman* landed a second time on the island.

"Bloody Spaniards," Clay spat.

"Do you think they found it yet?" Gail asked.

"No, we would see gold or crates if they did," Levi scanning for himself if they had anything.

"Ay, look there," Northrop pointed. A crew of men had a large piece of canvas rolled up and tied to be taken aboard.

"The bastards got the sail! I'm telling you, bloody Spaniards," Clay was ready to start throwing fists.

"Let's get the gold before they find us," Gail nudged.

"No," Northrop quick to turn down the idea. "Nay, we must make sure they can't find the gold."

"What are ye saying, old man?" Torie had a spyglass out.

"We need to get that map. Otherwise, they might find us. They'll kill us and make off with it all. We need to make sure they don't find where it is. For our own safety."

"Right," Levi nodded. "We'll wait till nightfall."

"Might not have till then before they figure it out," Northrop started lurching forward. "We have to get it now."

"No," Levi grabbed his collar. "They'll be with the map right now. I say it's best to wait till dark. We'll take it in hopes they haven't been able to figure it out."

"Aye, son. You're right."

Most of the old crew was half asleep on their raft, exhausted and cooked by the midday sun. Someone whistling the tune they sang repeatedly on their voyage. "Ay, what's that then?" Cook sat up when he saw movement under their boat. "In the water."

"Something be down there," Welham peered into the blue. The mass went under the string of rowboats and barrels, bumping the bottom of one boat, causing the men to at least open their eyes.

"Shark!" Jack hollered when he saw a blue dorsal fin piercing the surface. They jumped up as the shark circled the still water around them. Many of them had their feet or arms dangling over the edge of the raft. Jumping out of the water, the shark bite down on Crofton's leg. Tearing his foot and shin clean off. He screamed in agony. Soon, they all made themselves small, hiding every part of their body onboard.

"Back into abyss with ye!" Cook grabbed an oar and swatted the shark, now diving back into the water. Its back was blue, deep as the ocean. When it turned to make more passes at the sailors, the shark's white underside was revealed. Others took to the idea and grabbed their paddles and took cracks at shark, angerly looking for an opportunity to attack again.

"My leg! It took my bloody leg!" Crofton clenched his right knee as he screamed. His hands pulling on what was left of his leg, blood seeping through his fingers. Others held him down as they wrapped the wound with Harper's shirt, which had been lying in the boat for a little while.

"I got this one, lads!" Harper pulled out a fishing harpoon he had taken off the ship. He stood and got his balance on the crates he was on. "Oi," He turned back to Crofton, still conscious and in panic. "Stick yer leg in the water, draw him in."

"Piss off, mate! Stick yer own bloody foot in the water!" He cried from the corner of his mouth.

"He's coming your way, boy!" Welham announced. The shark swam under Harper and he drove the harpoon straight down. With his weight, he stuck the spear into its back, the barb hooking the shark's flesh. It kicked its tail and propelled forward, the sailor still gripping the harpoon. The man next to him grabbed his waist as he wrapped his legs around the barrel he was on.

"Someone kill it!" Harper cried, struggling to hold on as he was being pulled into the water, the shark trying to flurry itself loose. Jack climbed the pile of cargo and beat on the shark with his oar. It turned and sunk its teeth into the wood, trying to pull it away from him with what strength it had left.

"Bring it aboard!" The two sailors lifted their tools, raising the shark out of the water. They dropped it in one of the rowboats, now cleared of sailors. Harper came up with his cutlass and killed it as it was squirming to escape.

"To the Rowboats and Rum Mutiny Crew!" Welham called out instinctually. They cheered and hollered at their victory. Crofton passed out when he looked back at his missing limb.

The crew of the *Ave María* were mostly on the rocky beach to stretch their legs and to enjoy solid ground. They brought down crates of supplies they could need to make camp on the shore. Sailors used these barrels and boxes for tables and chairs to play cards on. Numerous lanterns dotted the beach, like little refuges to the dark beast of the island. In the shadows, the five snuck about, getting closer to the ship.

"We climb the anchor chain," Clay suggested.

"Could make a lot of noise, though," Gail mentioned.

"How else would ye board?"

"We could pose as their crew, just walk up."

"That there, lad. Is the single most stupid idea I've ever heard," Clay shook his head. "We take the anchor."

"I'm just worried old man Northrop won't be able to make the climb," Gail chuckled lightly.

"Speak for yourself, mate," Northrop glared over his shoulder. "Aye, the anchor."

They crawled into the water, the waves taking them out from shore. The iron chain hung down, moving with the bob of the ship over the waves. Clay was the first to start the ascent. He gripped the cold metal on the side of the link, stepping in the eyelet for footing. Levi followed, then Torie. Gail's arms shook as he began the climb.

"If you fall, boy…" Northrop threatened up to him as he grabbed the chain. "I'll gut you."

"Hold," Clay whispered down when he reached the deck. Each man relaying the message down to the next. Clay peered over the taffrail. As he scanned, Gail lost track of his hands. As the ship rose and tightened the chain, his fingers were pinched between the links.

"Ah!" Gail winced. Northrop scrambled up to try to cover the lad's mouth before he yelped in pain. When the ship sank, the links loosened. With two broken hands, Gail let go of the chain and fell backwards, knocking Northrop off with him. The two hit the shallow water, one after the other.

"¿*Qué?*" The boatmen on shore got up from their games or drinks to investigate the splashes.

"Up, lad," Clay whispered. He and Levi snuck over the railing. "Worry about them later, find cover."

The Spaniards below ran shin-deep into the water and surrounded the three. Torie calmly climbing down to join Northrop and Gail surrendering in the waves. Escorted at gunpoint back to shore, the three were put in manacles and left in the camp. After a few minutes, the Spaniards came back with their captain.

"I'm perplexed by your presence here," Amaro sat down across from the men "Your crew is far too small to take over the ship and no boat to carry away any cargo."

"Aye, three men can't do a whole lot," Gail joked. Amaro continued, unimpressed.

"So, what can you do? You're here for something, but what?" No one responded. "Do you know who I am?"

"Some Spanish bastard," Torie said under his breath.

"Not too far from that. I have been hired by Spain to hunt and destroy all who call themselves pirates. To wipe the seas of their scourge. Specifically, a wretched crew who claimed to have found the *Puerto Oro*. A crew who drew maps, like this one," He held up the small copy he had acquired. "Spain made sure *that* pirate crew above all others were put in the ground. But I know pirates when I see them, and you gentlemen are no pirates."

"Perhaps you were misinformed," Northrop coughed. "We are no pirates, but aye, we're the crew that found the island. The crew who drew maps."

"So, the question remains. Why board my ship? Perhaps you were attempting to commit an act of piracy, or somehow hinder our efforts, but I can assure you, your acts are in vain."

"So, I'm guessing you know how to read the map?" Clay leaned back from where he was sitting.

"Ah, you're after the *map*. Either you wanted to further study the map," He paused as he thought. "Or you already know where the gold is. So, which is it?"

"We aren't telling you nothing," Torie replied.

"Very well," Then Amaro turned to his men. "Take them to the brig. Get them to talk, just don't kill them. We could still need them yet if we can't read the map."

The line of chains clanked as the three were brought on board. Amaro remaining on shore to patrol the camp.

"Faster," The jailer pushed Gail from behind, who braced himself against the hull. He teared up in pain from his swollen, disfigured hands. "I'll be right outside this cell. Any of you wants to tell me your plan, you'd be free to walk," The jailed locked the steel cage, but no one spoke a word.

"Quickly, take it out the porthole," Clay opened the window in the back of the ship's cabin. Levi took the sail, still rolled, and put it on his shoulder.

"Christ, it's heavy," He staggered over to Clay and passed it out the window. Clay had already climbed the stern castle and had the aft rowboat lowered on its pullies. "Shut the porthole," Levi climbed out the window into the rowboat. They secured the map under the seats and lowered themselves down to the water. Levi and Clay rowed in the cover of night away from the vessel, stealing the map unnoticed.

Amaro eventually went back to his cabin to sleep. He took off his hat and coat and leather sheath for his rapier. Crossing the room, he went over to a cabinet to pour himself a drink. Turning back towards his bed, he noticed his desk lay barren. He gulped down his drink and pushed out of the room. He ran down to the brig, where the men were kept in repurposed livestock cages.

"Open it!" He ordered. The jailer shaking in fear, fumbled the key into the lock. Before the cage was fully unlocked, Amaro threw the door open and charged the closest man. "How many of you are there?" Amaro demanded. Grabbing Torie by the hair, Amaro threw him to the deck. "How many men are in your crew!?"

"It's just us," Gail stepped in. Amaro swung and hit him in the gut, knocking the young man to the ground.

"Lies! You came for the map and now it's gone!" He grabbed Gail by the collar. "So, where is it?"

Torie got up and charged Amaro, Gail quick to catch on. The two men tried to overpower him. The jailer stepped in and knocked Gail with the butt of his musket. Amaro yanked Torie's hair and put a knife under his throat.

"You really don't want to mess with me," Amaro pushed him to his feet, pinning Torie against the bars. Torie held his chin high, his lips trebling to stay shut.

"What could the navy do?" Gail petitioned as he was catching his breath from the floorboards.

"The navy would line you up and shoot you. Alas, I am far worse than them! I am Amaro Rodríguez-Felipe y Tejera Machado. In case you English swine haven't heard of me..." He began to press the blade into Torie's skin. "I've taken dozens of ships, cutting up hundreds of young men like you. Do you really think you could best me? So, I am going to ask again. Where is my map?"

"For Chrissake!" Northrop hollered. "Our men must have taken it. There are two more of us. Though, I don't know where they have gone."

"Stouthearted old man doesn't want to see any of his boys get hurt," The pirate mocked. "But it won't save them now."

Amaro drug Torie out of the cell and pulled him up the steps by his hair. Torie held his scalp in pain as he was thrown to the deck. Amaro's men quickly grabbed Torie and tied him to the mast, his shirt torn off and his back exposed. Lanterns around the ship shone faintly. Most of the deck lay in darkness except for this grave scene.

"You cross me," Amaro showed Torie the whip in his hand, the young man clenching to the mast in fear. "You pay the price."

Amaro circled back behind him, turning sharply to strike the first blow. Torie cried out, squeezing the wooden beam before him. Again, the captain struck, ripping up to the back of his neck open. Only a silhouette could be seen of Amaro against the dark night. He flailed the whip down on Torie with rage, his whole crew observing. Blood ran down his arms and shook off with each strike. The young man's whelps of pain were growing fainter with each continuous blow until there was no sound.

From the cell, the two could only picture the horrific sight above. After hearing the snap of the whip and their friend's cries, Northrop and Gail sat in frozen silence. Gail holding out his hands, not knowing what to do with the swollen clubs. Eventually the cracks stopped. Torie was thrown down the wooden steps, rolling over and landing on his back. The dirt and straw on the floor sticking to his open wounds. Torie now lay lifeless, as he was continuing to bleed out. Amaro stomped down the stairs and picked him up and dragged him to the jailcell.

"I hope your willingness improves," He dropped Torie's corpse on the deck and proceeded upstairs. Northrop scooped the young man up in his arms as the jailer locked the cage again.

"Set sail for Shorehaven!" Amaro stepped on deck and turned to his crew. "Come on, get up! If the local filth took it anywhere, it's there," He thundered back into his cabin.

"Not that I doubt your judgment, sir," One of Amaro's officers came in and spoke calmly. "But why are we sailing away from the island?"

"I've heard that the locals are very superstitious about this island and they would do anything to prevent someone finding the gold. I suspect those thieves were sent to sabotage us or to make off with the salvage themselves. If they took the map anywhere, it's back to their town on the other end of the island chain."

"If they aren't there? Say, they're still on the island?"

"The rest of the fleet is at hand. They'll find the bastards and snuff them out."

"They're leaving," Clay noted as the *Ave María* sailed passed the bay, where the two had hid the rowboat. The dawn light already illuminating over their left shoulders. "They know we took the map."

"So, let's use this opportunity to get to the gold," Levi turned to walk up the beach.

"Hey, our friends our in that ship," He protested, pointing behind him to the diminishing sails. "And you're not going to do anything about it?"

"What could we do?" Levi kept walking. "We don't stand blind chance against them in *our* ship."

"We have to at least try to rescue them!"

"We came for the gold, Clay!" Levi turned and let out. "Now let's finish the job," As Levi turned to march across the beach, he winced in pain. His chest cramped and burned, the veins in his hands turned dark. All of this, the young man ignored as he trudged through the soft sand.

"Boy, I won't leave them!" The tattooed man stood his ground. Levi turned back and glared at Clay.

"They're gone," He huffed. "Least we can do for them is finish what we set out to do." Levi turned to keep walking. Clay reluctantly followed, not able to find any words to say.

Going up to the *Gail Wickman*, the two grabbed the tools that had been thrown off the ship, still anchored in the sand. Levi cut down leaves with the machete as they trail blazed north through the jungle, east around the mountain. Clay, walking behind him, carried the shovels across his shoulders. They also had their backpacks to lug as much gold back in a trip as they could. Birds crowed over them as they went. As Levi swung to cut down the plants in front of him, he saw he had come across an existing trail. A faint line through the forest where plants no longer grew.

"This is the way," He pointed as he continued trekking.

"Maybe we should take a break," Clay stopped and caught his breath. "Get some water, yeah?"

"No," Levi kept on. "We have to make it."

Clay scoffed, wiped his brow, and followed behind. The trail followed a stream that snaked around them. Water running underneath them as they crossed over the steppingstones. Even when the river was out of sight, the waterfalls coming from the mountain could still be heard. The colorful birds sang to each other and leaves and palms rustled in the soft wind.

Yet Levi heard none of these. His heavy breathing took over his ears. He felt nothing except the pulse of his heart beating through his body. Blood pushing through his veins. Clay couldn't enjoy the nature around him like he had when he explored the west coast on their first voyage. The jungle was full of life, the sun in the east shining through the mist, but its beauty went unnoticed that day.

From the trees in front of them, Levi saw water. Gulls called from over their heads and settled on the sand beach. He ran to find a bay that was nestled on the northeast side of the island, quite smaller than the south bay.

"It shouldn't be like this," Levi panicked, looking out over the ocean. He recognized it, but something was off, something was missing. "The map didn't have water here; it should be land," He pointed repeatedly to his map in denial.

"Son, maybe we rest for a bit, clear our heads," Clay was exhausted not only from the hike, but from the constricting tension. "Maps can be wrong."

"No, we should go back to the original. See if we missed anything," Levi turned around to begin hiking back to the south bay.

"Boy!" Clay hollered, enough to get Levi to pause for a moment. "Let's just wait here," He panted. Sweat crossed over the lines of his tattoos and dripped off at the wrists. Water falling also off his chin and brow.

"Be my guest, I'm going back," Levi threw down his bad and trudged into the forest again.

"You rotten kid! You lost your head now, didn't you?" Levi did not stop to hear the storm of insults Clay hurled at him. "You're obsessed! Blast," He gave up, and sat down against a palm tree. Clay sat there for some time, gaining his energy, and looking over the still water. Clay built a small fire to keep himself busy during the day. He had a small camp for himself, stacking up starfruit and bananas he picked. By late afternoon, he noticed rocks began to appear from the bay. As he studied the water, more land began to rise.

"They buried it in a shoal," He realized. A bridge of land emerged from the water as the tides fell, leaving a pool of water trapped by the island. In the wall of stacks, peaking from the sand, hid a sea cave. Clay stood to get a better look at it. "That must be the entrance to the tomb," Clay concluded, impressed with himself, comparing it to the marked location on the map. He grabbed a shovel and, using it as a walking stick, hiked down to the beach. He walked the receding water, stepping on the solid rocks between stretches of muddy sand. The tides pulling at Clay's ankles. The water drained steadily, almost as if the island wanted to reveal its secret. The mouth of the cave deepened with the lowering waterline, unhinging its jaws. Water trickled down the steep cave. Clay stepped inside the rock and the darkness pulled him further into the cavern.

As Levi hiked through the jungle alone, he began to slow down. Allowing himself to breath, Levi sat on a boulder near the edge of a pond. He glanced down at his hands and quickly looked away when he saw their darkened color. His breathes grew choppy and his hands began to shake. He sniffed and wiped his eyes, a few tears falling off his face. As Levi scanned the scenery, trying to take his mind off of the setting Curse, he noticed something staring at him across the pond. Between the emerald leaves and rolling mist, stood a stone statue. It was light grey and covered in moss, vines hanging down from the creature's open mouth. The statue stood upright and wore a crown. It dripped with condensation, water rolling down the stone like beads of silver. It marked the last remnant of a more ancient people.

Levi got up to continue his path to the map. The hair on his neck shot up with the thought they might not be alone on the island. Suddenly, he heard the birds around him and noticed the bright flowers speckling the green foliage. Focusing his mind back to the task, he walked determined to the south beach. He was unsurprised to see the *Gail Wickman* still sitting in the sand, exactly where they left it. Going around to the west horn of the bay, Levi approached the rowboat. He unrolled the sail and laid it over the dinghy, the edges dipping into the sand. He studied the *T* on the map, trying to find any hint of faded markings or if there was anything else that he might have missed.

"Nothing," There was no hint near the mark. In fact, there was no border drawn between and sea. He took out at his smaller map, seeing where he connected the lines between the two shorelines. "It could be in water for all I know," He traced the shape of the bay with his hand, looking between his copy and the original. From the fog, out on the horizon, a black tower came into view. Levi stood to look at the incoming ship. More followed behind the vessel, a line of black ships stood out against the clouds. He looked at the flag, the faint red X coming into view. Levi nearly fell backwards as he began to run across the beach.

"The map," He turned about and went back to the map, still coving the rowboat. Levi threw the ends into the boat, then flipped the whole boat over. He began covering the rims in sand and grass, making it look like an old wreck. After he was done hiding the map, he got up to run back to the jungle to warn Clay.

10.

Retribution.

The *Ave María* pulled into port at Shorehaven. The frigate stood over all the other ships on the pier, dwarfing them with her height and guns. Amaro with some of his men stormed off the gangplank and met the sceptic welcome party.

Miss Mertie rushed to see the ship, thinking it might possibly be Levi in his new captured prize. From the edge of the street, she stood, witnessing the conversation between Segar and this other sea captain, who was unlike Levi in most attributes. The tall, black-haired man sported a red coat and wide brimmed hat.

"Been some time since anyone landed at our docks under their own flag," Segar confronted the pirate, no longer flying the Spanish flag, but his own colors. Half the flag was black with a skull in its sector, the outer half of the flag was red with a gold cross. Amaro knew better than to confront an English settlement under the Spanish flag.

"Where are they?" Amaro demanded. "The ones who went to the *Puerto Oro*, where are they?"

"No one has returned."

"Don't take me for a fool, Englishman. The men who went to the island, I know they've come back."

"We banished those filth to the island some time ago. None have come back," Segar waved off.

"Banished there," He chuckled to himself. "And while they're marooned on that island, they just decided to commit piracy and endanger their own lives?"

"Their actions are out of my control."

"Maybe so, but you're in control of this. If you return the thieves who withdrew here, I'll return the bodies that I have."

"Which bodies?" Segar said between his teeth.

"I caught three of this crew, but their captain has evaded me. He stole something very valuable. I suspect they have returned here. And I suspect you may be helping them hide."

"What are speaking of? We don't have anyone to give you. Besides, we wanted those rapscallions gone!"

"So, you wouldn't mind if we hanged them here, then? Finish their purgatory," The jailer brought the two onto the weather deck. Northrop carrying Torie's corpse.

"We don't have any gallows," Segar said hastily after seeing his nephew in chains.

"No bother, my ship has plenty of line. Unless, you have men you would like to exchange," Amaro pressed. "It's up to you, sir, who hangs."

"Alright," He caved, throwing up his arms. "A crew floated back, got here just before you."

"That wasn't so difficult. Bring them here," Amaro turned and called to his men on the ship. "Get the line! Sling it over the yardarms!"

Mertie followed the scene as attention was drawn inland. She studied each man aboard, recognizing Northrop and Gail, trying to find Levi's pointed face in the mass. Segar shook as he went up into the tavern. He rubbed his face, trying to stay calm at his own actions. The man was always confident in his decisions, but this time he was very unsure with what he was doing. Segar pushed open the door of the Rogue Star and took only a few steps inside.

112

"Hey!" He called to the crew who floated back on the rowboats. Crofton's stump leg had been patched by the town physician. His shin and foot replaced with a wooden peg. What was left of his quad was bruised black and blue. Crofton's pants cut at the mid-thigh on his amputated leg. The rowdy lot got quiet as they listened in to what Segar was telling them. "A ship be hiring your services," He muttered.

"Aye, aye cap'n!" Jack stood and saluted. The man's massive body moved the table he was seated at. The drunken bunch staggered out the door. Crofton especially unable to walk straight.

"The Mutiny Crew aweigh!" Welham laughed.

"Thanks for getting those blasted drunks outta here," Smithy joked, but Segar pushed out the door without a word. As he went down to the docks, Segar saw Amaro's crew preparing a line of nooses along the yardarm, where the sails would hang down. Stumbling towards the docks, the mutineers caught sight of the towering flag ship.

"Would you look at that!" Welham pointed. "We're making it big now," He laughed.

"Get on," Segar nudged them up the gangway. Amaro's crew quickly put them in shackles and stood them on barrels. "Now the prisoners," He demanded Amaro.

"Easy. I always honor my end of an accord," Amaro went up to the gallows on deck, ignoring Segar's request.

"Ay! What is this?" The Mutiny Crew sobered up and realized their predicament. Coarse line threatening to strangle their necks.

"You're about to be hanged," Northrop said bluntly.

"Where is the map?" Amaro addressed the five in all.

"Map? What are you talking of?" Jack blinked.

"Don't play games. The map you stole from me!"

"We's never seen you before, I swear," Harper called out, trying to struggle out of his restraints.

"Aye, you didn't see me. But this ship, might strike up a memory. Docked right off the Isla Maldito."

"We never made it to the island!" Cook called, Amaro turned to see face the sailor. "We mutinied and jumped ship, we's rowed back to port ourselves."

"I'll bet anything Captain Levi has it," Welham suggested. The others nodded along. "Surely come hell or high water, he was going to find that gold. Cursed be anyone who got in his way!" He shook his head. His red hair matching his face.

"Captain Levi?" Amaro questioned.

"Aye, he was with those lot," Crofton pointed with his shackles to Gail and Northrop. "Probably still on the island. His ship ain't here in port."

"Thank you, gentlemen," Amaro spoke softly as he glared down at Segar. His hat shading his fierce eyes. "You've earned your right to live, however much longer that may be. Put them in the brig with the others!" He turned. From the pier, Segar saw all of the men be taken out of sight into the depths of the massive ship.

"What of our deal?" Segar shouted, about to storm up the guarded gangway. Amaro held up his pistol, stopping Segar in his tracks.

"Harboring fugitives, accessory to piracy has the same ill fate as pirates themselves, both punishable by death. Only death may come howsoever justice seems fit."

Segar stepped back in horror. Amaro ordered his men to sail off from the docks. Lines were thrown down and oars pushed the ship into the sea.

"Get to my mansion," Segar quickly turned to the men with him. "Get everyone as inland as possible!"

"Prepare portside cannons!" Amaro went back to his men. The *Ave María* flared up, opening her gun ports, loading her cannons. "Burn down that nest."

The men on the docks ran to land, those on the streets quick to pick up their fright. Mertie in the scrabble of men on the ship and docks, still trying to survey to see if the young man she loved had returned for her.

"Get out! Everyone, inland as fast as you can!" Segar yelled, going around the streets.

Cannonballs blazed through the walls, shattering a building. Shaking of the ground and the whip of dirt, startled Mertie enough to save her from her trance. A barrage of steel ripped through the town as smoke flashed from the ship.

Hurley, from the shops, darted to the cannon, fortified behind low stone walls. The hardy man loaded and fired at the *Ave María*. Without thought, he began to load another round. The second shot struck the weather deck, where Amaro's crew was quick to take muskets and direct their fire at the merchant. Bullets chiseled away at the stone barrier as Hurley put out another shot.

"Fire every round into that scourge of a town!" Amaro commanded. The tavern windows were blown in, glass bottles shattering into sand. The market stalls were flattened, and the islanders were crushed in the rubble. Hurley looked up between shots, to see a couple stray cannonballs strike and splinter the lighthouse.

"No!" Northrop gasped. The islanders on the ship's jail were shouting in horror. They shook and rattled the cage, but they were helpless to stopping the slaughter. Amaro's crew continued to fire their muskets and cannons. A bullet connected and struck Hurley in the chest, bringing him to his back. The man already dead. Brick collapsed on the townsfolk who could not escape in time. Everyone heard the constant lighting of the cannons and the echo of buildings demolished to the ground.

The onslaught continued until Amaro gave orders to cease and to continue sailing on. He stood on deck, scanning his destruction in pride. Ruined houses continued to fail and collapse. Smoke filled the small town as blood crept into the dusty, ruined streets.

"No one cheats me," The Spaniard said to himself before receding into his cabin. *Ave María* following her captain's orders and cruising back to the cursed island.

Segar was in his mansion, looking onto the terror from his balcony. His town was destroyed, leveled to ruins. His people were in shock, if not laid slain on the earth. Dusty smoke rose while the destruction sank deep into the island. Shorehaven was torn apart; brought low enough to almost be washed away by the sea.

"Aye, the Curse?" One of the townsfolk coughed as Segar stepped out of his house and onto the road.

"No..." Segar cleared his throat. "Some men are just wicked. Evil."

Clay wandered in the sea cave, looking for anything other than damp rock. The series of pillars and connecting caverns created a labyrinth. As he aimlessly staggered further into the cave, he become increasingly unaware of how lost he was. The light coming in through the mouth became obstructed, but Clay was too far into the darkness to notice. He followed a wall of the cave, looking for a lever or sign of humanity, not sure exactly what he was looking for. He would work along a wall faithfully until he hit a dead end. Then he went back to try another tunnel.

"Wait, didn't I…" Clay said out loud. He turned about, trying to figure out which way he had come from. Shaking his head, he ran down one cave. His breathing grew heavy as he went back and forth. The foot of standing water splashed around his boots, as he surveyed all that was around him. Drops plinked into the water from the cave ceiling. Clay began to sweat, thrashing around, he realized he wandered so far into the dark, he could no longer see clearly. His vision became black and white, only faintly making out the stone pillars against the shadow of the cave. He wandered upwards, thinking that would lead him to the surface, but the trail began to slope down again. When Clay came to a crossroads, he turned from the path he was on. Dipping the down, the trail eventually bent and worked upwards. Then it sloped down and came to the same intersection.

"I'm going in circles," His words echoed, then were suffocated by the endless cave. He went down another tunnel, working further into the maze. The water at his feet moved, as if something else roamed the deep halls.

"Who's there?" He spun around, gripping the shovel in hand. He heard more water sloshing against the rock. Blind now, he put his hand on the wall and proceeded to walk forward, toward the source of the splashes. Something hit his ankle, floating in the water. As he moved his feet forward, he felt more of whatever was on the surface, hitting his ankles. His hand trembled as it slid down the cavern wall, wet with humidity. He swirled his hand around the black water until it came between his fingers. He grabbed the dead fish, knowing what it was immediately.

He dropped it in fear. Clay held out the spade as he advanced. His eyes trying to adjust. He poked into the blackness, occasionally clipping the stone pillars. As he jutted the shovel, he hit something, but it was not stone. It gave more and did not make a sound on impact. "Lord help me," He reached out his shaking hand to touch a body, standing over him.

"Where did he go?" Levi came back to the bay. He saw the fire pit, burnt to ashes, and their tools. He swiveled around, searching the brush and trees for any sign of Clay. He kept low and snuck around the area, suspecting Clay was either hiding from, or taken by, the Spanish. "God blind me," He gasped. Looking out to the open bay, he saw the body of his friend floating in the waves. Levi ran down the hill and waded through the shallow water to reach his friend. "No, no, no," He panicked as he turned the corpse over. "Clay, come on!" The body was clearly drowned and dead. "No!" Levi yelled and began to sob as he pulled him ashore. Sitting on the sand, drenched in saltwater, Levi screamed into his hands. He rocked as he continued to cry.

11.

The Crew of the Missing Captain.

"Long time no see," Welham called over to Gail from across the cell. "Last we were this close, you shot me."

"Surprised you survived. I wagered you wouldn't make it a league," Both men patched up from their wounds.

"Ha! Seems you didn't get too much further than we," The sailors chuckled. "So, what's your plan?"

"There is no plan," Gail sighed.

"Ay, there's gotta be a plan. Otherwise, we just get pushed wherever these swine take us. Left to be like them," Crofton pointed to the African slaves also held in the brig.

"Got any ideas then?" Gail shook his head.

"You know we're a scheming bunch," Welham replied. Northrop chuckled to himself at the joke. "They're only keeping us alive because they think we can lead them to the gold or lead them to Cap'n Levi, who can lead them to the gold."

"And?" Gail asked on.

"We offer Levi in exchange for our lives."

"All of us freed for one man?"

"The handful of some inconvenient waste of cargo space for the man who can get them all of the gold. We leave on yer ship and sail as far away from this bloody island! Back to England if we must," Cook added.

Amaro stood next to his helmsman as they sailed back into the Cursed Island's waters. As they arrived from the south, Amaro saw the bay that the other's stowed their ship. The island gave no fight to these men coming ashore, though it would not let them go untouched.

"What a pitiful little boat," The helmsman pointed out to the *Gail Wickman*, dry docked on shore.

"I don't think they realized how much gold is really on this island. Anchor here, we'll row in! And bring the prisoners," The *Ave María* obeyed to her captain as the men prepared to go ashore again. The crew in shackles were brought on deck and escorted to the rowboats.

"Hey, we have an offer!" Some of the mutineers were trying to get Amaro's attention, but he ignored them as he continued to give out orders. "What a cold-hearted man, he is," They gawked as they were loaded into the rowboats. "Ay, parlay! We want a parlay!"

They kept up until they were lowered into the water. After rowing in, Amaro's crew set up camp on the beach, next to the *Gail Wickman*. They built floors out of cut down palm trees and pitched tents upon them, like they had at their first camp. Amaro was having his captain's tent built as he fumed over the little counterfeit map he had taken.

"Captain, Admiral Esteban is requesting your presence. He's camped on the west shore, where we were before. I can escort you if you'd-"

"Sir, the prisoners are demanding a summit," Another sailor ran up and interrupted.

"I'll be with the admiral shortly," Amaro went to the tent the crew was now being held in. He looked down at the men, in chains on the sand. "I'm very interested to know what it is you think you can offer me in your current position."

"We'll give you Captain Levi. He's the only one of us that knows where your map is if he hasn't already found the treasure."

"And do you know where he is?"

"Aye," Harper blurted out. "He's in hiding, send one of us to fetch him. We can trick him to coming back, then he be all yours."

"Send one of the mutineers? I doubt he'd trust..." Amaro remained unamused.

"Send me," Northrop spoke up. "He trusts me. I get you Levi and you let them go."

"You have one day to find him. For every day you do not return, I will kill one of them," Amaro took out his dagger and spoke directly to Northrop. "You know I would."

"I'll bring him back," Northrop said sternly. Amaro motioned for his guard to unlock the old man's shackles. He stood and ran straight into the jungle.

"Are you sure he will come back?" The jailer asked Amaro.

"The way I see it, the island will kill him if he tries to run. He gains nothing from the bargain and only has everything to lose."

On the northeast beach, in the crest of the bay, Levi dug passionately with the shovel. The sand slowly filling in where he had meant to create a deeper well. He threw his full force with each stroke, throwing the dirt and sand aside. He grunted as he worked, tears collecting around his eyes. As he worked, he sped up, trying to stay ahead of the sand filling back in. Seeing his efforts undone, Levi dug furiously, faster, and more intense.

"No!" He yelled and threw his shovel, knocking against the trees. Levi collapsed in the sand, sweat dripping down. As he looked up, he saw Northrop standing in silence, observing the broken young man before him.

"Come on, son," He held out his hand. "I'll help you."

Levi crawled out of the pit he dug and retrieved his spade. He and the old man alternated as they dug their ovular hole. Neither one spoke a word. They got about the shovel's depth down when they stopped digging. Levi climbed up and helped Northrop out. They carried Clay's body over to the grave they dug and softly walked him down. After the two climbed out again, they grabbed their shovels and buried their friend.

"He drowned," Levi said, wiping his brow. "And I wasn't there for it. I wasn't there."

"You buried him, that's all that matters now."

"Did you escape?" Levi asked, changing the topic.

"No."

"They send you find me?"

"Aye," He nodded. "In order to let the others go."

"They think I know where the gold is?" Levi pondered.

"That's what your crew convinced them of."

"I thought I knew where it was," Levi looked out to the bay. Northrop catching where his gaze went. "But I'm not sure anymore."

"Oh, don't doubt now. You still know," Northrop turned and started back up the trail. "Now, come on. We'll free the others and then we'll figure out what to do."

Levi hid the tools under the large leafy plants and caught up to the old man. By his language, Levi knew Northrop would not abandon him.

"Have you found it, yet?" Esteban asked his mercenary upon the repaired *Nuestra Señora*. He sat at the gold trimmed desk, sipping his hot tea. He waved for his servant to pour Amaro a cup as well. The cabin was bright with the sun coming in through the windows. Admiral Esteban filled the cabin with his own luxuries. His many coats nearly overflowing the wardrobe.

"By my temperament, you should know we have not. Though, you're more than welcome to dig in the sand with us," Amaro said calmly. Esteban raised his eyebrows in offense.

"No, I don't think so. What have you found then? My men told me you had a lead at least."

"The crew I captured, who stole the map, they say their captain is on the island. He knows where the gold is."

"And you're sure he knows? A dastard's word isn't always trustworthy."

"He knows. They have nothing to gain from lying."

"Then for your sake, I should hope so."

"*My* sake, sir?"

"I don't want to have to explain why Spain wasted all this money to look for the gold, when we found none. Someone will have to take the hit for it."

"So, the crooked pirate takes the fall, while he did all the work?" Amaro set his cup down, trying to suppress his anger.

"It's the natural order of business. If the reward has a high risk to me, I just change the rules, minimize the risk."

"Cast it on others," Amaro corrected.

"It makes no difference, just find the gold. Spain gave you a letter of marque. *That* can go away. As you said, you are the crooked pirate," Esteban drank from his cup as Amaro left without a word. In the heat of the afternoon, he walked over the hill of the peninsula and back into the south bay.

"If that man comes back with Captain Levi, you report it to me immediately!" Amaro ordered the guard at his camp and stormed into his tent. It was lit only by the sun piercing through the fabric covering. He sat behind his desk, brooding over the copied map. Amaro then noticed his one hand on the desk began to darken. He studied it, the black dye spilling out from the veins. Lifting his other hand, he saw it, too, was darkening. He went up to his cabinet, taken from the ship, and poured himself a glass of liquor. Knocking it back quickly, he poured himself another. He set his glass down at his desk and resumed staring over the map.

"So, what's the plan if he doesn't know?" Harper asked the crowd in chains.

"They'd let us go by then, wouldn't be our necks," Welham stated bluntly.

"They wouldn't let us go. See, they were going to let him go in exchange for us," Harper pointed to Gail. "When the Spaniard found out we weren't who's he was looking for, he kept us all as prisoners."

"So, we need to convince Levi that he really does know where the gold is," Crofton thought, stroking his chin.

"What?" All the crew looked up at him.

"Now hear me out. We got the Spaniard to believe Levi knows where it is in order to set us free. All we have left is to convince Levi he knows where it is."

"Wouldn't he know if he knew where it was?" Welham debated. They all puzzled, trying to make sense of it all.

"Alright, if it all goes to soot, we push the *Gail Wickman* back into the water and sail off," Crofton announced their contingency plan, motioning with his hands.

"In chains?" Cook rattled the shackles around their wrists and ankles, then sat back in defeat.

"Captain, sir," A man pushed through the tent flap that evening. "Your asset has arrived." Amaro waved inward to let the men inside.

"You've returned quickly. Take a seat, *por favor*," Amaro addressed Levi and Northrop, standing behind his desk, and leaning on his knuckles. "You took something very valuable to me."

"It was mine before it was yours," Levi shrugged.

"And it was Hector's before you. That's the game of piracy," Amaro sat down.

"Glad we understand."

"It does not diminish the value it held, but now, I'm told we don't need it at all. After I wasted such an effort."

"So why call for me?" Levi questioned.

"Because I'm told you know all it has to reveal. You already know where the gold's buried. Why have a map when I can get a personal guide?" Amaro answered.

"And if I lead you around the island in circles?"

"Then you'll figure out how short my patience is," Amaro tapped the pistol on his desk. "I'm offering an accord. You take me to the gold, and I'll let you go free, you can even grab a few pieces on your way out."

"And your whole fleet of superiors would let me walk?" Levi folded his arms.

"I'm done running errands for them. You help my crew get the gold quickly, and we can all escape while they're still searching for the map."

"Deal," Levi said without hesitation. Northrop looked at the eager young man.

"Then it's an accord."

"Let it be bound," Northrop spoke up and turned to the pirate. "So that we all remain honest."

"Bound by what?" Amaro questioned.

"The Curse. It already has a grip on all of us," He held up his hand, which was dark along with Levi and Amaro's. Levi never noticed the old man's hand was cursed, being of tan complexion.

"As you wish," Amaro took out a pen and parchment and began to write. Under the candlelight, the wet ink reflected the golden flame before it dried to black. "Let it be so, that we each all aid in the finding and recovery of the gold," Amaro spoke aloud as he wrote. "That we are each to take of its plunder and free to walk away with it off the island. That none of us harm or kill another or that man be damned to the abyss."

Amaro took his knife and cut open his palm, letting ink drip onto the paper as his signature. He slid the contract across the table to Levi who also cut his palm and pressed his handprint into the paper.

"Let it be so," Northrop slit his palm and making a fist, pressed his mark of ink in the paper.

12.

The Tomb of the Four.

"How long have you been cursed?" Levi asked Northrop in the tent they were given. Both sitting on cots off the ground.

"Long time."

"It's because we want the gold. Like you told me?"

"Aye, the Curse infects those who seek the gold. Whose hearts are too hard to care for men."

"So why are *you* cursed?"

"In my heart, I always wanted it. I know I shouldn't. I tried to be caring and live a simple life, but the temptation was always there, trying to pull me back to sea. To go back for the gold."

"How long ago did you set out for it? If no one in town remembers it?" Levi asked, trying to piece together Northrop's connection to the island.

"Fifty years, I reckon. Most men in our town retired from privateering, too old or crippled for a life at sea and shooting. But I grounded myself so that I would never come back. I tried to shut it all out, but ink beneath my skin kept me from forgetting."

"I'm sorry I dragged you into this," Levi looked earnestly upon his old friend.

"Aye," He nodded as he laid down on his cot to sleep. "I'm sorry you were lured into this mess in the first place."

It was difficult to sleep easy on the island. Sounds from the jungle rained down on the beach. Animals unknown howled and chirped. Making the watchmen uneasy at their posts. Those from Shorehaven though, were more afraid of the water. They knew what lurked just off the shore in the old shipwreck. Crofton kept hearing the scratches of his sea ghosts, the hands of the undead scrapping the keel of their ship.

"Release the prisoners," Amaro went out to the tent they were being held in the next morning. The guard was asleep on his stool. "Show a leg, boy," Amaro kicked the chair from under him. He pushed through the flap to find the sailors were already gone. "Where did they go?" Amaro hit the guard. The jailer stammered.

"Captain, your prisoners," One of his crewmen ran to him and pointed across the camp to the *Gail Wickman*. The crew in chains trying to push the ship back into the water.

"Fools. Leave them," Amaro shook his head.

The chain gang was low in the sand, trying to push their ship into the rising tide. They climbed aboard at night and raised the anchor when they first snuck out.

"Gail you weakling, put your back into it!"

"I'll shoot you again, you bloody know it," He grunted, pushing with his shoulder, cautious not to put pressure on his hands. Crofton pushing from his left leg with his other simply off to the side. The men oblivious of how noticeable they were.

"We're leaving," Amaro threw open the flaps of Levi's tent. He and the old man were sitting on their cots talking. Levi put his journal and his jacket into his pack and set out. His white shirt was stained with sweat and his pants had sand collecting at the cuffs.

"I fail to understand the Curse completely," Amaro stated as the three walked down the trail, a line of Amaro's crew followed behind. "How does it work?"

"How it works," Northrop scoffed. "Is beyond me. The island isn't the thing that's cursed by nature. The gold, uh, became cursed because the ship went down without her captain. Which we know to be a condemnable act. Captain Hector buried it with him and his officers, trying to hold onto it all with his dying breath. And so, the Curse took form, bringing death with it, for that's all that follows from hunting the gold. The island plays along, aiding the Curse to kill off the men who seek her gold."

"And the ink?" Amaro kept on. "Will it kill you?"

"No. The ink alone won't," Northrop said through his beard. "But as I warned Levi, it's because no man with a beating heart would choose gold over the life of another man. Those of us who sought the gold to another's demise gets a heart of ink to the end of his days. The mark of a cursed man brings its own troubles."

"So, we are all alike then," Amaro concluded. To that, no one responded. The hike through the jungle was humid, the sun seeping through the leaves and palms. The dirt was packed down, sand mixing in the top from the boots of all the sailors who walked it. Red birds flew around them, singing and drinking the dew from flowers. Swarms of gnats formed clouds round the men. They swatted and tried not to inhale any of the little flies.

Levi led the line to the bay on the northeast of the island, where he had followed his map before. They passed by waterfalls trickling into pools of black water. The ponds linked together by the stream that snaked the path they walked. They crossed over the rivers, each taking their turn to jump from stone to stone that sat in the moving water. Turtles passed in and out of the pools, never minding the diverse environment around them. Lethargic fish, easily the length of a man's leg and as broad as a tree, lurked in the shallow lagoons. Their prehistoric scales paid tribute to the creatures' monstrosity. As Levi pressed on, he was not sure what he would find when he returned this time, but he was hoping something would appear for him.

"Look there," One of the sailors called from behind Levi, lost in thought. Coming in on the low tide, the shoal was above water with the cave exposed.

"Is that it?" Amaro pointed.

"Aye," Levi trusted his gut. He recognized this was the cave from his dreams. "That's it."

To the left of where the men emerged onto the beach, was the freshly dug grave. Levi went around it for the bushes where he stashed his tools. Finding the shovels, he led the crew around the pool. They walked on the stone path to the mouth of the cave. Below the surface were fish of color, brightly jeweled and reflecting the rays passing through the water's lens. Against the blue water and bright jungle, stood the black rock. The ominously dark cave seemed to breath with the flow of the waves. The cavern dove into the earth beneath the sea, delving deep below the world of the known.

"We have to go down there?" The sailors shivered at the sight.

"Aye," Amaro confirmed. "Get a torch, all of you. Mister Benson will show us the way."

They took out several torches and handed one up to Levi. He waved the flame around, getting a scope for how deep the cave was. After a pause, he stepped forward and the men followed behind. The black walls lit up from the torches spread out along the line. Levi led confidently until they came across the first branch out from the tunnel. Both tunnels dove deeper into the earth.

"Which way now, Mister Benson," Amaro assuming he knew this much. Before Levi could admit his ignorance, he saw from the ceiling speckles of gold, leading down the passage to the right.

"This way," He gestured with the torch without attracting any attention to his discovery. The faint trail of golden breadcrumbs led Levi through the maze. They spiraled downward, deeper into the heart of the island.

"Hurrah!" The chained crew shouted and cheered exuberantly. The *Gail Wickman* back in the water and floating out with the waves. The guards left at camp, by now, gathered to watch the Mutiny Crew struggle. They scrambled to chase after the boat, drifting further into the bay, still all shackled to one another. They ran through the chest-deep water to grab the ship.

"Got the net," Crofton grabbed the shroud, secured to the rail. He tried to pull up on the netting as the others weighed him down. "Christ, catch up already! You're pulling me arms off!"

Some of the others pulled themselves onto the rigging, the rest still trying to stay afloat. They had climbed the shroud, the net of line that supported the masts, when they snuck on at night. Being in the water now was an extra challenge. Gail hooked onto the rope with his elbows, making him more uncoordinated than he already was. As a unit, they hoisted themselves up the hull and onto the deck. They cheered again with chains at their feat, running around with what little mobility they had.

"Where's the caulking hammer?" Welham looked around.

"What?" Gail turned to him.

"My caulking hammer, to break out of these chains. I left it right here," Welham pointed out. "Wickman, did you move me hammer?"

"You mutinied!" Gail accused.

"Doesn't give you the right to touch another man's tool!" He wrestled Gail to the deck. The others cheered before they realized they were pulled down with them.

Amaro's crew marched slowly further into the cave. The men kept close to each other, not wanting to fall astray, but also afraid of what else the cave could behold.

"What's that stink?" One pirate asked. "Jonesy?"

"Very funny! Dead fish, that is," The other replied.

"Be on your guard," Northrop looked at his feet to see there were dead fish scattering the ground. "We may not be alone."

"Who else would be down here?" One seaman asked. Footsteps and splashes then echoed from the caverns and holes around them. "What is that?"

"Arm yourselves!" Amaro ordered as he unsheathed his rapier. Levi passed the torch to his left hand and drew his pistol. The sailors grouped up, turning their backs to each other, peering into the series of tunnels around them. The dark corridors seemed to close in around them. Men spinning in panic. An albatross cried as it flew out of one shadow and into another.

"No!" One man ducked and shook. "That scared me guts out."

"Not as much as that will," Another pointed into the blackness, trembling, as a set of boots walked out from the water. With them, the blue corpse of a sailor, armed with a sword and dead in the eyes. More shambled out from the caverns, surrounding the men.

"Don't just stand there, lassies! Send em back to the grave!" Amaro shouted as he slashed at one, who parried with its sword then struck back. The others quick to action, clashing swords with the drowned. The rusted blades of the undead crew tore sourly through the flesh of the pirates. The living men fought with grater skill, but the dead were resilient and seemed to register no pain.

Levi shot one in the forehead, but the hollowed-out brain did not stop his attacker. He quickly dropped his pistol and swung at it with the torch. Its turquoise skin bleed water from its wounds.

"Stab the bastards in the heart!" One man called out. Between glances of swords, the men thrusted for the chests of their opponents. Once pierced, the hearts leaked out all its water, drying the cadavers to a crumble. After the skirmish was over, the men began to notice their wounds and tend themselves.

"There'll be more," Northrop grabbed a torch from the ground. "We must keep moving."

"Like the ship, boys. There's still work to be done," Amaro ordered as he waved his sword. His crew was used to fighting in battles and jumping immediately back into tending the rigging and sailing. Those who could not bounce back or keep up either jumped ship or died. "Keep yourselves armed! The old man's right, more may come."

Levi went back to following his trail of gold dust. The tunnel leveled out and began to climb again, winding around corners and pillars as it made its way.

"How does a cave like this not flood? I reckon the water would fill in," One of the pirates asked.

"Mate, after the dead sailors, I stopped asking questions," The crew chattered here and there to keep themselves occupied.

The tunnel eventually opened up to a cavern. It was high and spacious; the torchlight could barely reach the other end. Water fell in from the ceiling and made a series of pools, all continuing to flow into the ground. In the center was a great mausoleum. A light stone tomb covered in cobwebs. Etched columns and a stone roof boxed in the two slates on the front that appeared to be a door. An inscription above the door read:

What beneath the earth was whelved,
Fools and thieves now only delve
To seek the treasure cold
Behold the Port of Gold

"This is it," Northrop confirmed as he stood. "The tomb of the four..."

"What happened to the fifth one?" One pirate asked himself, knowing the legend of five officers surviving.

"The fifth had to bury the other four and seal the tomb," Levi answered. "To live out the rest of his life on the island."

13.

The Port of Gold.

"Don't trust Amaro," Northrop whispered to Levi as the men made camp to rest before trying to open the tomb. Not that anyone could tell time down in the abyss of stone. They only could assume it was night by their level of exhaustion.

"Surely, but why?"

"You haven't seen what I have, lad. He killed Torie and…" He sighed and shook his head. "And bombed Shorehaven. Obliterated the town looking for you."

Levi swore under his breath and looked away sharply.

"We were all held prisoner. He's not a part of the Spanish navy, he's a pirate. You keep watch."

The two sat against the rock wall, seeing the whole camp between them and the tomb. Most men slept with an eye open, waiting until their shipmates were asleep to sneak into the tomb and slip away. When the first man attempted this, he jammed his shovel between the two rock slates and tried to pry them apart. The spade broke off from the handle and clattered loudly against the rock environment. Defeated and embarrassed, he went back to where he was laying. Amaro glaring at him. Others who got the same idea, sank back into their place, not wanting to face their captain's wrath.

"Ay, get up," Amaro woke Levi. "It's time to open the tomb," The men slowly got to their feet and collected their things, fastening holsters and buckling boots. Levi circled the mausoleum, hoping for a sign to once again show him the way. No gold flakes, no signs, or levers of any sort. The only thing other than the building itself was a pedestal with a bowl, collecting water droplets from the cave's ceiling.

"Well?" One sailor demanded. His voice echoing throughout the cave. "Open it already."

"I'm thinking," Levi replied quietly.

"Enough messing around boy, open the tomb," Amaro pulled out his pistol.

"You can't hurt me, remember?" Levi held up his hand, revealing the scar on his palm.

"You're hindering us from getting the gold, I say it's a wash!" Amaro pulled the hammer back.

"He doesn't know how to open it," Northrop defended. "You know he hasn't made it all the way to the gold yet."

"The pact was to be taken *all the way.*"

"But not necessarily by him," Northrop walked up to the slates that guarded the mausoleum's entrance. "Four of the five officers were buried here. The fifth had to seal the tomb and only one cursed like him can open it."

"So, what have we been wasting our time for?" A sailor called out. Northrop unwrapped the bandage around his wounded hand and pulled his dagger again.

"You seem to know a curious amount of detail, Mister Northrop," Amaro accused.

"Aye," He broke open the scab on his hand and went to the bowl of water. He let the ink from his wound dye the water, the dark cloud filling the bowl. Then the ink seeped out of the bowl and was absorbed into the pedestal. The two slates began to shake and slide apart. "Curious."

Men grabbed their torches and went over to the opening. A deep set of stone stairs descended further into the belly of the island. The stairway breathed as it was opened, low rumbles echoing from within. Even Amaro shivered at this above all else they had seen.

"The gold is just down these steps," Northrop wrapped his hand again. The men all frozen in fear. Amaro grabbed a torch from one of his crew and then holstered his gun.

"Lead on," He gestured toward Northrop. The old man was the first to step down the crypt, Levi close to follow. Amaro stopped his men before proceeding. He pointed to one man's flintlock and then pointed down the stairway before he took his first steps down. They descended into a significantly larger cavern. The steps carved a corner out of the rock's edge. More water dribbled in from the walls and fell from where the pools collected in the room above.

On the floor off from the bottom of the steps was a singular stone tomb. '*Teniente de navío Marcos Romero*,' the engraving read. "A lieutenant," One man translated. An antique rapier was placed upon the lid, but age had gotten the better of it. The stone box stood seemingly alone in the cavern from what their torches lit up. But as the men with lights pushed further into the black room, they spotted another tomb.

"Gustavo Abasto," One of the crew read. His tomb was the same in size as the first, but surrounded by ponds that the waterfalls fed. A path of rocks, high enough out of the water, reached the tomb. On his grave were a pair of signaling flags, each red and white checkered.

"Ahoy, there's another," The men, taking their time at each tomb, went on to the third. Not that the pirates were ones to pay respects, but the solemnness of the scene hushed their usual rowdy nature. None of them spoke to another. The third tomb was higher than the first couple. It was built on a ledge that overlooked the cave. The steep path up to it was worn from erosion, but it was still accessible.

"César de la Cruz was buried here, another lieutenant," One sailor spoke aloud. On his grave was a spyglass. The brass was oxidized, and lens was warped.

These tombs were an old echo of a story perhaps far more wicked than the journey Levi found himself on. They were eerie as they stood in the deepest reaches of earth these men had ever delved in. Far below the surface and society, the tombs were a reminder of all that is nefarious and dark, lurking in the world.

From the vantage point of the third tomb, far across the cavern, a glimpse of red could be seen. Levi wandered over to it, most men too distracted from the findings to notice. Northrop was still at the first tomb, not daring to go any further. Laid across the fourth and final grave, larger than the rest, was the flag of Spain. Red and gold fabric covering the stone box that read, '*Capitán Hector de la Caballería.*'

Levi looked up from the tomb and saw a glisten from the shadows. Like the gold flakes in the cave far above. He walked around the grave to venture deeper into the offshoot. Levi paused when he heard a scratching under his boots. He knelt down and picked up what he had walked over. As his eyes were adjusting to the blackness, he could see what he was holding. A single gold coin. The crest of the Spanish crown marked it.

He reached out and felt more of them piled up. Amaro came up from behind. His torchlight exploded the massive piles of golden and silver coins. The reflection shone out into the rest of the cavern, turning everyone's attention. The gold pieces were piled high like dunes of sand. The tunnel behind Hector's tomb flowed with the legendary treasure. The metal reflected the fiery light of the torches, each coin flaming into life, brighter than the sun. There were chests filled to the brim with gold, underneath the piles of loose doubloons. There were not just coins, but crowns, chalices, and jewelry all casted from gold and adorned with jewels. Men tried grabbing chests for themselves, but they were far too heavy to carry alone. They filled their pockets and found every spare compartment on their clothes to possibly hold the endless golden coins.

Northrop started walking over to the bright scene, when he noticed something off to the side, tucked away from the rest of the cavern. He walked over to the lonesome tomb, finished except for a lid. Etched into it, 'Alférez Harvey Northrop.' Away from the merriment of riches, the old man stood alone and wept. The grave made for himself was never used. He was the last of his comrades, all laid to rest.

A gunshot pierced the scene and rang loudly in the cavern's corridor. Amaro holstered his pistol after getting his crew's attention.

"Two of you to a chest. We start hauling them up to the surface. Four of you run back to the Ave María and at nightfall, sail it to back to us. The rest of you keep making trips. Mister Benson, Mister Northrop, I suggest you take your chest and part ways."

Northrop was just walking to the scene after hearing the gunshot. He and Levi grabbed a chest, and fastened it shut. They lit a spare torch and began carrying the chest to the stairs, enshrouded in darkness compared to the treasure's light. The rest of the men trying to load as much in as possible, testing to see if they could lift more before starting the walk for themselves.

On the hike up, the torch was beginning to fail. Levi was surprised the old man was keeping up, he figured all the stairs while working in the lighthouse made him equipped for this. There was a haste to escape, they both felt it. They were not sure if they were free from Amaro and they knew the Spanish were still at hand. Behind them, they saw the lights of the pirates also on their way out of the cave.

"Watch out!" Levi called. A sword swung from the shadows. "The swamped bastards."

Northrop dropped his end of the crate and drew his sword. The old man fenced and parried. Another drowned sailor shambled out of the darkness as well. Levi dropped his handle and began to fight, the chest sitting in the standing water, with the torch laying on the lid. Levi lunged at his target's chest. He struck, but not without taking a slash to the arm with the rusty blade. Black dye stained his white shirt as he bled. Levi winced in pain before he took his weapon out of the corpse.

"Run," Northrop yelled as more came from the side. Levi darted for the chest. Reluctantly, Northrop grabbed the other end and carried it with them as they ran. The dead followed them, thrashing across the pools of water on the cave floor. Levi thrusted his sword at oncoming creatures, all bleeding water and covered in algae or seaweed. Yet the two kept their pace, not stopping. They heard the pirates behind them firing shots and yelling as they fought the dead sailors the two had escaped. Amaro's crew left behind a trail to follow back, sometimes leaving a boot or shovel at a turn, since they did not catch on to Levi's trick.

"Blast, these fiends are everywhere!" Levi dropped the trunk again as he was blindsided by an encroaching enemy. He fought with just his right arm. His left stung from the tear as he crossed swords with the dead. While he and Northrop were fighting off the constant raid of dead sailors, two of Amaro's men came up behind them. One pulled his pistol and grinned as he raised it toward Levi. Northrop heard the click of the hammer and turned to slash at the pirates. The gun aimed at the young man fired. The explosion of gunpowder permeated throughout the cavern. Levi looked down in shock to see the bullet had not hit him.

On the other end of the cave, Amaro dropped down. He coughed up bloody ink. His side gashed open, as if a bullet had pierced him.

"Seize those men!" He ordered, spitting black ink through his teeth. "I want them alive! Don't let them escape," He clenched his abdomen as he pushed himself back up.

Levi and Northrop dueled the pirates, in between defending themselves from the oncoming dead. One grabbed Northrop from behind, he ducked and flipped the creature onto his attacker. Staggered, Northrop lunged and pierced the man's leg. He then joined Levi in fighting off the other. The two cut and slashed unevenly at the man, making it impossible for him to defend. After several cuts to the arms and ribs, he dropped his sword and cowered. Levi grabbed the pirate's pistol and tucked it into his belt. The two then grabbed their chest of gold and ran for the way out. When they came to the cave's mouth. They saw it was completely submerged, but the water was not flooding into the cavern. It just stopped, refusing to flow. Levi stood pondering the ocean wall, seeing the waves just above the mouth of the cave. Fish swan passed them, not acknowledging the anomaly.

"Come on, Levi," Northrop urged. "We have to go."

"Right," He snapped out of his amusement. The two dove into the water wall. They swam upward, their heads just bobbing out of the water, keeping the chest of gold below. Treading water, the two looked around for any signs of the Spanish before swimming ashore. Soaking, the two men dragged themselves onto the sand, the chest limping along with them.

"Ye bastards!" Amaro's crew yelled. The pirates appeared in the water, their over loaded gear and trunks pulling them under. "Come back here!" The two scrambled into the forest as the pirates trudged through the water to get ashore. They ran along the trail back to the south bay. They ignored the steppingstones and rushed straight through the shallow rivers in their path. They couldn't see anyone behind them, but the two refused to stop running. When they were almost to the south bay, Levi darted into the jungle, pulling the old man with him.

"Where are we going?" Northrop questioned.

"Obviously, we need to hide," Levi trampled through the bushes and under leaves, careful not to let the chest snag on any plant. "The map room is only other place I know."

"Good thinking."

Amaro kicked the sand and turned over one of the chests that had been brought up upon hearing the news the men had escaped. His crew standing off from him. "Someone get my ship!" He ordered to the crowd. All too scared to move. Eventually, some broke loose of their fear and ran down the trail toward their camp. "What are you all standing around for? Go and get more!" He screamed, pointing to the cave with his blackened hand, his other clenching his bleeding side.

The Port of Gold

14.

Marooned.

"Our ship is gone," Levi came back from scouting the bay. "The others must've taken it when they were freed," Northrop did not answer. He sat on a cot inside the cave and smoked his pipe. Levi squatted down, across from him. "We have to get off the island."

"Possibly."

"There's a rowboat on the beach. We could *still* get away," Levi planned.

"Row twenty-five leagues back to Shorehaven — which is ruins remember — then what? They would lynch you on spot. If they even had the patience to do so."

"We have to get off the island."

"Lad," He huffed out a small cloud of smoke. "This island has taken so much from me. Can't you see it's taken from you? Have you no integrity? Curse the ground, let it kill us both!"

"No. I'm not dying here. *Especially* because of what it's taken from us. I have to leave with the gold, otherwise it was for not."

"And then? You live a long life and ye die anyway! People died for that blasted chest and even if it buys you the world, it be for not!" Northrop shouted. "That gold can't take away all this. It can't buy Clay back, it can't even buy the words to tell his own lady, if'n she's still alive. God dammit, Levi! What good will that little chest do ye? The rest of our lives are condemned because of that. The curse's been laid upon you. There's no going back."

"Move back to New England. Leave this all behind."

"You can't leave this! Don't you hear? Listen to what I've been telling you," Northrop pleaded, his eyes streaming tears. "You can't leave behind a town slaughtered because of you. You can't leave Clay or Torie or Tanner. You can't undo the harm you put that lassie, Miss Mertie, through. You *never* leave the island. Even if you move a thousand leagues away, you'll never escape it! It'll haunt you and torment you more than that cursed heart of yours will. You think Captain Hector didn't commit atrocities for that treasure? You think I didn't kill for it? You never move on."

"I hear you, but we are not dying here. Even if they hanged me on sight, they could use the gold to rebuild."

"They would never touch a single coin. You know that. Doesn't matter what you do with that gold. There's no moving on from this," The old man inhaled another puff of smoke. Levi stood and turned away from the old man. Northrop calmed himself before speaking again. "I was on this island for years."

"What?"

"Levi, I was the officer who sealed the tomb. One of five to abandon hundreds of loyal men and betray them all to save some of the gold. We coveted the treasure more than life. The crew wanted to lighten the load and sail back, but we would not part with it. As the hull began to break, we offloaded the entire treasure on the beach. That night, us officers camped on shore with the gold. And while everyone was asleep, the ship sank, drowning every man aboard.

"Yet the captain had no remorse. He was vexed on protecting his prize. I watched each man go mad for the gold. They would have killed each other if the Curse had not gotten to them first. One after the other, the island killed them. They elected whoever was the last to survive would seal it all away and guard the tomb with his dying breath! Only after I buried em did I realize how little it was worth."

Levi didn't say anything.

"So, believe you me, kid. This never leaves you."

On the northeast beach, Amaro stood over the crates and chests, being loaded into the *Ave María*. His men, exhausted and wounded, spoke no words, and never lifted an eye. They hoisted the pullies and continued to bring up gold from the seemingly endless hoard in the cave. At that point, they had slain all the drowned sailors in the cavern and worked relentlessly for their captain.

Around the bay, a foresail could be seen, followed by the rest of a ship and then more ships. The Spanish fleet closed in the bay. All opening their gun ports showing off their cannons. Amaro and his men stopped to see the ships trapping them in the bay.

"Run a shot across the bow. If they don't think we're serious, they will soon," Esteban commanded sternly. A single cannon was fired and landed near the *Ave María*.

"Keep working," Amaro hissed.

Esteban was rowed to the beach from his blockade. Amaro standing to meet him. Both men glaring the other down.

"I hoped you had gone through the trouble of retrieving the gold, but I'm curious why you didn't tell me," Admiral Esteban started. Amaro said nothing, which confessed his guilt. "I am confiscating all your gold, all your men, and your ship."

"You have no comprehension of the work it took to retrieve this. The audacity to take everything from me!"

"That's what real power is, Amaro. You may be the most feared *pirata* from Spain, but as you can see, you are powerless. You crossed me and I warned you what would happen. If you played by the rules, you would have gotten away with a fine slice of the treasure. Instead, you reverted back to your pathetic piratical nature. You think you can take whatever you want."

"So, you and I are not so different."

"There is a distinction between us," Esteban looked to his line of five ships. "I have the backing of a country. That power, the confines of rules do not outweigh."

"Rot in hell," Amaro punched the dignified man. The guards with Esteban, seized the pirate who was unsheathing his saber. They beat him down with their muskets.

"I'm sure you'll get there before I do," The admiral covered his bloody nose. "Tie him up and get the whip from his ship."

"Aye, Admiral."

Amaro's crew halted their work and looked onto the scene. The whip their captain had used on them would be used against him now. Esteban took off his coat and laid it on the rowboat. Amaro was on his knees in the sand. His hands were bound to a palm tree just on shore. His coat and shirt were stripped from him. Without a warning or word, Esteban brought the whip upon the captain's back, lacerating his skin. Amaro held in his pain.

"By God," Esteban saw the black pitch gushing out of Amaro's back. But again, the admiral whipped him. With each strike, Amaro becoming less able to keep it in. The cuts crossed into each other, some deepening old wounds, others marking his back with fresh gouges. Eventually the man screamed in pain as the admiral beat him with all his ferocity.

"Don't waste your breath trying to escape, there's already bounties for you being posted in every harbor," Esteban said to the dying man. Amaro spat on Esteban's shoes in reply. The admiral turned away from his foe. "Keep loading!" He snapped at the crew. He threw the whip into the sand and went back for his rowboat. Amaro's crew stood in terror. Seeing their captain brought low and humiliated was an intentional part of Amaro's torture.

The admiral had the *Ave María* tied to one of his ships to be towed. Worried for an uprising, he took Amaro's crew and split them up into the brigs on the various ships. His slaves were forced to continue loading gold into the two ships now ashore. They worked the rest of the day and into the night. The gold they brought up was simply unending. The next day, Esteban had his other four ships loaded as well. The bounty beneath the island spread out between the six ships in all. Amaro was left as his ship, crew, and all that he owned, were hauled away with the fleet.

Northrop sat at the stern of the rowboat, facing the mountain island. He had sailed away from this place once, he never thought he would live to endure its wrath again. Levi was at the bow, rowing south off the coast. The unassuming chest sat between them with the map rolled and tucked under the seats.

"We don't have to go back to Shorehaven," Levi suggested. Northrop turned to face Levi and waited for him to continue. "We could just sail. You're right that we wouldn't be accepted anywhere, especially home. But we don't have to settle for land. We could get a ship and live out on the sea."

"Doing what?"

"Anything. We could fish or whale. Start transporting goods. Maybe do nothing? Change our names if you think people would be after us."

"Son, I'm far too old to live on the ocean. Why do you think you don't see any curmudgeons like me working the line? We all died not much older than you. I lived long because I was on land. Out here, in the water, it's a dangerous life. Even when you're not chasing gold, men will be after you. Trouble will never cease."

"How is that different from the land? People are after each other there, as well. There are thieves on land, just as on the sea. Instead of drowning, you're just buried in dirt."

"I don't know, boy. I don't think I can start over."

"You're right that we'll never escape this, but that doesn't mean we can't move forward. We can still live and thrive and be out where we love. On the water."

"You can sail forever, but eventually there'll be no place to run. The globe doesn't go on forever. One day, you'll run out of places to hide and end up back here."

"You told me you grounded yourself and you lived a good quiet life. Is that repentance not available to me?"

"You're still after the gold," Northrop interrupted himself, gripping his chest in pain. Levi was struck with it too, their hearts enflamed, and their veins burned. The black in their hands darkened and spread up to the forearm.

"Amaro," Levi guessed. The old man nodded, knowing the bind of the Curse must still be on them. Levi brought the dingy around and rushed back ashore. They could not get to the beach fast enough; their chests were searing with pain. Breathing became harder as their chests closed in. The two pulled the boat ashore and went for the trail to the north bay.

They ran down the path, Northrop falling behind. Their legs were exhausted from the spelunking up and down the cave. Levi ran past his burning legs, wanting nothing more than this all to end for good. He knew they all had to make it off the island alive to be free from their contract, to what end, he did not know.

"Jesus," Levi found Amaro, still breathing and slumped against the tree. Sand sticking to his scabs and covering his black wounds. Levi took his sword and cut through the binds, Amaro's arms collapsing to the ground. "He's still alive."

Northrop sighed as he came upon the beaten man. They put Amaro's arms around their shoulders and carried him back to the south bay. His feet dragged along the ground, running over roots and rocks that made the trail. His head limp and his long black hair covered his face. They did not see the blackness in their hands turning to normal.

"A rest, son," Northrop grunted. His legs shook as he walked.

"Alright," Levi huffed as they set their foe down, Amaro still unconscious. Looking around, Levi saw he was at the pond with the tall stone statue hidden in the leaves. Northrop looked over his shoulder to see what caught Levi's attention. "Were there natives on the island?"

"Once," The old man grunted. Levi didn't bother to ask further. He saw how hurt Northrop was, reliving his past. "We should go."

When they got back to the beach, they laid Amaro down in the rowboat and pushed off again. Levi and Northrop each took an oar and rowed in sync. Amaro woke up and became aware of where he was, sitting alone on the stern and facing the two men driving them away from the island.

"Why did you save me?" The pirate asked.

"Certainly, not out of stout heart," Northrop replied, keeping his eyes down as he rowed.

"We're bound to each other, remember? We all have to make it off the island," Levi added. Amaro did not say anything else, he crossed his arms and hunched over in complete exhaustion. His shirtless back being warmed in the sun. The canyons of scar tissue across his spine were raw and continued to bleed.

They kept on in silence, rowing without any particular direction. Away from the island was their only heading and for all intents and purposes, the three were okay with that. As they rowed further, the island was slowly consumed in fog and disappeared from sight, fading into the cloudy horizon.

They stood out like a dot on the ocean, lonely and calling out. The craft bobbed with the low waves, waiting for anything other than clouds to pass by. As the afternoon sun turned to evening, Amaro spoke up.

"Where are you taking us?"

"There is nowhere to go," Northrop said, he and Levi were still rowing. Their arms burned, but they kept on, not knowing what else to do. "Maybe land at Crooked Island and part there."

The sun began to set on the watery horizon. From the bright light, a white sail took form, like a mirage. It grew as it moved toward the castaways.

"There's a ship," Levi looked out. Amaro looked into the water but knew he couldn't swim away in his condition. The merchant ship spotted the rowboat and stirred toward the three.

"Men overboard! Heave them up!" A sailor called from above. The merchant vessel threw down lines and pulled up the three men, burnt and drained from exposure. The crew was especially courteous in helping them over the railing.

"Lord help us," One man gasped, seeing Amaro's whipped back. Their captain quick to approach the scene.

"Take them below deck," He ordered to those standing over the men. "Fetch em some water, too."

The three sat in the galley where other sailors congregated. Amaro was passed out and sat away from the old man and Levi, who slowly sipped the water they were given.

"I don't like this, bringing a *Jonah* on board," One sailor said to the others as he dealt a hand of cards.

"This be something far greater than Jonah. Look at em, all three of em look plagued," The sailors on the merchant ship discussed to themselves as they gambled. Levi watched them from across the room. They played the same game as he had seen in the tavern, except these men were wagering money. Whereas the unemployed privateers had nothing to gamble.

"We should have never taken them on," The dealer continued. "They're cursed men."

"Aye, I say we hurl them back into the sea before they sicken the rest of us," The other added his opinion as he played his hand.

"To what evil will they bring? The one is clearly a fugitive. The others with em, they didn't seem to own him as their prisoner. They be accomplices, I say."

"What do you think is wrong with em? You saw the man, his wounds were black, and their hands and feet are darkened, too."

The men quietly debated with themselves. Above them, another crew member went to the captain.

"Sir, we're worried about these men. They're sickly…"

"And?" The captain asked. He was an Irishman, red hair and muscular.

"The beaten one, I recognize him from a bounty we saw," The sailor got quiet. "I think he's a pirate."

"A pirate?" The captain thought. "Be some reward for em, then? We'll keep them locked in the galley."

"We don't want them on deck, sir. Throw them overboard, be done with them," He suggested. "We cannot risk getting sick."

"No. We're turning them in. We need the money. Tomorrow we will see who they really are. For now, see to it they're under a watch tonight. If they are pirates, they may try to overtake us," The captain went to his quarters below deck, in the stern of the ship. His sailors stayed up that night to keep an eye on the three, who were all now asleep.

"Where are you from, sailor?" The captain of the schooner asked Amaro the next day.

"Kingston," He lied. They were still below deck in the galley. The crew above was now preparing the sails to take off again.

"So, you are not the wanted man in Havana? There's a poster that looks very much like you."

"No, sir," he said quietly.

"What is your name?"

"George."

"Hmph," The captain grunted. "And you two, where are you from?" He turned to Levi and Northrop.

"Kingston. All of us," Northrop responded.

"And how was it I found you so far from Jamaica?"

"Our ship went down, heading for New Providence. We escaped on the rowboat. Though it was night, so we could not see if there were any other survivors," Levi added.

"Compelling," The captain started. "Unfortunately, your accent deceives you, Mister *George*. Put them in in the cargo bay and tie them up," He turned to his men. "We sail for Havana."

"Yes, captain," A crewman came from the crowd surrounding them. Amaro got up to fight, but the large number of men overpowered him, and bound him with line. Levi followed Northrop's lead and surrendered willingly.

The Port of Gold

15.

Hurricane.

Admiral Esteban was overseeing the cargo being transferred to his larger fleet of vessels to brought to Spain. He had commanded the treasure fleet for years, racking in a profitable amount of gold himself. In his office, he purposely underestimated their loot for the ledgers as to take more for himself. Several chests of gold were brought to him in his Havana mansion. The rest of the treasure joined the countless crates of silver and jewels onboard the fleet of twelve flagships.

"Sir. Some men are here to collect a bounty," An officer entered. Esteban waved for the men to come in, not taking his eyes off his paperwork. "Sir, they claim to have Amaro."

"How?" He trembled in rage, dropping his quill.

"I don't know, sir," The officer stammered.

"Bring them in!" Esteban snapped. The decorated sailor left Esteban's office. Esteban shut the ledger book and sat back in his chair. He pointed at his empty glass, queuing his servant to pour him another drink.

"I have this one, thought he matched the description on your flyers," The Irish captain brought in Amaro, his arms were tied behind his back. "Knew he was a fugitive just by looking at em, beat and all. Picked up a few others with him, actually. My men told me they's were bounties for someone else," He gloated.

"Where are they?"

"Well, back on my ship, I have to sail them over yet to collect their reward," He gestured out the window toward the docks.

"Bring them here, I'll pay you double," Esteban said sternly.

"Ho," The burly man laughed. "That's a fine deal. Saves me a trip back that way. I should warn you though, I think these men are sick. An infection or something."

"Never mind that, bring them here," Esteban insisted. The captain left, leaving the two alone in his office, except for the admiral's stationed guards and servants. "How did you possibly escape?"

"The fools untied me. Don't worry Esteban, when I escape these binds too, I'll come for you," Amaro jeered.

"I don't doubt you'll try," Esteban took a sip of his drink.

The captain came back with Northrop and Levi, also tied with line. Esteban handed the man a reward from his newfound gold and dismissed him.

"Now, you I haven't been introduced to yet," The admiral looked up and down the two men with Amaro. "Crew members of his? Fellow pirates on the run?"

"No," Levi spoke, holding his chin up. "Twas my crew that first made it to the island. Found the map before any of you Spaniards."

"The locals, then. Yes, I was told some had made it there before us. Though, I'll admit at this point, it doesn't matter who you were. You are all prisoners of Spain now. And since you, Amaro, have been such a wretch in my life, I'm taking you all back to Spain so that the king himself can oversee your execution."

"What an honor," Amaro hissed. His black, unkept hair hanging over his face.

"It's ironic, isn't it? You all sought after the gold with such tenacity only to be left with nothing. Such is the life of pirates."

"We're not pirates," Levi spoke up.

"And yet you share the same fate as him," Admiral Esteban went back to his desk. "Load them up on a ship. Prepare to leave as scheduled this morning," He ordered the guardsmen in the office. The soldier promptly escorted Amaro, Northrop, and Levi to the docks. Havana was bright that morning, the sky still red with the dawn. Soldiers walked the prisoners down the stone streets. The three were brought on board a ship named *El Dorado* and escorted below deck. Amaro placed in a cell by himself, with the other two in a cell together.

"I'm sorry," Levi whispered over to Northrop.

"This has been out of our control, son."

"Do you think this is what we deserve?"

"If they hang us…" The old man thought aloud. "Then we got off easy."

"Cast off the moorings! Lower the sails!" The twelve ships were all pushing off from the port of Havana. Navy men worked the line as the sails caught wind. Slaves washed the decks and tended to the aristocratic officers in each of their cabins. The armada traveled straight north toward Florida, keeping their eye on the compass as they sailed.

Down below, Amaro glared across the brig at Levi.

"This was your doing," He hissed, sweat dripping from his brow. "I had everything, and you took that away!" He stood and pounded the bars, yelling across the deck at the two, who only glared back at him. "You stole the map and look where that got us! Are you happy? Did you succeed in your plan? None of us got anything! And now that we're unbound from our pact, I can kill you. Dice you up and eat you myself!"

The creak of the ship as it rolled and yawed over the waves was the only reply given to the enraged man. Not even the guards said anything in this. His hands out of the cell as his forehead pressed against the bars.

"I had an empire before you. Whole crews and ships! I was feared, respected even, for paying my tithes to the king and to God. Any port would bend if I stepped foot on their pier and now that's dead! King Philip won't even get the chance to condemn you, because as soon as I get out of this cell, you're dead, mate."

With no reply, Amaro sunk back into his cell and leaned his shoulder against the hull. Rain started dripping in from the top decks, the waves were gradually getting more powerful. The wooden deck and iron bars grew cold, not even the lanterns provided any heat for the men. The three shivered with the slaves below deck as the storm progressed. All of them wearing light clothes, Amaro still without a shirt.

"Best get some sleep," Northrop turned to Levi. "We have nothing else to do," He crossed his arms and sat back against the corner of the cell. Levi doing the same. Thunder was soft in the distance and the steady rocking of the boat kept the prisoners calm.

Lightning cracked like a whip against the ships' masts. The men below deck woken by the wind, now exponentially louder. *El Dorado* dipped over a wave and took on another. Water flooding in the portholes. Levi knocked off the cot and onto the deck with the violent pitch of the ship. On board all the ships, men pulled line to furl the sails.

"Get them up!" One captain far from Levi's ship, cried through the downpour. A wave came from the side and beat the men against the deck, many letting go of the freezing line. The sail dropped unevenly as the rope was quickly taken up the pulley.

"Batten down the hatches, be ready for worse!" Wind caught the funnel of material. The mast twisting and breaking right off the deck. Like a tree, the timber dropped onto the deck. Its crash broke the taffrail and down into the lower decks as the waves took hold and tore it from the ship.

"Water coming in port side!" Men worked to patch the immense breakage with the spare lumber they had aboard. They tried to hammer boards over the hole, but each wave undid their efforts. The element of water was against them.

"Keep her straight on!" Another captain ordered the coxswain of his ship. Sailors begun to throw over their fishing tackle and nets, trying to lighten the load. "Not the cargo!" That captain cried when he saw a man bring a chest on deck to jettison. "Not the cargo. Get rid of the barrels!" Powder kegs and barrels of liquor were rolled off, anything not tied down slid off the deck on its own. With the changing winds, waves were coming from unpredictable angles. Trying to ride down and over another wave, they were hit from the side. The opposing waves warped the wooden ship and spun it around. The ship's wheel cracked from pressure on the rudder. With no control, the waves tossed the ship where it willed. Men threw lost overboard, who hadn't secured themselves to the ship. The last thing lost into the sea was their hope. Rolling with a wave, the ship's masts dipped into water and began to weigh the vessel down. As it capsized, the hull filled with water and eventually sunk to the bottom of the sea.

The guard on *El Dorado* was knocked backwards with a sudden surge of a wave. His back slammed against the cell Amaro was in. The pirate pulled himself up and hooked his forearm against the guard's throat. As the man was choking and kicking, Amaro reached for the keys on his belt. After he pulled the set of keys off the leather tie, Amaro reached out with his other hand and snapped the guard's neck. He fell limp to the deck.

Levi and Northrop bracing themselves in their cell as the ship continued to roll freely over the crossing waves. Amaro unlocked his cage and slipped forward with the sharp pitch of the boat going down a wave. Drenched from the water coming in through the deck and portholes, Amaro crawled to his feet. He looked at Levi briefly before turning away. He went to the bow of the ship, where the slaves were bound and chained to the deck.

"We're commandeering this vessel," Amaro stated. "Any issues with that?" They shook their heads, frightened to speak. Amaro unlocked their chains and led the men up the stairs to the weather deck. One slave kicked the keys over to Levi's cage and then ran up the wooden steps. Levi grabbed them before they slid away.

"Arise, Admiral!" An officer burst through the captain's cabin on yet another ship as Admiral Esteban was belching his seasickness into a bucket. "Get up, call out to your men what they should do!" Esteban paid the officer no mind and laid back down in agony. The officer went out to give orders himself. The tempest storm beat on the sea so that the ship began to break. The heavy waves shook and strained the boat, as the storm rose up against them.

"What are you doing?" Esteban staggered on deck. The motion of the ship turning him green. He saw his men hoisting up the sails and tying their equipment down. "No! Lower the sails! Get us out of here!" Esteban waved and braced himself.

"Sir, we won't be able to sail in this!"

"Do as I say, swab!" Esteban pushed the young sailor and went on up to the helm, commanding his ship. He hurled from his vertigo, the washing of rains quickly dispelled Esteban's mess. His officers did not have time to comment on their admiral's weak stomach, as they fought the sea and all her fury. They fought against the wind and rain as the storm encompassed them. His ship rose with a surging tide and was dropped on a rock near the shore. His ship split in half as waves heavy like lead slammed against them, further breaking them against the rocks. Esteban was thrown against the stone, each pulsing wave beating him further until he had no life.

On each ship in the fleet, men fought against the hurricane and were driven along by its mighty winds. Some captains saw land and tried to run aground; others were forced deeper out to sea. They looked for the leeward side of an island to shelter in, but the storm was too monstrous. There was no bay that could possibly shelter the Treasure Fleet. One by one, the ships were swallowed by the ocean until only one remained.

"Get his sword," Northrop said as Levi unlocked the cell. "I'm more worried about Amaro than the Spanish."

"Aye," Levi armed himself with the rapier off the guard. They heard brawling on the deck above them as well as the constant crashing of waves. The two pulled themselves up the steps and observed the chaos. Sailors fighting the slaves, mostly with their fists. Some of the mariners were still trying to control the ship, all of them battling against the rain and whitecaps roaring onboard. "Get to the helm," Levi ordered. "I'm going after Amaro."

"Levi!" Northrop warned.

"It's the only way," The young man pushed off toward the bow. Northrop holding the railing for dear life as he went back towards the helm. Amaro dueling the naval officers with a sword he had taken from them. He slashed at them and dodged their attacks. Kicking one overboard and fighting to keep his own balance with the constant movement of the ship.

"Benson!" Amaro saw his foe walking intently toward him, dragging his blade with him.

"You have a threat to deliver on," Levi readied his cold steel sword. "So, let's have it!" He shouted through the shivering rain.

"It's your doom, then!" Amaro ran and swung down with his sword. Levi blocked and threw him off only to be faced with a series of flurries. They crossed swords and circled each other, keeping on their feet with the motion of the ship. The metal blades struck against each other like lighting in the storm surrounding them. Amaro attacked with rage, relentlessly swiping at Levi. The young man side stepped from his attacked and slashed at Amaro's back. He screamed in pain, then turned to deliver another stream of attacks. Their swords met again, Levi forcing them to turn downward. Amaro flicked his blade up, cutting Levi's cheek.

Northrop went up to the wheel. Seeing it was unoccupied, he quickly seized the helm and began to straighten the ship out. "Reef the sails!" He called out, hoping there were able men to carry out the order. "Reef the sails!" Some of the slaves and sailors took hold of the line and lowered the sails part way. The winds caught the ship and began to propel it forward. Roars came from the foaming sea below and the wuthering sky above. The fighting had all ended, most seeing it more worth to keep the ship afloat than to die fighting for control.

"Broad off the starboard, it's clear!" Someone called to Northrop who looked to see where the clouds ended near the horizon. He turned the wheel and pointed the ship cross wind to get them out of the storm. The waves were far too violent, and the day was far too dark to see if any other ships were around.

Levi yelled as Amaro cut at his hand and disarmed him. The pirate grinned through his rugged face and began to swing at the defenseless man. Levi dropped and tackled Amaro, dislodging his feet. Levi punched Amaro in the face, who pulled on Levi's hair and struck back. Amaro threw him off and scrambled to find his sword. He found Levi holding himself against the taffrail, trying to stand. Amaro charged and stabbed with the blade. Levi caught the man's arm and turned to throw him overboard. The young man watched his enemy be taken by waves and swallowed by the sea before he realized his side had been slashed.

"Where are we going?" Levi limped up to Northrop at the helm, gripping his side. "We can still go back and take another ship," Levi stopped after seeing the old man wouldn't reply. "Northrop, the gold," He pleaded.

"Let it go, son," he said softy. The old man sailed toward the seascape. Strong waves continue to rage from the wells of the deep and rain poured ever on them. Levi leaned against the rail. They rode the storm, not knowing whether or not they might survive.

Act II

The Port of Gold

16.

Rumors.

In an island town of Jamaica, many listened to music and drank at an open tavern. Birds flew about, picking at fruit on the trees. Seagulls scavenged the town, competing with rats to pick up scraps that were discarded or forgotten.

"Might I have a word with ye hearties?" One man approached two middle aged sailors who were drinking their rum in peace. They set down their green glass pints and turned. The two had seen this man before, wearing his felt tricorn hat and strutting in his bright coat with bravado. He was a popular sea captain in Kingston. Long black wig and finely trimmed mustache. "I have a proposal for a quest if you're interested. Lots of gold to be had."

"Heard it before, Henry, we ain't joining your mob," One went back to his drink, wiping the sweat off the glass.

"Nay, this be different. I have here a letter of marque from Lord Hamilton for the heist. It all be set."

"What heist would this be then? Sacking a Spanish port? Robbing the French plantations?"

"Tis not wise for a captain to reveal too much about a job to those not on board."

"Forget it then. We're not getting our limbs blown off for some money," One joked.

"What happened to Thompkins is unlikely to repeat itself," The captain murmured and shrugged. "This is a mighty fortune."

"Said forget it, Henry. We won't be swindled into your crew," The two got up to find a place to continue without interruption. Henry sat in the vacant seat put his boots on the table and sighed.

"Tough bunch," Another man observed. He was thirty-five, roughly the same age as Henry. His black coat was just as fancy as Henry's but did not have the same largely decorated hat that Henry wore proudly. "You're asking the wrong lot, mate."

"Do tell," Henry kept his feet up as the man sat down across from him. "I've asked a lot of lots."

"Sailors, aye. Not all of them easily corruptible as you hope."

"Corruptible?"

"Not everyone is keen on plundering as up front as you speak. They'd prefer an honest wage. Maybe more reliable wage."

"Nothing dishonest about privateering or treasure hunting. I have a right commission and all."

"Perhaps. You just need men who also see it that way or who don't care where their money comes from. You've been trying to recruit prey, captain. It's those sailors who will end up plundered by men like us, the predators," Henry put his feet down and leaned forward to study the man speaking to him.

"Us?"

"Pirates," The man confirmed. "A new brand of men, raising out of the ranks of these filthy empires. Molting out of our confined privateers' shell into free men. We take what we want, give nothing back to those men in their castles."

"I take it you think ye be the man I need for the job?"

"Benjamin Hornigold," He went to shake Henry's hand.

"Henry Jennings."

"I'll help you find your gold. Got my own ship and all, but I suppose that doesn't help your disposition."

"I'm a few hands short on my own."

"Well, as I was saying, you're asking the wrong crowds. These are working folk here. What you need are the scum of the seas I have on my ships. Breakaways, criminals, refugees, the people who got a rotten deal and need somewhere to run."

"Sounds like a lousy replacement for seamen."

"Oh, you'd be wrong. Any man can work the line if you teach em or promise them enough. I've been at this for a while now, Mister Jennings. I consider myself a mentor to those like us."

"Didn't know you could teach a man to commit piracy."

"Why do you think I recruit criminals?" Benjamin laughed. "They don't think twice when I give the orders."

"Say I bite, run with your kind, where do I find these racketeers of yours?"

"I'd head for Tortuga just north of Hispaniola. Any slave run off from big plantations head there, same with the crooks. The island be filled with wretches hiding from society. After that, sail forth to Nassau in New Providence and I'll meet you there."

"What's in that town?"

"I'm starting a little *country* of my own, I'd think you'd be interested in. For now, I use it for a rendezvous point."

"A country for predators?"

"Aye, black flags need to establish themselves or we'll be picked off one after the other. You may not see yourself as piratical, but I've heard of ye. A man with such ambition and pomp, you're cut from the same black cloth as I. Meet me in Nassau, I'll have more men who'd want to join us in this raid of yours"

"Let it be so," The Englishmen toasted.

"What are you worrying about?" Welham, the grizzly sailor asked the man next to him, shaking as he sipped his drink. Both men seated on stools taken off their ship.

"Don't you ever think they'll find us? This hut doesn't provide much cover given we used all the trees on the islet to build it," Gail practically looking over his shoulder. There was no land in sight of the tiny island they were on. He still had on his brown vest over his white shirt, though his pristine clothes were now tarnished months of being stranded. Their ship sat tilted and beat on the sand.

"What's a bounty gonna do to you?"

"I'm not bluffing mate, they'll skin us if the see any of our faces," He trembled.

"Well, come here," Welham his dagger around. "I'll change that face for you!"

"They'd still recognize your ugly mug," Gail bantered. "Why don't we just turn ourselves in?"

"What a fantastic idea! We'll tie the nooses for em as well!"

"I don't see you men doing anything to better our position."

"I'll gut you; I swear I will."

"Well come at me then, Welham!" Gail Wickman stood up, raising his unsteady fists. Both men practically healed from their respective injuries.

"Oi, it's no use," Welham sighed. Gail lowered his hands and nodded in content with him. Then Welham turned to punch Gail while his guard was down. They crashed onto the sand floor of their hut and wrestled out into the beach of their deserted island.

"Enough," Gail scurried away and threw out sand to ward off his attacker. "We've been stranded here for too long! We need to be finding food, not getting piss drunk on our ship's supplies every day! What'll do when those barrels run empty?"

"Hope I'd die by then," Welham sat up and brushed the sand from his shorts. "We can start eating our friend over there," He pointed to the whale that had beached itself not long after the *Gail Wickman* ran aground on the same remote island. "Heard them's good eating. Last us longer than these frickin' crabs," He scoffed.

"Got any guns left aboard? We could shoot the seagulls down, before they start picking at us."

"Not a terrible idea. Too bad the Spanish took em all before we got out. Surprised they left the grog."

"Huh," Gail sat down next to Welham. The two men looking out into the ocean, the other five in the lean-to hut they made. "We really going to die like this?"

"Maybe. You were right though. Bounties on all of us. Even if we do push the ship back into the water, none of us knows where to go."

Tortuga was a crowded city. Taverns seemed more numerous than houses. French guards were stationed there, but they often were too mixed up with the towns cahoots to stand an effective post. Women outside of brothels catcalled the drunkards across the street to follow them inside. The French government that had been established there moved to Port de Paix on the mainland of Hispaniola, not wanting to waste energy suppressing the ramble. They ignored the island, giving it no support save for the few coastguardsmen stationed there to remind people who still reluctantly owned the land.

"I'm very unsure about this, cap," Thompkins said to Jennings as they landed in the filthy city. The man on the docks meant to tie off ship's moorings was blacked out and leaning against some barrels, only a breeze away from falling off into the ocean.

"I'm rethinking my faith in that man," Henry said as he saw the collection of low lives that made up the city.

"Truly. I'd say he *is* a man of faith to let these bastards run his ship. Jesus Christ, look at this place," One of the taverns made use of the local tortoises and used their shells to serve drinks to those around. The slow-moving animal never strayed too far from the inns, not that anyone knew who actually owned the beast.

Jennings was afraid to sit down, lest he get his bright clothes covered in dirt and muck that coated just about everything. Thompkins limped behind him on his wooden leg, making him shorter than he already was. He wore simpler clothes than his captain, a striped shirt, and plain breeches. A bandana covered his head and grim covered his tanned skin. When he walked, he was slow to put his weight on his wooden leg, then quick to step with his other, grunting with every step. Tompkins had thick, yet short beard lining his wide jaw.

"Well, look at this aristocrat, strutting in here with big hat and long coat. You get lost, your highness?" One drunk stood up, blocking Henry from walking further into the tavern.

"Afraid not. I sailed to this rat's nest by choice."

"Ha," He smirked and let them pass. "What business have you here? Delivering more wenches, I hope?"

"Oh no, I'm not delivering. I'm here to pick up..." Henry turned to the rest of the room who gave him their attention. "Any man with three limbs and a thirst for gold.

I have a job and a need for men in my crew. Easy coin if'n we get there soon."

"Aye, I could use the fresh air," One stood up and walked out the door. Others mumbled to themselves, many of them getting up and walking out.

"Ay! You're stealing me patrons!" The bartender hollered.

"We weren't gonna pay you's anyway!" The mob laughed as the left the dingy tavern. Henry led the mob to his ship, called *Bersheba*.

"Speak with Thompkins, here, to enlist," Henry ordered. The men from the tavern lined up as Thompkins took out some parchment and wrote down their names.

"So, cap'n," One of the new recruits called out as he was reclining on top of some crates. "What's this prize we're after? Not that we're much to ask questions. Just curious, see."

"We're wrecking the Spanish treasure fleet. The whole twelve ships went down in a storm."

"I heard it was eleven," Another joined the conversation.

"Pretty sure I know the size of the fleet," Jennings refuted.

"Oh yea, the fleet was twelve, but only eleven of em went under. I heard one was commandeered and escaped."

"Truly?"

"Aye. If you're looking for men, might as well ask *them*."

"You know where they are?" Jennings inquired.

"Oi, Rory," The sailor called another over. "Where'd you say that Captain Benson was from?"

"Benson? You mean the one with the Spanish ship?"

"Yeah. Shore-something, wasn't it?"

"Aye. Uh, Shore-rock, Shore-hill. Oh! Shorehaven. That's what it was, Shorehaven."

"You know he's there?" Jennings asked.

"No," He scratched his head. "You see, I met him on his way through, not a month ago. I only recognized em from his wanted poster up at the inn. The bounty was to be collected in Shorehaven."

"So why would he be there if they wanted him?" Captain Jennings tried to piece together.

"Who knows? But if you're looking for a man, where he's wanted might be a good place to start looking."

"Aye," A few others on deck agreed. Jennings wide eyed at the realization his operation was in the hands of criminals.

"Alright, Rory, was it? Can you show me on my charts where this town is?" Jennings gestured to his cabin where the maps were.

"Oh sure, it's on our way if we're heading over to Nassau."

The Port of Gold

17.

The Town of Ashes.

"Ay, Cook," Welham called to his shipmate who ran the galley. "Why's this grog taste worse than it did yesterday?"

"Fresh batch, you'll get used to it."

"Fresh batch?" He burped. "We don't want to get used to it; we want to get drunk. It's like seawater!"

"Aye, it is sea water. Little bit of rum, lot a bit seawater," He replied, not adverting his attention from the food he was preparing.

"Is that all grog is?"

"Aye, we drink straight rum, we'd've out before we ported. Mix it with water, the liquor lasts longer. Each day we're here, I'm having to thin it out more. We don't have more than one-barrel left. Maybe less if you's been serving yeselves."

"Christ, we need to get off this island," Welham spoke aloud to his sobering thought.

"Aye, and soon. This whale meat will rot before we can cook it all. Soon we'll all look like him," Cook said, pointing his knife out to the skeleton of the beast. Gulls picking at the bones as its guts were being pulled out by the tide.

"Maybe we could salt it and store it in the empty kegs. We got plenty of salt from the water you's boiling."

"Could work."

The survivors of the Mutiny Crew scattered around the sand barge, looking for something to do. The lowland was flat enough to see someone from any side. Some stood by their ship, thinking of ways to get it to sea again. They beached on high tide, wind driving the sails further inland. Their lack of knowing where to go next fueled their lazy motivation to escape. Crofton was laying in the sand, sunburned like most. Ants crawled on his remining foot, callused, and torn. He and the other castaways had no regard for the bugs that bit them from beneath the sands and settled into their unshorn hair. Seagulls hovered above, almost wagering which castaway would drop first.

"What if we dug a trench straight through the island? Water would fill it up, we lower the sails and the wind pushes us across to the other side," Crofton visualized. Those with him were unsure how to respond, giving him only blank stares as they tried to picture in their heads how it would work. "That or Jack can just push it out."

"Hey, Jack! Come over here," Harper called to his crewmate from across the island. "You might finally be useful!"

Jennings threw down the lines to be tied to the pier of Shorehaven. The men worked quietly as they observed the ruins. The light house stood low, collapsed in on itself and most the other buildings lay in rubble. The roads were filled with sandy dirt and many open yards grew crops and weeds.

"Ahoy," Segar waved quickly as he tied the ship off. Jennings walked off the gangplank and looked around before responding. People moved in the dust, sitting in the old buildings with caved in roofs and wrecked walls.

"Is this Shorehaven?" Henry asked.

"Was," Segar sighed as he scanned his town. "It's no longer..."

"What happened here?"

"Spanish pirates."

"Bastards. My apologies from one Englishman to another."

"They hit us springtime. We just, uh, haven't got it in us to rebuild. Lost that peacefulness we had."

"That's darn near an act of war," Jennings followed Segar into town. The market square was covered in dirt and sand, chickens picked the unkept ground.

"Aye. We used to be a pretty bustling town. Trade ships would come and go from that pier, but after word got out that the Spanish obliterated our city, merchants stopped coming. We started farming to survive. No fish left in the water anyhow."

"They just attacked for no reason?"

"No," Segar replied quickly. "Most say it was God punishing us, but we were tied up in business we should have never been in. The Spanish were after some other pirates, thought we were keeping them fugitives. I told them the men they were after weren't here, but they, uh, they didn't believe me. Blew up the town in retaliation. Anyway, you stopped at my dock. Was there something I could do for you? Seemed you had specific business."

"I'm looking for a pirate," Jennings said, frankly. "Was told he was wanted here."

"Levi," Segar said sternly. "Is that your man, Levi Benson?"

"Aye. Captain Benson."

"Captain," Segar mocked and spat on the ground. "He isn't here. If he were, he'd be nothing but a corpse."

"Where is he?"

"I don't even know," Segar sighed out his anger. "There's one man here who *might*, but I can't get him to talk."

"Bring me to him."

Segar led Henry back toward the docks. They turned around the Rogue Star, which was partially rebuilt. From its door hung wanted posters for Levi and his old crew. Segar pointed to the lighthouse that sat apart from the rest of town. Henry looked at Segar before going the rest of the way. He took off his large hat as he entered the ruined building.

"I'm looking for Levi Benson," Jennings spoke softly to the old man who sat inside the lighthouse. The house still stood, but the tower had fallen in on itself. It was dimly lit through the pile of bricks. Sunlight beamed through the dust in the air.

"You and everyone else."

"Do you know where he is?" Jennings pushed, but Northrop did not say a word. "I need his help. I'm after a large sum of gold and I believe he knows where it is. I'll be sure you get rewarded if you help me in this."

"I don't want that gold," he said sternly. "Gold is the reason our town was blown to shred. Gold is the reason Levi went into hiding. Godforsaken gold, God curse every last coin," He exhaled smoke from his pipe, adding to the dusty air.

"You want to protect him, don't you?"

"The kid can take care of himself."

"But you want him safe. Otherwise, you wouldn't care to keep him hidden," Jennings continued. "He helps me with this one job, I can settle him an estate. I have land all over the new world, he can hide in peace, in safety. Just as long as he helps me find the gold," Northrop sat for a while, breathing through his pipe.

"He captains a ship out of Nassau. Small sloop, yellow sails, the *Sun Dew*," Northrop sighed. Jennings was about to turn and leave when Northrop caught his forearm. "After this job, you leave him be. He doesn't need to get mixed up with your like."

"But as you said, the kid takes care of himself," Jennings grinned as he walked away. "Sounds like he's already my like."

Henry Jennings walked from the rubble and down to the docks. The townsfolk rarely looked up from their work to notice the ship's passing. They tilled the ground, using the dirt of the old road to grow food. The white and brown sails of the *Bersheba* dropped, and they sailed away from the island chain, west toward Nassau.

"What did they want with the boy?" Smith came into the lighthouse, leaning against the doorframe.

"To recruit him," He coughed. "They need his help to run a job, I guess."

"More treasure hunting?"

Northrop shook his head before responding. "He didn't say. I'm beginning to think Segar was right."

"Never thought you'd be the one to say that."

"He should have never stayed here," Northrop said slowly as he smoked. "I should've never taken him in. I just wanted to make up for some past mistakes, but I created new ones."

"We couldn't have known it would end like this," Smith admitted in a huff.

"But we all knew it would end badly. That blasted gold only ever brings pain," He brought his pipe to his mouth.

"Now don't get teary on me," Smith said. "We thought we could live quietly, but our world's always been dangerous. We were both dangerous men in our day. We've lived that life, the ambition. He just reminded us of that world. It was the Spaniard that blew up the town. Not Levi."

"He was a good kid. I thought I could make a man after myself. I let him slip into this madness that's taken over. That man looking for him, and the Spaniard, they all were cursed. Not from the island, from this new plague. It kills men, leaves nothing but monsters. Pirates," Northrop grieved over Levi as father would his child.

"Levi's still a kid, he's not yet a man. Nor a monster. I wouldn't give up on him," Smith stood to leave. "Even if the rest of them have."

A gaff-rigged sloop cut through the shallow water. It sailed at an angle as the wind took the bright sails. The *Sun Dew* capered smoothly, skipping with the bounce of the waves. The yellow sailcloth reflecting off the clear blue water.

"Keep her close to shore, we'll get around the horn faster!" Levi stood on the rail at the bow of his ship, looking ahead of them.

"Aye, cap'n!" The man at the helm called, turning the wheel. A cannon shot hit the water beside them and exploded a splash on deck. The men continued unphased.

"Hold your lines," Roger, the bosun called out. He was roughly the same age as Levi. He was tall with short dark hair. Stubble grew on his pointed chin which matched the black of his eyes. Men worked at their stations; water washing in evaporated in the heat of day. Another blast came from behind them as a cannonball yet again missed their ship. The frigate was slow compared to the cutter

Levi sailed. It had no cannons but was able to outrun and outmaneuver the larger ships protecting the coast.

"There's a channel between the trees," Levi cried back to the coxswain. "Take her in there, we'll lose em."

"Aye, aye!" The sloop banked around the bend in the coast and took the channel between the mainland and the smaller island. Tall trees on either side hid the small ship.

"Furl the sails," Levi commanded quietly. "Slow us down," The *Sun Dew* drifted silently over the shallow blue water. The men looked around in anticipation, peering between the trees and looking fore and aft for their pursuer.

"I say we sneak up behind frigate and take it," A shipman suggested, getting fidgety.

"No, we have far too few men for that. Far too guns fewer," Levi refuted, still at the fore lookout.

"Behind us!" Another man cried, seeing the bowsprit of the ship appear from the trees. "She's following us inland."

"Lower sails, come on!" Levi called out to his crew, quick to get their ship catching wind again. "Get us moving!"

"They're gonna run aground," Roger pointed out. "We're only sledding the sand now."

"Aye. Let them. Fat bastards should've known better," Levi called. He watched as the ship crunched to a halt. The frigate's sails pushed and strained the masts, digging itself deeper into the sand. Men aboard fired muskets at the sloop, now evading them yet again. After they sailed out from the channel, Levi went below deck to his private quarters.

November 1715

Picked up another shipment from a Spanish wreck. Crates spices and silk that we can sell off when we port this evening. Also, a chest of silver plate and coin. We can't carry too much in a job, so it helps the ship can run them quick. Almost thinking of getting a bigger vessel. A caravel like Wickman's would be a good step up from this sloop. Many other freelancers have even larger ships in their possession.

We've hit sporadically, trying to stay out of notice of both the English and the Spanish. The jobs come to us even more randomly. A deckhand hears a rumor or 'accidentally' intercepts shipping information, we're quick to act. Mainly sneaking in and robbing camps or ships at night. Sometimes running goods already commandeered in or out of Nassau.

That city is a haven for men working between commissions like myself. Plenty of shops and taverns, plenty of people. Safe, it may not be. The English navy has a fair presence in the area and immediate islands. They used to control the island until a group of privateers took it over several years back. They're making their own country, as I've heard. Many think the English want to snuff the place out. It's an unsettling fear that lingers over the merriment of the town.

18.

Rendezvous.

"Captain Levi?" Jennings walked over to the young man on the docks, who was standing aboard a ship. From the railing hung a wooden sign that had inscribed, '*Sun Dew*: Ship for hire.' "Is there a Captain Levi on deck?"

"Depends, who are you with?" He stood in a blue jacket and a brown leather tricorn hat, breathing in the fresh morning mist. As he was leaning against the taffrail, a tattoo of an octopus could be seen wrapping his right forearm.

"A man answers that way, you know he's the right one for the job," Jennings laughed as he stepped up the gangplank. The young man tensed up. "At ease, I'm with no navy."

"Alright then. What do you need?"

"I'm rallying a few crews to recover some sunken treasure. Was told this captain was very familiar with the wrecks."

"You'll have to shed some detail. My shipmates have wrecked quite a few ships. Plenty ruined boats out there to plunder. Might not have heard of this run you're planning."

"Not too many haven't heard of the Spanish Treasure fleet taken down this summer. Till recent I, with the rest of the new world, assumed all twelve went under. Yet a rumor told me that one of the ships was overthrown by a prisoner and sailed out of the storm. A man named Levi Benson."

"Aye. I've heard that rumor," The young man nodded.

"Tis true, then? I was told he be captain of this ship."

"Some days, aye."

"When he decides to return, can you relay my offer? I'm in need of good men more than ships as of now. Him and the other captains will all get their fair share to distribute to their crews. Benson would be a valuable asset, being he knows about where the ships went down. Maybe he'll get a bonus for his knowledge."

"I'll let him know," Levi said. He stayed on deck, waiting for Jennings to leave. Henry walked back to the pier and across the rough planks back into town.

Nassau was a particularly rough looking town. Once the pirates took ownership, very little, if at all, was maintained. Sand from the beaches, under the docks, flowed into the stone streets that were once neatly swept. Broken glass polluted the ground, cutting those who wandered the streets barefooted. Paint on the buildings were once bright, now faded and peeling away. Palms grew on the beaches, some trees even sprouting up in the roads.

The civilized Englishmen who lived there before either fled with the last retreating soldiers or converted to the new anarchic lifestyle. Hundreds of men, all serving different captains flooded the once small town. Most lived in camps on the beaches. Some stayed in the many taverns. Other still, found comfort in the brothels that were already in place. Almost none of the men were married, but those who were lived off the island, wanting to keep their wives as far away from town as possible. There was truly no governance there, only people surviving together in the shambled houses. The only rules were orders given out by captains.

"Who was that?" Roger came from below deck, eating an apple he took from the galley.

"He didn't say. He had a commission for us, though."

"And you said yes?"

"No, I didn't agree just yet."

"Forgive me cap'n, but are ye crazy? We need the gold. The men aren't even going into town on leave because they haven't the spare money to drink away."

"He asked for me by name. That makes me uneasy."

"So? Any sea captain worth his spit has a name known across the world. Given nicknames and legends. You should be flattered not scared," Roger joked, looking down to his captain.

"We're wanted men, boatswain. It's something we need to consider. If there's men out there knowing where we are, some of those might be bounty hunters."

"What is it ye tell us? No gold has no risk. There's an inherent hazard to who we are. You know that as well as any of us, you taught us that. Let's take the bait. We're treasure hunters, for Chrissake. Even if it gets us into a bind, it'll give us something to do."

"You listen too closely," Levi smirked.

"Just following orders sir," Roger shrugged as he went back below deck to the galley, ducking himself under the boards. The galley was where the crew's hammocks were hung at night and while they were in port. They communed their if they had truly nowhere else to go.

Levi stayed on deck, now going to the opposite railing, looking out to sea. From his pocket, he pulled a gold piece, one he took from Isla Maldito. The rough cut, almost square coin moved between his ash-colored fingers.

"There'll never be enough of you," he said to the piece. He scratched the scruff on his face and went down to the pier into town. He saw the man from before sitting on a porch, drinking with a few other finely dressed sailors. The tavern was named the *Shark Bait Saloon*. The old building was close to the docks. The bar itself was inside, but sailors often sat out of the porch that overlooked the bay. Wind blew through the palms that hung as a canopy from the trees. Colorful birds glided from the forest to any spot they could find to perch on. Men drank from the compilation of bottles and glasses the tavern had acquired over the years. They drank light and spent more time talking in the earliness of the day.

"Ahoy again," Jennings called out to Levi who approached the grouping of mariners.

"Morning again. My captain brings his response to your offer," The men at the table turned more intently. "He'll lend you his men to man your ship. Though he regrettably has business to tend to elsewhere, he's appointed me to boatswain his men and to relay any information you may need."

"You hear that, mates? More men rallying to the cause," Jennings said to Benjamin and the other sailor.

"What captain doesn't want a slice at some fortune, but sends his men to grab a piece for themselves? Where are we going anyway? Wasn't this captain the man who was supposed give us our heading?" The other scoffed. Samuel Bellamy was his name. He was only a little older than Jennings. He wore a black coat which matched his dark curls. He'd been treasure hunting for years in New Providence, wrecking old ships for goods, before joining up with Hornigold's crew.

"We all have our matters," Benjamin spoke up. "We'll honor his decision, tis only at his loss."

"I'm afraid he didn't give me any exact coordinates. He sailed with the fleet, aye, but the storm scattered the ships and no navigator had the peace to find their position," Levi sighed, acting as though he wasn't the captain they needed.

"Very well," Benjamin shot Jennings a look of annoyance the turned back to Levi. "Deckhand send your shipmates to meet at the *Bersheba* tomorrow afternoon.

Captain Jennings here will direct you from there," He shoed the young man away with a dignified sense of superiority.

"I was told he would know where it was," Jennings defended immediately.

"You knave, how are we supposed to plunder the gold if we don't know where it is?" Samuel threw down his pint.

"Information that specific just can't be acquired," Jennings stated. "Can you give me the coordinates of any prize you took? Were you given an exact map to any treasure?"

"Aye, I found the Williamson Fortune off Barracuda Cape. The treasure of Sir-"

"We know they're along the coast," Jennings interrupted Samuel, tired of being proven wrong. "We just sail up the shore and who knows how much we can find."

"Oh, shut it! You said this was an easy job, 'guaranteed money,'" Samuel got up to leave. "We haven't had pay in months. My men needed this."

"We can still take it," Benjamin stepped in, the other stood to hear. "We have to sail north along the coast regardless. Any private ship we cross, we're commissioned to take to find the gold. Perhaps we can get some Spaniard to tell us where the wrecks are."

"See? It's not a lost cause," Jennings shrugged.

"But that is if they haven't already been scavenged. The Spanish knew about it before your governor did. You're not out of this just yet, Henry," Benjamin turned.

"So, it's my head if the job is a bust?"

"Aye, that's a good plan," Samuel pointed to Jennings. "I'll hang you meself before my men will."

"Oh, quiet up, Bellamy! I'll shoot you."

"Men," Benjamin interjected. "Be more civilized. If Jennings delivers on his promise, like he says he will, then there be nothing to worry about."

"In all my years..." Samuel shook his head. He left, taking his pint with him, forgetting he was still gripping the handle. The two remaining sailors did not add another word to the conversation. They sat, breathing heavy until they were calmed, and took in the ocean view.

"What are you doing?" Gail ran over to his ship. Men hung down from the stern castle and chipped at the woodcut letters on the stern with shovels and daggers.

"Well, it's not the *Gail Wickman* anymore," Cook called down. "Not since it was commandeered from you."

"Aye, but then we all took it back from the Spanish."

"The group, aye. And as you can see, the group wanted to rename the vessel."

"To what?" Gail threw his hands up.

"*The Whale*," Cook pointed to the carcass across the beach. "After our friend there. After all, he's the reason we ain't starved to death."

"You haven't the letters to spell *The Whale*."

"What?" They all stopped.

"You could take the *H* and the *E* from *The*, but then it would just be called *Whale*."

"Where's the *H*?" Crofton looked at it.

"Am I the only one on this island that can read?" Gail looked around him to the others who sat in confusion.

"It's not that we can't read," Welham joined. "We just can't spell. We know what we need to know to sail a ship, the rest is just useless rubbish!"

"Aye!" The others laughed along.

"How would you spell *The Whale* then? I take it you can't carve your own letters, since you don't know any," Gail continued.

"Look, just because I don't know no flipping letters, doesn't mean I can't still gut you."

"You truly are a barbarian," He looked at Welham in disgust.

"Isn't it just *W. A. L.*?" Harper called from on top the ship, still beached on the sand barge.

"The *Wall*?" Cook refuted.

"Way-Ill," Crofton tried to over annunciate to figure out its spelling. "Wall-Illy."

"Crofton give me your wood leg. We'll use that to carve the other letters," Leatherneck Jack grinned. Crofton scrambled up to his foot and hobbled away from the encroaching man.

"Look, it's *W. H. A. L. E.*! The *Whale*," Gail snapped. "Just put *Whale* on the ship, we'll call it *The Whale* and we can finally go about getting off this bloody island!"

"Are you sure there's not an *I* in there?" Cook asked.

The Mutiny Crew took the bones from the whale and dragged them over to the ship. They used the cargo crane to move the heavy bones, insisting the whale become a part of the ship for feeding them those weeks. From the taffrail, its ribs dangled from bowlines and hitches, and from the bowsprit, its skull was knotted. They'd all grown too attached to the mammal, who was stranded on the same remote island. It was almost as if they felt that it, too, needed to escape with them.

"There she be! *The Whale*," Welham stood back in amazement at their beloved ship. "As seaworthy as they come," Even after they rechristened the ship, breaking an empty bottle at the keel, the Mutiny Crew was still stuck waiting.

It was only days before waves began to rise and grow. The sky darkened and wind swept the seas over their little island. Drops of rain woke the men who were passed out on the beach, their legs in the rising water.

"Storm tide," Welham scrambled up to his feet. "The water's surging! Weigh anchor, let's go!" The men around him got up and climbed the shroud onto the haunting ship. Sails were dropped and the anchor was hoisted up from the ground. "Wickman," He snapped as Gail was getting on deck. "Take the helm."

"Aye, aye!" Gail called then muttered, "You son of a gun," He turned to run up to the wheel.

"Climb down and dig us loose, lads!" Welham ordered some of the others. Gail smirked at how well Welham suited the position of captain, though he would never let anyone know of it.

The *Whale* dug its way out of the sand, being pulled by the heavy winds, and began to float on water.

"The Rowboats and Rum Mutiny Crew!" They hollered and yelled in excitement.

"Where to?" Gail called down.

"The heck if I know, just get us away from that island," Welham replied.

"Very well, onward it is."

"Captain Jennings," Levi along with his men went up to the *Bersheba*, docked on the opposite pier from their small vessel. Levi now wore simpler clothes, black blouse, and plain grey trousers. Clothes worthy to be worked in. "We're ready when you are."

"Stow your things below deck and help with the lines. We push off in an hour. You'll report to Mister Vane, me first mate, from now on," Henry pointed to a man on deck before receding into his cabin. Charles Vane was strong and lean with short hair that he cut himself. He had an angry look to him, a look he knew of and played into. He was a cunning man, serving under Jennings for several years, but often swayed his captain into his own motives.

"Captain Jennings, I didn't know you were married."

"Are you comfortable, Samuel?" Henry snapped at the man reclining at his own desk. Sam held a picture of Jennings and a woman that he found in his desk drawer.

"Remarkably," He replied as he got up, setting the picture down. "Captain Hornigold wanted me to check in, make sure everything was in order."

"As head of this raid, I should be the one sending men to check your ships. Who does this Benjamin think he is?"

"You may not know it yet, but he is captain of this port. He runs this town."

"Yes, I'm aware of his self-proclaimed rule."

"I would watch your tongue. He got his rule through killings and nasty ones there. He may look like and act like the kings, but he is a monster. This may be your expedition, captain, but it is his men and his name that's also on the line. So, if you would, get your ship in order," Samuel walked to the door. "And pray we find your gold."

19.

La Florida Coast.

Bersheba led the small armada from Nassau north west around the Bahamas to the Florida peninsula. Henry Jennings kept true on his course with Benjamin Hornigold and Samuel Bellamy keeping their ship, *Marianne*, tight behind. The third ship, *Eagle*, sailed by another gentleman from Jamaica, a Mister John Wills.

"I reviewed your letters from Governor Hamilton," Vane approached Jennings on the top deck.

"Aye?"

"Just thought I would clarify, there's restrictions in here. Says 'Execute all manner of acts of hostility *against* pyrates according to the Law of Arms.'"

"That was the commission."

"Do they know that?" Vane pointed the paper off the stern to the other ships. "This assumes if the gold was reclaimed, it was plundered by privateers, not the Spanish."

"Hamilton can't say in writing that we're free to attack the Spanish. That'd start another war."

"So, we're going against his orders, then?"

"In writing, he says attack pirates. But when he handed that marque to me, 'anyone not under King's colours is free game.' Whatever it takes to get this gold."

"It's just a bit bold for you, sir. Attacking the Spaniards outright. Perhaps there *is* some malice in ye."

"You've always urged me on to it," Henry Jennings turned to his first mate.

"Oh, I'm not against it, captain. Just affirming you know what it is you're doing. We're in the same lot as them now."

"A pirate is a matter of perspective. To their employer, they are marques-men. To the victim, a pirate, indeed."

"That's how it were, years ago. These men are pirates to all. You know they have no affiliation to the King. They say Hornigold is their Governor."

"As long as they help us with the raid, it doesn't matter who they are. Don't tell me Benjamin's been lecturing you."

"I hear what the man has to say. You will always be my captain, but if our crew lived like his, we'd be a lot richer. And isn't that what we're after?"

"I'd like to consider myself a good man of class, I'll always be different from them."

"In manner, yes."

They sailed on for days, keeping a spyglass' view from shore. The lookouts scanned for shipwrecks or camps on the beaches. Men who were not currently needed communed in the galley. They ate from the stash of food they brought aboard, some gambled, some got rest for their coming shift.

"What's your name, kid?" A sailor looked up at Levi who sat across him.

"James," Levi replied.

"You're with that crew that pier jumped?"

"Aye, just for the job."

"Just for the job," The man nodded then his eyes caught Levi's cursed skin. "What's wrong with your hands, mate?"

"Squid," he said hastily. "You kill enough squid, the ink seeps into your skin."

"That it might," He thought to himself. "Is that why you got yer tattoo, there?" He pointed to the octopus. Its dark marks fading into Levi's ink-filled skin.

"Aye," Levi lifted his right hand slightly.

"Name's Rory, by the way."

"Pleasure."

"You, uh, look familiar, no? Have we worked together?"

"Not unless you're in the squid business."

"No," Rory laughed. "You sail with the same crew for too long, every stranger starts to look the same."

"That could be."

A Spanish packet boat came from the north and was passing between *Bersheba* and the shore. The small vessel hailed over to Jennings, who waved courteously in return from the top deck.

"Sir, Hornigold is moving to cut it off," Vane called, looking aft off the ship.

"What? It's a mail ship, why would they attack?"

"Wills is following them to blockade."

"Bring her around!" Henry called to the coxswain. The *Bersheba* banked left and circled behind the small ship, who lowered sails to slow down before reaching the blockade. It shot a white flag up the main mast as the unarmed vessel was quickly surrounded. "What on earth, Benjamin?"

The *Bersheba* pulled up alongside the mail ship as Hornigold had already hooked and boarded. Benjamin had the captain at gunpoint when Henry stepped on deck. Levi and the other crew members went up to see what the abrupt maneuver was about.

"What is this?" Jennings asked.

"Information," Hornigold pulled the hammer back on his flintlock pistol. "This kind sir was just explaining something of importance."

"*Sí, sí!*" He pleaded. "I just came from the fort, Palma de Ayz."

"And the gold is there?"

"What's left," The captain shuttered.

"How much?" Benjamin pushed, inching the barrel closer to the crying man. "How much gold is left?"

"*No se! No se cuanto!*" He shook his head as tears came from his face. "*Nunca he visto el oro!*" Benjamin grunted in frustration.

"Where is Palma de Ayz? *Donde?*" Henry asked. The man nodded and pointed back to his cabin. Benjamin motioned with his pistol to let him go. The Spaniard led the two into the cabin and took out a map of the coast. He tapped on the fort; whose name was marked on the parchment. Then he moved his shaking hand just north of the fort. "*Velero.*"

"Twenty-seven and a half degrees north," Henry said, translating the markings. "Not far from where we are," Benjamin took the map off the desk, rolled it, and forced it on Henry.

"Lead on, Jennings. Now that we've found your gold," He turned back to the man, still cowering from the pirate. "*Gracias.*"

The *Bersheba* lowered its brown and white striped sails and came about. The *Marianne* and *Eagle* were close behind. They let the packet boat sail on, her captain insisting he would not tell a word of the interception. Levi was still on deck, taking in the ocean mist and feeling them ride over the waves. Behind him, Rory stopped Captain Jennings to exchange a few words before descending back to the galley.

"Sir," Roger came to Levi.

"Yeah?"

"Did ye ever find out why these men were looking for you?"

"Aye, they thought I knew just where wrecks were."

"Why would that be?"

"I was on one of 'em, mate. All that gold these men are after, I was there when it was found. Bought our ship with my slice of what we took."

"So, you really sailed out of that hurricane?"

"Don't go starting legends now," Levi smirked as he pushed off from the railing to head below deck to get some rest. Evening would come and Levi had the night shift. Before going to sleep that night, he took out his notebook and journaled under the flickering candlelight.

December 1715

I've been aboard the Bersheba a week now, under Captain Henry Jennings. He seems agreeable enough, though as it were, the other captains seem to be taking charge more than him. I'm still suspicious of him knowing who I am. Rumors spread fast, but they're easily corruptible. My name being spoken around the world is an uneasy feeling.

We're close to the gold now. I feel it, the black pitch in my blood running to life again. I feel my veins invigorate and my heart pump the ink through my body. It's uncomfortable, like it was when I was first cursed. Whatever vexed me on that island, didn't stay. It's the gold itself that's condemned.

Despite that, I've always wanted to return. My heart has longed to reclaim the gold. It may be just another treasure to these men, but it's nonetheless priceless to me. I don't know why it's more valuable than regular pay, perhaps it feels personal. As if the pain I endured for this treasure, I'm owed.

Bells rang from the deck and men hollered in the morning. Sailors stowed their hammocks and prepared their stations.

"Dress yourselves for action," Thompkins cried down the stairs. "Get ready for the battle."

"Battle?" Some said aloud. As the men rallied on deck, guns, and swords in hand, they saw the camp on shore. Spanish soldiers marched the beach, unaware of the incoming fleet's purpose. The small stone fort had only a few buildings and guns. Tents were put up on the beach. Further up the beach, hidden between rocks and trees was a wrecked ship.

"Just like the navy, boys," Thompkins limped down the line. "Or whatever else you did to find trouble," The thrown-together crew had a variety of experience. They grabbed whatever weapons they brought aboard themselves. Some carried guns, others had tools like harpoons or hooks. They wore breeches or shorts with simple tops. Clothes that fit tight were better for working the lines and in the present case, battle. They wore heavy belts that holstered pistols, hung powder flasks, tucked away swords.

"Privateers, navy men," Vane came alongside Thompkins. "You'll be the first wave on the beach; ready your guns. Rest of you will follow behind. Get an idea of what a Spaniard looks like and kill some of those!" Some of the men shouted and raised their weapons.

"On your orders, sir," Thompkins turned to Jennings who stepped on deck in his finest clothes. A bright red felt jacket and a large hat that covered his usual black powdered wig. He gazed out at the camp, then turned to the other ships, seeing their men assembled as well.

"Bring us some gold, men!" He laughed.

Men hurried to the rowboats and lowered themselves into the crashing water. Shouting came from the fort as they were noticed. The Spanish quick to fire at the attackers with their mounted cannon and gunmen. The mariners rowed hard to the shore, ducking under occasional musket shots from the fort walls. The crew of the other two ships did the same. Hornigold fired several cannons that gave cover to the rowboats below. Once the men reached the sand, they charged with their guns to front gate. Spanish soldiers fired over the walls at the oncoming attacks.

Levi was among the first wave in the longboats, the other attackers close behind in what crafts were left. The sailors yelled as they swarmed the beach. Jumping into the salty water, they trashed to dry land. The soft sand was rough to run on, some tripping over themselves. Yet, the overwhelming numbers staggering on shore was enough to get the Spanish to lock themselves into the stone fort. The invaders soon rushed to the gate, breaking down the wooden doors. Before entering, Levi fired at a Spaniard on the ramparts. After firing his shot, he drew his sword for battle. The Spanish took turns firing down from the high walls between loading rounds. The muzzle loaders taking time to pour and ram gunpowder before being able to fire another round.

Roger ran in behind the first wave. As he turned the corner into the fort, he was hit with the stock of a gun and laid on his back. He drew his sword from his belt and crawled backwards to gain some distance. He pushed off the ground and lurched at the Spaniard, who was now occupied with another pirate. Roger swung at the soldier, the barrel of the gun blocking the attack. The Spaniard turned back to the other pirate and fired his musket, tearing off some of that man's shoulder. Using the bayonet, he sliced up at Roger and continued a series of jabs. Jumping back, Roger dodged them until he hit the fortress wall. Grinning, the Spanish soldier lunged at his pinned opponent. Roger dove to the side and brought his sword across as he did. He flinched as he turned back to see the Spaniard on the ground, his throat bleeding open.

"Out the back gate, they're getting away!" Vane yelled as two soldiers opened the doors and ran with a chest. Levi sprinted through the rumble to catch them. He tackled one and quickly got up to meet the other. Their swords connected and crossed as they each took swings at the other. The man on the ground was getting up to his knees when Levi turned to kick him back down. His opponent lunged, Levi stepped to the side and cut his stomach. Around him the few dozen soldiers that were left ran into the jungle, leaving even their weapons behind. Charles Vane continuing to fire gunshots into the fleeing enemy. Levi picked up the chest and carried it back to the fort, now captured by the pirates. Others were stockpiling the plunder in the center. A handful of chests and several crates worth of goods was all that could be found.

"What's this?" An exhausted sailor asked Jennings as he was standing up on the pile.

"This is the gold, men," Jennings said slowly, realizing himself how little was left.

"Twelve ships of gold, and that's all we find?" They grumbled and began to holler at the man.

"Look, this is still a considerable amount. Each of ye could get a year's wage or more, just from this. Plus, anything the Spanish left is fair game. It doesn't look like it, but there's a lot there!"

"Aye, lads," Hornigold stood up. His voice was low and hoarse. "We were promised whatever was left, and Jennings delivered. We'll have our quartermasters all count it and split it. You'll collect your pay when you get back to port. Those with injuries come forward so ye can be compensated. Cause we will hang you on the way if you keep grumbling like dogs. Hear?"

"Aye," Some of the mob nodded.

"Good," Jennings nodded to himself. "Vane! Take some men up the shore to that shipwreck. See what's left."

"Aye, sir," Charles nodded and proceeded out the fort with a handful of followers.

Charles Vane led the men up the beach. With him was Rory and several others, all off *Bersheba*'s crew. Plants grew towards the water that pushed up against shore, forcing the line of men to walk shin-deep in the waves. As they rounded the bend, there laid a ship. It was on its side with the masts dug into the sand. A hole in the keel invited them to venture into the wreck. Vane took out his pistol and stepped on the broken planks. Sunlight seeped through the boards and gun ports which were now on the ceiling. The few men silently followed behind, peering into each compartment. A clatter came from stern as if a box full of items had just been dropped. Vane made an airy motion with his gun toward the noise to order his men to investigate. Rory held his rifle as he slowly walked to the back of the ship. Planks creaked beneath him with each soft step. He breathed once before turning the corner sharply and raising his gun. At the other end of the barrel were three black men in rags.

"Pick up that box," Rory said to them. They stood silent and calm. One man squatted down and scooped the lockbox he had dropped. Looking across the floor, the slave had noticed the key had landed at Rory's feet. "I find any more of you in here?"

"No," one said, looking down, slowly reaching for the large skeleton key before standing back up.

"What is your name?" Vane came into the room, both white men still holding their guns.

"We're property of the Spanish captain here. Méndez. I am Terek. These are my brothers, Keon, and Akia," Terek was a muscular man, tallest in the room. His younger brothers were also lean, all of them with shaved heads. Terek also had a long, full beard.

"Captain Mendez took a leave of absence. You'll be aboard our ship from now on," Vane stated plainly. "Take whatever you've found and meet me on the beach," Charles and the others carried what little was left on the ship. The lockbox, gunpowder, some firearms, and a stack of papers, which the men only assumed Jennings would want, not knowing what they were.

"Found some ledgers in the fort's office along some charts, I thought you might add to the book," Thompkins handed Jennings the papers back on the *Bersheba*. "Most of the gold was recovered and sent back to Havana months ago. The Spanish were obviously quicker to hear of the wreck than we. This was just what they stripped from that last boat, the one north of here."

"The ends would have justified the means. I'm not a man who would commit crimes like this lightly, Thompkins. Now that we're sitting on our puny plunder, makes me wonder if'n was worth it."

"We all hoped there would be more gold, sir. Perhaps this isn't the end just yet. If you read the ledgers, they shipped most of what they found, but they haven't found everything. There was a lot of gold on that fleet, they only recovered a fraction. After we pay the compensations and the surgeon, I would think each of us might still have a good chunk of coin, you know?"

"Bring me that man who brought his crew on, from Nassau," Jennings said, thinking more on the subject. "From the *Sun Dew*."

"Aye, sir," Thompkins limped away, his peg leg knocked on the wooden boards beneath him. Jennings didn't bother to look at the papers, he knew they couldn't bring more gold. He put the charts in with the others in the heavy leather-bound book. Then, Henry got up and poured himself a drink as he waited for the young man.

"You requested me, sir?" Levi entered, not a few minutes after Thompkins left.

"Yes, sit. Your captain, remind me, how much gold did he make off with?" Jennings still seated in his cushioned chair.

"He never had it all counted," Levi started. "Hasn't even spent it through."

"But was it more than what we pulled out of here today? He took a whole ship, where did all that gold go? Gold that took *days* to fill up in port."

"Yes," Levi nodded. "Yes, there was more on that ship than what we found today."

"It's humiliating; leading a job, recruiting all over the New World to find such a pitiful reward."

"That's the game. There's no reward without risk. That is why there's so much ambition among men. The more chances we take, the more likely we get the prize."

"Maybe so. Hard to find an honest wage, isn't it?"

"No, that's not hard. It's hard to find an honest wage that pays as well as this. Or as near exciting."

"Hmm," Henry nodded. "So, if we plundered the coast in search of more gold, ye'd be on board?"

"Very likely, captain."

"Thank you, that's all," Jennings dismissed him. "And Levi…" The young man turned back. "Next time make it known you're a captain. You'll earn a captain's wage."

"Fire the chase guns!" Henry called out. The *Bersheba* pursued a Spanish frigate, both firing at each other with their respective fore and aft cannons. Simply due to the motion, the Spaniards connected more shots than Jennings. "Signal the others to flank!"

"Aye!" Thompkins hobbled to the stern of their ship and waved the signal flags to the *Marianne* and the *Eagle*. The ships were slow to pass the *Bersheba*, already gaining on the Spanish. Now, with three ships overtaking and firing, the Spanish ship was slowed. Cannons from a sweeping range fired in and broke the hull of the Spaniard's ship. As the two attacking ships came along both sides of the Spanish, they quickly threw up their white flag. The damaged keel slowly breaking apart as Hornigold and Wills' crews hooked on to board. The *Marianne* and the *Eagle* squished the frigate from either side. The dozen or so navy men had their hands up, already standing in ranks. Hornigold was chuckling to himself as he neared the defeated captain, amused on how easy their victory was.

"*Disparad!*" The Spaniard yelled and stomped on the hatch leading below deck. Cannons thundered from both port and starboard sides, borrowing into the pirate's ships.

Hornigold took his pistol and shot the captain in throat. His men quick to join the retaliation as they slaughtered the unarmed sailors. Hornigold's men charged below deck and cut at the remaining crew, still carrying out orders to fire until death.

"Gah!" Benjamin yelled after he had killed the last of the men up top. He breathed with heat; anger filled his eyes as he looked around at the damage. "What the devil are you standing around for? Damage control, let's move!" He screamed at his crew, who was staring at him. They were quick to scramble back to their ships and repair the damages. The Spanish vessel was taking in water, slowly lowering into the sea. Ben cut the lines between the two ships, so the deadweight would not drag his own ships under.

"Edward, Samuel!" He called to his first mates. "Help me check the cabins," They went into the officer's quarters in the stern on the ship. Jennings with Vane and Levi, and a handful of other men, came in rowboats to help loot the sinking ship. The top deck was beginning to swamp, having six inches of standing water. The men thrashed from room to room, tearing apart desks and turning over tables. Any chest or purse they found was thrown onto the deck and quickly loaded into the boats floating above.

"Let's go or we'll be taken with her!" Edward hollered. He was towering and had a thick black beard on his face. The officers waded back to the boats and rowed back to their ships, already drifting away.

20.

The Betrayal.

Henry sat outside the tavern on the pier in Nassau, wearing his formal attire. Levi was at his right, wearing his own bright blue coat. Both men drinking from steins and enjoying the merriment that the gold brought to the town. Men across the saloon were singing a powerful yet slow tune as they drank.

> *I've drift'd away lads, for far too long*
> *I've oft not seen my wife or son.*
> *I joined a crew that promised me gold*
> *I sailed into that ocean cold*
>
> *Think of home then let it go*
> *Now, sail into that setting sun*
> *Think of how you let her go, lads*
> *You'll not return till the day is won*

"One of my favorites," Henry smiled softly and closed his eyes. "The boys would sing this in Jamaica. A sailor leaving home in search of riches. Familiar, no?"

> *A storm of wind and flooding water*
> *"Do not avast but keep her onward"*
> *Davey Jones now, to the depths, oh!*
> *Say her name as my final breath*
>
> *Think of home then let it go*
> *Now, sail into that setting sun*
> *Think of how you let her go, lads*
> *You'll not return till the day is won*

"I didn't leave home," Levi looked to the pirate, who listened intently. "I was lost at sea, washed up in these islands. Hardly remember where I came from. I had some sophisticated life in the colonies before. Though now that this life at sea found me, I can see how others would choose to seek it. The adventure, the glory."

"I think you and I are very similar," Henry grinned as he took a drink. "Most men took up this life in order to earn money for their wives or had nowhere else to run. I left my *sophisticated* family for the thrill of being a privateer, leading my own quests."

"There's no better life, I'd say."

"Aye, adventure, and glory... No better a life," The two men reminisced in the music and the stories. Stories being told at every table of grand, dramatized adventures. One man remained singing the chorus solemnly to himself in the hum of the evening.

Think of home then let it go
Now, sail into that setting sun
Think of how you let her go, lads
You'll not return till the day is won

"Wills left yesterday," Henry picked up the forgotten conversation. "Heading back to Jamaica to return Hamilton's cut of the raid."

"What'll you do?" Levi asked, also wearing his blue coat.

"I've told you, lad. After they finish careening my ship, I am going to keep making runs up the coast. Now that we know there's gold there, surely some men will come back with me."

"Some, aye. I heard Hornigold wants to stay here and establish his republic."

"Yes, he's told me. Offered me some position with the other high-up captains; 'governors of the New Providence.' Even if the fist raid was a disappointment, he admitted it's brought in more coin than his men's latest attempts. Think we're going to divide our territories."

"How so? Will he be staying south as you keep going up the coast?" Levi took a drink.

"I suspect. And what of you?"

"That gold is personal to me. You know I will sail with you to find it. I'll probably leave the *Sun Dew* in the command of my boatswain. My men enjoyed a break, but bootlegging is their calling. They'll make a steady income for us, here."

"Seems like we are making a county of our own. Our own navy and commerce completely independent of the British Empire."

"Not completely independent. We need someone to steal from," Levi chuckled.

"That we do, kid," Jennings stopped and gazed at the sight pulling into port. It was a rundown caravel, worn sails and scratched keel, with horrendous bones hanging over the edge. "What in the devil is that thing?" Levi turned to see the men on board who were throwing down the mooring lines.

"God blind me," The young man got up and walked from the table. "I know those men."

"Levi Benson?" A familiar voice shot over.

"Wickman. Never thought I'd see you again," They shook hands at greeting. "You sailing with these bums?" Levi asked, noticing the mutineers with him.

"Aye, we've gotten quite a band now. Helps when you're marooned and imprisoned together, really *bonds* the crew."

"Well then, what are you doing here?"

"Heard there were jobs here. For those who, uh, could do a variety of things."

"Aye, lots of men looking to hire muscle or commission a ship. Mines docked on the other end; make pretty good money myself running jobs."

"You have your own ship now?"

"After I-" Levi paused, realizing Gail and the lot had only just reached civilization after escaping the island. "Well, I found the treasure, see. Got myself a boat to keep making income."

"You found it?" Gail laughed, in shock.

"Aye. It's been some time."

"That it has, friend."

"Let me get you a drink," Levi took Gail by the shoulder. "Looks like you could use one."

"Fire on that sloop!" Jennings called. He and Levi were on the *Bersheba*, with Charles Vane on another ship, engaging a small Spanish vessel not far north of Nassau. Cannons rocked the ship as they bombed their target. The thunder echoed across the calm water. It banked around and returned shots. "Raise the colors," Thompkins went to the mainmast and raised a red flag, warning the enemy they would give no quarter.

"You see that, men?" Vane shouted to his crew. "Kill 'em all!" The two ships charged the sloop head on. The Spanish could not put out more than a few shots before the two frigates were able to engage with their rifles and harpoons. Men swung from lines hanging off the masts, others jumped over the railings onto the ship now pinched between the two.

"Come on, you scum!" The loosely uniformed sailors fired back against their attackers. Steel swords clashed as bullets flew through the air. Jennings had a pistol in each hand, firing them into the throng of Spanish sailors. Levi also wielded his sword and pistol. Firing when needed and reloading when he found a break. He ducked under an oncoming swing, slashing at his attacker's bare feet. As the Spaniard fell, Levi stood and cut down to strike his opponent.

Terek and his brothers fought with their bare hands. They wrestled men to the ground and beat them unconscious with their blunt fists. The three had become cabin boys, Terek sailing with Vane while the younger two served on Jennings's boat. Jennings had two hundred men between his two ships. Most new recruits in Nassau joining after hearing of his raid in Florida. They quickly took over the smaller boat and killed all of the sailors aboard. Thompkins, being not much use in battle anymore, came on deck as men were collecting themselves after the fight. He went into the cabin to search for letters and manifests, as Jennings was looking for other valuables.

"Captain..." Tompkins stammered.

"Yes," He looked up. Whatever Tompkins had just read, left him in horror. "Out with it, lad."

"This was no Spanish ship."

"What do you mean?" Henry walked up to him.

"It wasn't employed by Spain. It's disguised. It's... Hornigold's, sir," He handed over the ship's log.

Jennings turned scratching his neck. His face flushed its color, he could feel himself begin to sweat. "God!" He pounded his hands on the table, fastened to the deck. He stormed to the window, looking out for a bit. "We don't tell the men."

"What?"

"They cannot know we took a ship from Hornigold. Some of these men might have sailed together."

"What do we do? Hornigold will be back in port soon."

"We sail for Jamaica. We'll sell the sloop there and the men will think nothing of it," Henry shook. "Then we pray Benjamin never finds out."

"Aye, sir."

The flotilla remained anchored overnight. Men drank and reveled in their victory as repairs were being made. The captured sloop was filled with sailors from the overcrowded frigates, giving relief to Jennings quickly growing crew. Away from the partying on deck, Henry shook; cold sweats taking over his body. From his bed, he bent over and threw up onto the floor. He wiped his mouth and stumbled out of the cabin to throw up over the taffrail, into the water.

"You feeling well, sir?" A sailor asked him, only knowing it was his captain even in the pitch black.

"Drank too much, mate," He coughed and spat out.

"Aye, sir," The sailor chuckled and left him be. Henry belched onto the deck as he was walking back to his quarters. His throat stung as he tried to catch his breath. In the lantern light, he saw he had expelled an eel, lying dead among the waste.

"By God," He shivered. "What is happening?"

"Captain?" Levi entered the cabin early that morning. Jennings was wrapped in a blanket, sitting at his desk. "Jesus, what did you eat, you look awful."

"You never told me what sickened your hands," Henry looked up at him.

"Squid ink, sir. Dyed from working all my years with them."

"And yet, I never met another man with hands blackened like yours. It is a sickness, no?"

"Why should it matter?" Levi adjusted his posture.

"Because, now it's afflicted me," Henry took off his gloves and showed his greying hands. His veins were black beneath his skin. "I was throwing up eels last night and this morning, my hands and feet were turning black. A black spot above my heart, too. What plague did you bring?" He asked sternly.

"It's followed us," Levi mumbled in awe.

"What, boy?"

"This gold the Spanish lost, it's cursed," Levi showed his hand.

"Cursed you say?" Jennings eyes widened.

"Aye. Wretchery surrounds the gold. Brings the dead back to life, possesses men into doing unspeakable acts. Slowing killing them or driving them mad. All for the gold."

"Shorehaven?" Henry assumed.

"Shorehaven. The whole town blown in because the man looking for us needed to be sure he could find the gold."

"What can be done?" Henry reached across the desk at the young man. "How do I get rid of this?"

"Nothing as far as I know. The gold was vexed decades ago and anyone who seeks it with such zeal, killing for it, is cursed for life. Ink replacing blood, the very essence of a man no longer in 'em."

"I realize now not all quests are so exciting… I took that ship and killed those men, thinking it might carry more of the treasure. Is that what did this?" Henry asked earnestly.

"I can't say. I buried a good friend in search of it. But even now, after all it's taken, it calls out. You know we'll always want more."

"How long will you be gone? I thought you intended to stay."

"Things change, Levi," Jennings said. The three ships had only docked that morning and were already planning to leave as soon as possible. "I have to return to Jamaica."

"Hope it's not this curse that's spooked you," Levi spoke quietly as men around them were working. "It's uncomfortable at worst."

"No," He sighed, still wearing cloves to hide his skin. "But trust me, this is what I must do. I'll return though and when I do, you better have a fortune waiting for me."

"Don't bet on that."

"You take care, Levi."

"You as well, Henry," He saluted from his leather tricorn hat.

Later, Levi sat outside the Shark Bait Saloon in the hot evening. He enjoyed hearing the music from town and the rush of waves against the armada of ships at bay. He smiled faintly between sips, looking out to the darkening sky over the water. The waves were still and shown like glass. Yellow and red glowed and mirrored the clouds, on fire in the western sky.

"Captain?" Roger came over. "You sure about these men? Joining up with these crews? I know what we do isn't honest, but some of these captains," He diminished his voice. "They're wicked," Levi kicked back some more of his rum.

"I've thought of it. I could go back to Charleston, live as some snob, never see the outside of a mansion again. Could work in a lighthouse, hidden away from the world, kept out of trouble that way. Or I could do the only noble thing left in this world."

"You've changed, cap'n. When did it stop being about laying low and earning a modest wage? When did it become piracy?"

"Look around you, mate. The city we serve is changing. It's... well it's more than bootlegging and treasure hunting. These captains have ambitions, real taste for gold," Levi grinned. "That's the adventure I want to live. Those are the men I want to sail with. It isn't just the money, it's exciting. 'It's a predatory world,' they say. We'll be eaten up if we don't adapt."

"So, you're a pirate then?" Roger looked at his captain.

"Don't act like you're above this. We've been stealing for months, mate. *You* urged me to take the job. Now we have a whole trail ahead of us. Reclaim the gold!"

"That's before I knew these men were killers. Murderous men. Is that who we are now? That battle on the beach, it's really gotten to me, you know. Never killed a man before that day."

"Men die, we all know this. It's the world we live in," Levi glared. Roger was at a loss of words.

"The crew and I want to leave. Nassau is getting too radical," Roger eventually cleared his throat. "If you would like to captain us, we'd welcome you. If not, it's been a pleasure. The men agreed to pool their shares to give you something for the boat. We'll give you time to clean out your cabin. We respect you for serving us well."

"You're leaving me?"

"We'll go no further, Levi," Roger stood and left.

21.

The Crooks of Kingston.

"Strike sail!" Henry called over. The Spanish ship quickly lowered its flag in compliance, knowing they stood no chance against the *Bersheba*.

"No blood has to be shed, sailor!" Her captain hollered to Henry, whose men were hooking onto the smaller ship. The Spanish hand their hands up and stood calmly. The merchant ship only held maybe ten sailors, compared to the crew of over a hundred.

"Aye, perhaps you're right. Hand over ye cargo and maybe we won't kill you!" Henry declared as he stepped on deck of the Spanish ship.

"Fair enough," The Spaniard said reluctantly. Between the Bahamas and Jamaica, was a vast territory of Spanish water. The island of Cuba sat between the two isolated pieces of English land.

"Thompkins take a look through their paperwork. Make for sure they's giving us all they have."

"Aye, sir," He hobbled over to their stern castle and escorted the Spaniard at gun point, to hand over the legers.

"Rest of ye, get those crates moving!" Henry called again, showing his own guns. His men behind him also revealing their weapons. The Spanish looked to their captain who nodded mournfully. They began moving up and down the decks, bringing over all the barrels and crates they had.

"Sir, that is our food. Leave us that at least. We'll starve before porting again," The Spanish captain pleaded with

Henry. The privateer stared at the man, his large hat shadowing his face from the noon sun. "I'll hand over my personal treasury."

"What is your name, Spaniard?"

"Diego," He muttered in his accent.

"You are altruistic, Diego. Looking after your crew over yourself. You have a deal," Henry smirked. "Give em their food back," He ordered to his men who had already taken the boxes aboard the *Bersheba*. "We'll let you go, captain. Just fer being so compliant."

"*Gracias*," He thanked and nodded. Diego ran back into his cabin and brought out a chest he had hidden in his wardrobe. Henry and Tompkins took it and went back to their own ship. With oars, Henry's men pushed away from the Spanish ship.

"All the cargo accounted for, cap'n," Tompkins counted as he double checked the papers.

"Very good Mister Tompkins. Onwards, men! Continue to the Windward Passage; shouldn't be after nightfall," Jennings went back into his quarters as his ship dropped sail and continued their southward course.

The *Bersheba* sailed east along the coast of Cuba and south around the horn before resting for the night. Hornigold's old sloop sailing behind. The men fastened the lines, holding up the striped sails, and dropped the anchors into the shallow water. They rolled out their hammocks and secured them to the support beams below deck. Those on the captured ship did the same.

"A hundred and twenty thousand pieces. Counted em meself."

"Thank you, Thompkins. Suppose we ended up with a fair prize. We'll see how much we have left after Hamilton takes his tax. Surely enough to keep the crew on. Spur them to keep searching for treasure with me."

"Aye, sir. Not bad. Plus, the goods can be sold off, I reckon. If we don't want to keep em on deck for our own use. Besides, we still have that sloop to sell."

"Well, you're the one with the books. Figure out how much we used and what's necessary. I trust you to sell the rest off."

"Aye. Then what's the plan? You said you want to keep the crew if they're itching for gold."

"We'll keep requesting marques from the Governor," Henry shrugged. "After he sees our catch, he may be more confident to send us out again."

"And not go back to Nassau?"

"We can never go back."

"There's power there, though. Gold all up the coast. Are we goin' to let that out of our grip because of Hornigold?"

"We may have started something we can't win. He has power there already, influence. We have one scrappy vessel."

"Ye got men loyal to you though."

"Whoso?"

"Well, that boy Levi. He's a fierce fighter, brave lad. He's got men to back you up."

"If Hornigold hasn't already swept him into his crew."

"That'd be on you, you left him there," Thompkins reminded. Henry gave his crewmate a dirty eye. "Look, all I'm saying is that if we went back, we'd have a chance. Maybe Hornigold has not figured out yet. This empire he's building, as mucky as it is, there's gold there."

"Aye," Henry thought.

"There's power in being your own man. Not have to worry about ol' Hamilton."

"Now you're starting to sound like Vane."

"Him and I both think that republic is what's best for our crew. We may not have the backing of the English, but when have we ever? They've never come to our aid, only sent us out for their errands."

"Alright, mate. I'll think about it."

"Your excellency, Henry Jennings here to see you," The escort bowed as the privateer entered the room. Henry also gave a cordial bow. He wore his fine coat, and his tricorn hat. He also had black cloves over his withered looking hands.

"Henry, my boy! Come in," Governor Hamilton chuckled. "I trust you bring the rest of what Wills reported?"

"Yes, your excellency. My yeoman reports a hundred and twenty thousand Spanish pieces," Henry handed the log over to the decorated Governor. He had a grey wig and layers of expensive arrayments. His African servants catered him plenty of water and often dabbed his forehead of sweat. Overheating was a common issue among the upper class, wearing heavy garments in the heat of the Caribbean day.

"You did well to bring this much. This will be most pleasing to the king, God save him. I'll have my accountants go through your treasury with your yeoman and divide the spoils rightly."

"Of course, your excellency."

"Now, you and Wills and the rest of your privateers deserve a rest. Enjoy town for a while, maybe remember what dry land feels like. You've earned it."

"Thank you, your excellency," Jennings bowed. "If you should ever need anything else, I and my men are honored to serve."

"Of course, Henry. You know you are my best asset," Hamilton brought a glass over to the man. "Now, enough business. I am sure we'll discuss future exploits. For now, have a drink," He chuckled. "It's on the king."

Jennings enjoyed the quiet celebration with the governor more than the rowdy drunken parties his men were throwing on the docks. They toasted and sang, enjoying their victory and awaiting their pay. Men who have not seen a woman in the weeks they have been gone, stumbled into town to find comfort in some of the local establishments.

"No, you don't," Vane caught Jennings as he was sneaking back to his ship. He dragged his captain to the riot. "To Henry, the hero of the town!" His men cheered and clanked their pints together. They danced to their own music, someone on the mandolin, another sailor on the accordion, yet another from town brought down a fiddle. Jennings joined the dancing, showing off what he had learned from his wealthy childhood of going to balls.

Those living in town celebrated with the hundreds a part of Henry's crew. That much gold and supplies fueled commerce for them. On top of that, they wouldn't be able to sleep with all the noise the riot created. Men joined up with old friends, woman went down to meet their husbands who had been away. They all drank and sang. The celebration stretched across the docks and wide across town.

When Henry awoke the next morning, not knowing where exactly he had fallen asleep, he expected the festivities to have died in the night. Yet the markets were as lively and loud as ever. Rubbing his temple to ease his headache, Henry staggered to the noise to see what was going on at that hour of day. He passed by a bowl, collecting water, and splashed his face to wake himself up.

"What in the devil?" He winced in the bright sunlight to make sure he was seeing right. "Thompkins, what are doing?"

"Selling the stock, me captain!" He was behind a table he had acquired throughout the night and making sales with the local townsmen. Jennings' privateers were taking the commandeered containers off *Bersheba* and piling them in the market. "Everyone's too bloody excited to see we've returned with goods and gold to notice how bad our prices are," He chuckled. "Fresh wine! Fine silk and flavorful spices! All right here!"

"Carry on," Jennings sighed. He walked back to his ship, passing by his crew scattered asleep mixed with the locals who joined in their merriment.

"Laureano, your excellency," A Spanish navy man came into a large mansion in Havana.

"Couldn't you wait until after my dinner," He gave his inferior a stern look before wiping his mouth and rising from his seat. He used a cane to pull himself to his old legs.

"I was told to have you called right away, sir."

"Yes, I'm sure you were. Now what?" The military official snapped, now face to face with the man.

"More reports of a certain Henry Jennings, sir. He was tracked back to Jamaica. Kingston."

"Tracked? How so?"

"A Captain Diego says he was stopped and plundered by the pirates. Only, Jennings let them go. That is how he was followed, sir. Other ships have reported hits as well, all Englishmen. Not everyone was fortunate to sail away. Some crews lost completely."

"We'll send those Englishmen into the abyss," he said between his teeth.

"We do not wish to start war, Viceroy," Another officer who was at dinner also chimed in. "We just need to settle things better than out late friend, Esteban. Fool, he was."

"What do you suggest?" Laureano turned back to the table, pointing his cane at the officer.

"This issue isn't inherently Spanish. English as well are being targeted by this new *pirate republic*. Even the French have reported the black flags. You say Jennings went to Kingston? Then I say we pay our English friend a visit. Make sure the old governor isn't harboring any pirates."

"And if these assaults are under Hamilton's orders?"

"Then the English stand no chance in another war. Not in the Caribbean. I will get my ship ready. We can sail first thing in the morning if you'd like."

"Very well," The old man grunted. "Thank you, boy," He dismissed the navy man. Laureano was just over seventy, serving his second time as colonial governor of Cuba. Before that, he was viceroy of Florida. With pain, he walked to his bedroom, limping on his cane. The stone corridor was open to the courtyard in the middle of the estate. Nights were still warm enough to let the fresh ocean air in.

"Payment out-front. As you can see, I've made quite a profit. If you would sail with me again, there will be plenty more," Levi stood over a chest of gold doubloons.

"You know, I always liked you. No hard feelings things didn't work the first time," Welham lit up at the sight of the money. "No reason we can't make it work now."

"Aye," Cook shook Levi's hand.

"Might I ask?" Gail interjected. "Why us? You seem plenty tied up with the high ups round here."

"There's something about having my own ship and crew. I can run with the big dogs, but sometimes I need to sail on my own. Now, about this... *fine* ship," Levi gestured toward the *Whale*, bones still roughly hanging over the taffrail, tied with spare rope. "We'll get it fixed up right and good. The keel's been through a lot. And in the meanwhile, you men can start scrubbing the decks. Can't sail proper on a grimy ship, can we?"

"Aye, captain," Crofton, who was sitting on the railing, kicked his peg leg over and began to work on the deck. They took sandstone and water to wear down the dirt and salt building up on the wooden boards. Jack took a block and scrubbed with him.

"Wickman," Levi called again. "Take inventory, see what we need. You know the ship best."

"Aye, aye."

Over the next days, Levi outfitted the *Whale* to his standard. Using the cranes off the masts, they brought eight cannons aboard. Cutting holes in the solid taffrail, they secured the guns to the weather deck. He even hired some craftsmen from town to better mount the whale ribs and skull. They remade the crudely placed name, officially turning what remained of the *Gail Wickman* into the crew's new ship, the *Whale*.

"What do I owe the pleasure, Señor Laureano?" Hamilton was just being served his midmorning coffee when the Spanish viceroy and his own naval escorts came into the mansion in Kingston.

"I'm afraid it's some matter of urgency, your excellency," The Spaniard knew to be formal and polite, even when addressing an English man nearly thirty years younger than he.

"Do tell," The governor sipped from his fine glass.

"Many reports are coming back to me that my ships, naval and civilian, are being targeted by a particular pirate. An *English* pirate, mind you."

"I assure you; piracy is not taken lightly here. It is our law, as it is yours, that pirates be hanged till death."

"Then do it," The old man leaned forward on his cane.

"I'm afraid I don't know what you mean, Viceroy."

"Turn over your pirate," he said blatantly. "We know he hails from Kingston."

"If we knew of any such a man-"

"You'd have him give you a tithe of what he stole from us?" Laureano raised his voice. "Huh?"

"I'd have him strung up like a dead weight to be eaten by the gulls," Hamilton replied calmly. "What are you after?"

"Don't play games with me," He hit his cane on the ground. "Either you are incompetent as governor or you have these thieves under your employment!"

"I am speaking the truth," Hamilton clenched his jaw.

"For every day you do not turn over the corpse of a Mister Henry Jennings, we will hang an Englishman in Havana!"

"There's a lot more Spaniards here. I'll flog every one of them myself if you touch a single English subject!" Hamilton shouted. Laureano breathed deeply before speaking again.

"Perhaps we are getting heated. Calmly now, we can continue, lest we burn down the New World," he said softly.

"If I find any pirate, he's yours."

"Very well, Mister Hamilton," The Spaniard bowed before leaving. The officers walked slowly behind their master, limping with his cane. Hamilton watched out the balcony to see the men depart of their wagon.

In the cover of night, Governor Hamilton prepared his horse and rode to the docks, hiding himself in a cloak. He rarely was allowed to go anywhere without a carriage, being the town's most important official. He rode down the cobble streets, between alleys to the piers. The horse's shoes clipping the stone ground. Hitching his brown horse, Hamilton walked out on the dock. He whispered to the watchman on the *Bersheba*. Hamilton was escorted by the sailor, who recognized him.

"Henry," The governor took off his hood.

"My lord, what are you doing here?" Jennings was caught off guard by the informality of the visit. They were in his cabin; Henry had been writing at his desk.

"You need to leave."

"I don't understand. What has happened?"

"The Spanish are looking for you, you cannot stay here. If you do, you will be found out and I'll be forced to deliver you to them. God help me if you died on my hands."

"I was just following orders, your excellency," He stammered.

"And then some. You made too much noise and they noticed. Henry, you're a good man to me. But you have to go now. I'll be putting up wanted posters for you."

"But Jamaica is my home," He shook his head.

"You cannot come back. You have been warned."

22.

The Beast.

January 1716

Edward and I have been sailing now for a couple days on the Marianne. We're following Hornigold in his new prize, the Ranger, south of the Bahamas. He hopes to intercept a few merchant sloops to take back to Nassau. Now that the city is growing, it needs more trade of its own.

Benjamin says he take the sloops and rigs them with his own men. They go into port to pick up supplies for whatever the intended destination is, except they end up in Nassau. He says it's a much longer term and efficient form of piracy. "Leeching off of the empires who are too rich to notice."

"Alright lads!" Edward hollered through his beard in his thick, low accent. "Let's show em the devil!" The crew he had begun captaining, raised a black flag with a horned skeleton spearing a heart. The monstrous banner waved to their enemy; whose tiny ship cowered. "Fire some shots over, men! Make em scared" Cannons were fired at the ship, most shots missing and exploding near the ship they had chased down. Edward took out his pistols and started shooting at the surrendering vessel. The crew did the same until they were actually close enough to make a shot.

The *Marianne* captured the sloop with a web of lines and hooks, beginning to pull it along. Levi led the crew onto the vessel, screaming as they boarded, as ordered. They waved weapons and beat their chests. Running around the cowering merchants. Then Edward followed, dressed in a black coat with a large tricorn hat.

"Yarrr!" He screamed at the whimpering crew, giving way for his crooked, stained teeth. Edward was broad and tallest of any man on deck, even some of his men were scarred of his appearance. He stomped towards one of the merchants, they were all sitting with their hands up, being held at gunpoint. "Where be your captain?" He shook a man to his feet. Trembling, too afraid to talk, the man glanced over at the stern on the ship, to the cabin. Edward dropped him and strode over. Kicking the port hatch open, Edward found the captain. He was sitting at his desk, holding out a pistol with his shaking hand. Edward did not flinch but walked right up to the man. Pulling his own flintlock, Edward shot him square between the eyes. Taking a small lockbox out of the cabin, Edward looked at his crew.

"Do likewise," His men fired on the unarmed sailors. Levi looked for a moment at the killings, but then he too joined the firing squad. The bodies fell limp on the deck, blood staining the boards. Pirates quickly began searching through their enemy's pockets, picking out medallions or weapons.

"Clean em up," One of Edward's men hollered. Pairs grabbed and threw the corpses overboard. The current below scattering them out in the ocean. Edward finished rummaging through the cabin, picking out gold jewelry and silver tableware.

"Benson," He called. "Take charge of the ship. I'll spare you some men to work."

"Aye, aye. You there!" Levi quickly turned to some men on deck. "Check the cargo hold, see what we have aboard."

Later, some men stood in silence as Levi went down to the galley. "At ease, men. I'm not your captain," He went up to the chef, got his bowl of stew and bread, and sat at table with the others.

"Sorry sir," One began. "It's just that captains don't eat with their crew."

"Why is that?" Levi replied.

"They're superior. To eat with us is saying we's equals."

"Hmm," He thought. "Any crew I've captained has been so small we all ate chow together."

"Not these dogs," He shook his head. "Hornigold is too proud to ever eat with his men, most are. They's rather be dinning in their cushioned quarters. As for Edward Thatch, the man's so monstrous, we'd be too scared to sit with him."

"Suppose you're right. Edward might be an apprentice, but he's mighty good at it. By all rights, a pirate of his own."

"Aye, a pirate by nature, he is. Rest of us, even you other captains were once fishermen, craftsmen, maybe privateers. Captain Thatch was born a predator. Some of us think he could just overthrow Hornigold, being as vicious as he is."

"That may be," Levi stopped to take a bite.

Levi sailed the sloop behind Thatch and Hornigold. There were few men on the smaller vessel, leaving more on the big ships to be used in another assault. The bright sun reflected off the spring water, shining into the boat.

"Sir," A watchman came to Levi, at the helm. "Ship off the port side, it's signaling for help. The other ships haven't noticed."

"Well, let's just see what the damage is," Levi grinned. "Signal over to Benjamin, we're making a stop," He turned the wheel and brought the ship around. They furled sails and dragged line to slow next to the other vessel. It was a sloop of similar size, anchored in the open water.

"Ahoy!" A man called over.

"Hail, sailor," Levi nodded, at the railing. "What seems to be your trouble?"

"Who us? We haven't any trouble," The man shrugged. Levi peered at him, studying the man's smirk and posture. "In fact, I'd say you're the ones who's found trouble!" His crew pulled pistols and muskets out from buckets and various nooks they were hidden in. Levi laughed. His crew started to chuckle as well, grinning as they drew their sabers and pistols.

"Well, come on then!" Levi fired at the sailor, caught off guard that they were attempting to rob other pirates. The young man vaulted the railing and landed on the bow of the enemy ship. With his sword, Levi swung to attack. His men followed, colliding with the opposing crew also attempting to board their vessel. Men swung in on lines from both masts, cutting at each other as they passed.

Their captain dueled with Levi, easily a foot taller than the young man. Both smiled with clenched teeth, enjoying the exhilaration of combat. The captain threw a left hook between strikes with his sword, initially throwing Levi off. The next time he threw a punch, Levi flicked his sword up, slicing the man's forearm. He clenched and screamed in anger, no longer grinning at the fight. The captain swung furiously in retaliation, ignoring his damaged arm. The captain eventually slashed Levi's right arm. The young man grunted as he had to keep defending himself. Levi parried and forced the ends of their swords to the deck, then swung a punch of his own. The tall man grunted in pain. Levi dropped his blade and delivered a blow with his right fist. With his enemy staggering backwards, Levi picked up his saber and cut down, striking his opponent dead. Levi pulled his pistol and shot down a man from behind. Stowing his gun, he joined the brawl, cutting at his opponents mercilessly.

"Anyone else?" He panted for a moment, catching his breath. The battle had died down, most men only brawling with their fists after firing their guns. Once they saw their captain was vanquished, the smaller crew surrendered.

"No, sir," The opposing crew stood in horror.

"Outstanding," Levi sheathed his sword. "Hook up the towing lines, we'll drag this sloop behind ours."

"Aye, captain," The men promptly went to work, untangling the ships' hooks and fastening the two with one solid line.

"Call over to Hornigold, get that surgeon on deck," Levi pointed to the man who ran the semaphore flags. "Those of you wounded, we'll have you taken care of in a while. For now, just don't bleed on our deck."

John Howell rowed over from the *Marianne* to the two sloops anchored still where the battle took place. John was a thin gentleman, a head full of white hair and a set of glasses on his nose. He had on a long vest and was in all respects a well-mannered man.

"How'd you get in with this lot? You don't seem like the type to join Hornigold's crew," Levi asked as he was being stitched up.

"Didn't have a lot of choice," John did not glance from his work. "I was the surgeon in town back when the Brits owned it. Once Hornigold and his men took over, they forced me aboard to work their med bay."

"Sorry to hear that. Running with this crew is one thing. Being forced is another. I'd imagine you don't sleep easy."

"Quite the contrary. They know they need me on their ship, and they treat me as one of the officers at this point. They're an uncivilized bunch, but after patching so many of them back together, they treat me well."

"So, you stay?"

"More or less. At first, yes, they did force me on. Hornigold offered to sell me to some French marauder, cannibals. So, I told him I was content on the *Marianne* and now it's been three years."

"Do you enjoy it?" Levi inquired. At first, he asked for sake of conversation during the timely task, but now he was genuine. "I sail with Hornigold because it excites me. I love being on the water, taking prizes. Gambling to find the fortune."

"Enjoy isn't the right word. I don't much care for battle or agree with thieving, but this I enjoy," He gestured to his equipment. "The stories, too. I write em all down if they're adventurous enough. Perhaps exaggerate some detail. Maybe one day I'll sell it back in England, 'The True Tales of a Life on a Pirate Ship.' They'd love it, I'm sure of it."

"Perhaps you could share, tell some stories to the crews. *They* would really enjoy that," Levi nodded. "Given they've drank enough."

"Then came on deck, Edward, the bearded devil, maddest man on these seas," John was standing on a table outside the Shark Bait Saloon in Nassau. It was a hot night and many of Hornigold's crew were out drinking after returning to port. "He towered over his prey, his yellow eyes putting fear into their very bones! With a pistol he drew, and firing, killed three men. All with one shot!" The crew, far from sober, was enthralled with this man's stories.

"Boom!" He yelled; the men shook. "Another shot, another six men dead. With one hand, Edward ripped open the cargo hold. He jumped to the lower deck, the whole ship shaking under his weight! There before him lay a chest, filled with Spanish silver. Each piece of eight cut finely and shone bright as the moon. He hoisted the crate to the weather deck and through his great black beard yelled, 'Arrg, we found the treasure!'" The sailors clapped and shouted. Levi sitting in the back laughed and shook his head. The other captains not present.

"Now, a newer tale. Some of you may have even witnessed it with your very eyes," John began again, reading from his journal. "The story of a captain with the prowess of a great beast, the leviathan, Captain Levi Benson! The gunfire was thick, and smoke rolled through the air as Levi swung to the deck of his opponent. The enemy captain was six, no seven, feet tall and with a grimace smile, challenged Levi to a duel. But the leviathan has never lost at sea! With a gun and a sword, Levi took on this fearsome fighter. He shot the man in the gut, but the bullet did no damage! Levi would have to kill him with a blade," John motioned with his hand as if he were sparring with a sword. "All throughout the ship, the captains dueled. Then, in a single swing, Levi cut off his left arm at the elbow! His opponent still did not stagger, so they crossed swords some more until Levi put his blade right through the man's heart!"

23.

Flying New Colors.

Brown and white sails fell and filed with wind. The masts' timber shivered at the pulling of the canvas. The *Bersheba* left Kingston in haste at twilight. Men worked in the chill morning, moving enough to warm themselves from the cold splashing sea.

"Excommunicated, are we?" Charles Vane went up to Jennings, who stood at the helm.

"Aye, Hamilton advised us to leave. He'd hang us if we came back. Outlaws we are now."

"Coward for not backing us. After all the faith ye put in him."

"Aye," Jennings said soberly.

"That's betrayal, the way I see it," Thompkins came up the steps, gripping the railing to pull himself. "We risked life and limb for the governor, and what does he do? Throws us out to be trampled!"

"Betrayal indeed," Vane nodded. Jennings looked at each of the men. "It shouldn't go unpunished."

"Punish?" Henry asked. "How?"

"We show him just how powerful of an asset he lost," Vane leaned in. "Take it out on one of his own ships. Perhaps he'd regret letting us go."

"Take one of his own pieces?"

"Aye, captain," Thompkins added. "The crew's angry. Show them ye are as well."

"He warned us," Jennings stated. "He is letting us escape."

"The crew is angry," Vane said sternly. "We are, too. We gave him our treasure and now he is throwing us out."

"One ship," Jennings nodded. "Then we go for gold. This time, there will be no room for mercy. We showed those Spanish mercy and look what's come on us. This time is different."

"A wise plan, my captain," Vane bowed casually as he snickered and left. Jennings kept their ship heading north. He sailed them back toward the Windward Passage, the water between Cuba and Hispaniola. The day gradually warmed up with the rising sun, bringing comfort to the men working on deck.

"Merchants, sir," A watchman called down. "Just off the nose," Jennings handed the wheel off to another sailor. He took out his spyglass and, walking to the bow, looked off at the incoming ship.

"Battle stations, this one will do! Remember, men. We're keeping these sailors alive. We need to teach Hamilton a right lesson!" Henry called looking over at their prey. The sloop was flying the English jack off the bowsprit.

"What colors should we raise then, sir? We haven't any other flags," Thompkins went to his captain as Henry usually flew the English flag as well.

"Dip the Red Duster in the wine."

"Sir?" Thompkins was taken back.

"Then we'll set it ablaze, let the wind take it over to them. They'll get the message," Henry stood at the bow, holding a torch over their English flag hanging downward. As the other boat passed, they waved at their fellow countrymen. Just then Henry lit their red flag on fire. The other sailors staggered back in shock. "Light em up, me hearties!" Henry hollered then unhooked the burning flag and let it fly over towards the other ship. Cannons shot at the top decks. The *Bersheba* steered to get as close to the sloop as possible. Henry's men threw over lines and hooks, capturing the smaller ship. They jumped over with their guns, yelling and cackling.

"We're unarmed!" One man cried.

"Mercy!" Another called. Jennings went aboard, wearing his decorative hat and coat as was his routine. He strutted the length of the deck, simply looking the sailors in their fearful eyes.

"Everything you own," Henry began slowly, holding his own bright sword. "On my ship," Then he waited. Soon the sailors went down to their cargo hold and brought up their deliveries. Crates of spices and fabrics. Barrels of liquor and chests of silver and gold. Henry noticed their captain was the only one not moving. He stood watching the pillaging without a word. "You as well," said Henry, pointing his saber at the man's face. He was about to move back to his cabin. "Not so fast. I said everything you own," With his sword he pointed up and down the man's well decorated body.

"I will not stand this," He protested with clenched teeth.

"Vane," Henry called, without his gaze leaving the other captain. Charles took his pistol and shot one of the crew members who were working diligently. The body of the older boy collapsed onto the deck, cracking open the crate he was carrying.

"Alright, Jesus!" The captain muttered. He removed first, his coat. Then his shoes with brass buckles. Next his blouse and trousers, leaving only his long underwear.

"Everything," Henry said again. The captain shuttered at the humiliation but looking at Vane, who still held out his gun, he complied. Henry's men came through and scavenged the captain's quarters.

"The rest of you," The captain called to his own crew and simply pointed at his pile of clothes on the deck, unwilling to be humbled alone.

"What happened?" Hamilton demanded as sloop came into port, the whole crew in nude.

"Jennings," The captain spat, covering himself with a map he had in his office. "That pirate!" Hamilton's shocked expression quickly tensed into anger.

"Send word," Hamilton turned to his servants with him. "Anyone who brings Henry Jennings back to me will be well compensated."

"Trouble?" Laureano was walking past to his ship.

"We found your pirate," Hamilton sneered as he mounted his horse. "He's all yours if you can catch him!" Hamilton rode up the street to his house. Laureano walked as fast as he could on his cane back to his ship.

"Anchors up, send her out!" He barked as he hobbled up the gangplank.

"Where to, Señor?"

"To Jennings, you fool! Get moving!"

Laureano's ship pushed off from the docks in Kingston and made way toward Cuba. They rushed, full sail northeast, where the viceroy suspected Henry to be heading back through the way he came. They rolled over the waves, the wind on their side. Laureano was banking on catching up to the Englishman, thinking he would be plundering all along his way.

"Ship, ho, sir!" The Spanish watchman shouted down the main mast. "Right on the cape."

"What ship is it?"

"Cannot read the name. It's an English frigate though, there's another anchored with her."

"Jennings," The old man grunted.

"You sure it's him?" One of his officers asked.

"I'm sure of it," Laureano walked away, leaning on his cane. "Bring us in!" He yelled up to the helmsman. The Spanish frigate turned toward Hispaniola and went for the beach that the two English ships were anchored on. Englishmen were cutting trees and bringing lumber onto their ships.

"Neither of these ships are *Bersheba*, your excellency," Laureano's officer said to him as the sailors rowed in from their frigate. The old man huffed.

"Could be associates of his," Laureano said, refusing to believe they were not on track. When they arrived on shore, he had his men pull the rowboat as far out of the water as possible before getting out. Some men working on the beach stopped at the sight of the Spanish authorities. "Henry Jennings!" He hollered to the men, who all now had stopped. "Where is Henry Jennings?"

"Who?" Some of the Englishmen asked.

"Captain Henry Jennings!" The Spaniard said sternly. "Notorious pirate. Where is he?"

"He's not here," Someone stepped forward. "We've been here for days."

"Where is your captain?" Laureano demanded.

"On deck," The Englishman turned and pointed to the dry-docked ship behind him. He led Laureano up a large ramp to one of the ships, where the two captains sat.

"The audacity to make me walk," Laureano glared at the two men.

"Apologies, what can we do you for?"

"Are you joking me? You're off your land, you Brit. Tell me where Jennings is and I'll forget to report you to the French, who by all accounts are much crueler than I."

"He's in Kingston. I'm sure of it," One responded without hesitation.

"You're sure of it, eh?" Laureano leaned in. "I just came from there. Nowhere to be seen. So, I will ask you boys again. Where is he? Where is Jennings?"

"Then we don't know."

"Liar," Laureano's officers grabbed the men from their chairs and threw them to the deck. "Bind them," He turned and went to the bow. The Englishmen struggled, but his officers outnumbered the two, tying their hands and feet.

"Look here!" He shouted to the men on the beach. "I'll give you one last chance. Where is Henry Jennings?" He only got blank stares in return. "So be it," Laureano took out his flintlock and held it against the first captain, who was brought forward. He shot the man, the captain falling backwards off the ship into the shallow water below. The other captain was brought up. One officer handed the old man another pistol, already loaded. "Anyone now?" The men below shouted, naming dozens of towns. "You don't know," He mocked as he blasted the last captain. He fell to the deck but was thrown overboard on top of the other.

"Burn their ships," Laureano said without another word, walking toward the gangway. The men on the beach had built a ramp up to their ship, to haul lumber more easily into their damaged boats. The Spanish officers found their alcohol and dripped it out across the deck leading to the powder kegs. Last they knocked over the oil-burning torches and ran down the ramp as the ships quickly caught fire. With their guns ready, they escorted their master back to the rowboat and left the men stranded. They shouted and ran around, but the flames couldn't be put out.

Under no flag, *Bersheba* continued north. They were officially outlaws, their own navy with no allies. Henry Jennings literally burned their last tie to their home country. A ship full of guns and a crew who had made their enemies, this is how Jennings' men saw themselves. Though they were not remorseful. England had neglected to pay her privateers, many of whom were sailing under Henry now. They partied on their ship that night, toasting.

"To new life and new wealth!" Henry shouted as he stood on a crate on the top deck. Many of Henry's men dressed themselves in the clothes of the pillaged sailors. They gambled for other belongings they pulled from the merchants. The crew drank on the softly rocking deck, dancing when they weren't bracing on the wooden ship for balance. Vane took the garments the English captain had been wearing. He ripped the seams and tied the ends together. Raising his craft up the main mast, the long banner flew against the dark sky. Tompkins was sitting on the deck, surrounded by a few bottles of confiscated wine. He moved his one foot with the beat of the music the men played. Lifting a bottle to his mouth, he saw a light from the bottom of the glass.

"Huh?" He held it up to his winking eye. The liquid in the clear glass shone a little. He drank the last of it then looked into the bottle like a spyglass. Thompkins scanned the length of the deck until he found the light again. Taking the bottle off his face, he saw the faint light on the horizon. "Captain!" He barked, not attempting to get up from the floor. "Cap'n!"

"What is it, mate?" Henry walked over. Thompkins pointed, more or less, in the direction of the light.

Following his finger, Henry went over to look starboard off the ship. Taking out his spyglass, he studied the light. "Tis a fire. Watchman!" He yelled up the mast.

"Aye sir?" A cracked voice came from the dark mess of lines and rolled sails.

"Starboard side, what is that light?"

"Fire, sir. Looks like a building on the beach," He called back.

"Cap'n," Thompkins stood up. "Let's go to the fire."

"In the morning," Henry patted the man on the shoulder, causing him to stumble back to his seat. "Hopefully, you'll be back with us by then."

At dawn, the crew untied the sails and moved eastward toward the shoreline. Most men grumbled at their headaches if they were not still throwing up. Thompkins still lay asleep on the deck, the bottles rolling around him with the motion of the ship. Henry walked out of his cabin and threw a bucket of eels overboard. As they neared the land, Henry went to the bow and looked out at the wreck.

"It's a ship," Henry said to himself. "...Or two?"

"What's the move, cap'n?" Vane walked up to where Jennings was standing. The burned ships lay barren and alone on the sand only a few hundred meters from the *Bersheba*, which at this time was not moving.

"We'll row in. See what's left that can be looted."

"Aye," Charles nodded as he was walking away. "I'll rally some guns to bring with us."

"Very well."

They lowered the longboats into the waves and rowed toward the beach. The bow of the ruined ship had collapsed inward on the rest of the body. Most of the yardarms were broken off and the sails were disintegrated.

"Who goes there?" A voice echoed from the wreck. Jennings and his men looked around as they landed but saw no one.

"Ye English?" Jennings called back.

"Well, we're certainly not with the Spanish after what they's done to us," Vane crept closer to the ship, trying to track down the source. "We don't want any more trouble."

"The name's Jennings," Henry complied. "We won't harm you. Just come on out to speak, will ye?"

"Alright," A mob of men came from the rubble.

"How many have ye?" Henry asked.

"Forty strong," One replied. "Our captains were killed by some Spanish officials. Others lost in the fires they set herein. Says they were looking for a *Henry* Jennings."

"Aye. That's who you be speaking to now."

"So it is," The marooned sailor nodded and looked off. "We don't much know why they were looking for you but judging by yer colors and the looks of you all, I'd guess."

"We are what you think we are," Henry confirmed.

"Well, we have nothing to take. But if you want some more men," He looked to those stranded with him. "We could use a way off this island."

"What's your name, sailor?"

"Edric Shore, sir."

"Well Mister Shore, whatever trade you knew, ye might as well forget it. You're a pirate now," Henry tipped his hat. "Welcome aboard."

24.

Crossed Swords.

"Sir," Samuel Bellamy walked in on Hornigold in his mansion. Benjamin took the house when Nassau was captured from the British. He used it as his first display of authority to gain governorship over the forming republic. "A letter from Hamilton was sent to you."

"What?" Benjamin looked up from his large mahogany dining table. Sam placed the sealed envelope in front of his captain. Benjamin wiped his mouth with a silk cloth and motioned for his black servant to clean up his lunch. "A Proclamation. By the..." Ben stopped reading aloud when he saw what was on the page.

"Something important?" Sam was leaning in ever slightly to try and catch a glimpse of what Hornigold was reading.

"Nothing," He folded the paper and stuffed it into his pocket. "Rubbish, that's all," Benjamin stood, buttoned his coat, and took a swig of the brandy he was enjoying. "What else do you have for me, Samuel?"

"Edward's still on his voyage to the North American colonies. Scheduled to be back in a fortnight, but you know how is. He will take his time with each kill. My crew just returned from Hispaniola, where you got that letter. We'll have your share of the spoils counted and brought up to you. But once Thatch returns, we'll head up to New England as well."

"What of my missing piece? Has that been found yet?"

"Yes, your excellency," Samuel gulped. "We caught it sailing to Jamaica during our voyage."

"Who in the devil who steal a ship from me?"

"Well, Jennings, sir."

"What?"

"Your sloop was following behind *Bersheba*."

"The fool wants war, does he?" Benjamin huffed, then collected himself. "No, not yet. Thank you for this information, Samuel. What of Benson?"

"He's been attacking Florida, sir, in his new ship."

"That ugly beast? I'm surprised Edward hasn't tried to buy from him," Hornigold chuckled slightly. "Thank you, Samuel, you may go," He waved the man away. Bellamy nodded to himself and turned to leave. The mansion had polished stone floors and many rooms that were once highly decorated and filled with people, but now lay nearly barren.

A crash of water came onto the deck of the *Whale*. Its sails filled with the stormy wind, pushing hard against the roaring waves. Rain cut down at the men who pulled hard on the rigging.

"Fire, let's go!" Levi commanded. Cook and Welham loaded the heavy cannon, pointing forward and lit the end. The gun fired and rolled back on its wheels. The two grunted as they pulled on the ropes to keep it in place and push it back against the hull. Wind howled through the wooden ship and salt sprayed up from the dark water. They were gaining on a ship, caught leaving a suspected salvage camp. The Spanish brig shot back, a bomb diving into the sea just off the bow.

"Keep her to the side! They'll sink us if we're right behind!" Levi cried up to Gail, who had control of the helm. He turned the wheel, deviating their bearing. "It's turning to shore, keep on the inside and we'll catch her!"

"I see it!" Gail called over the wind. Grey rolling waves mirrored the clouded sky above them. Cook and Welham put out another shot, loading it with the lighter ammunition, as to more likely reach their fleeing target.

"They're turning back toward us!" Levi yelled from the fore lookout. Gail then turned the wheel the other way as to avoid running into the other.

"Stations, everyone!" Levi had picked up more men from town, taking advise not to run a ship short-handed. Harper brought out a chest of swords, arming himself before others took up their weapons. "We may be out gunned, but we have more manpower here than the Spanish fleet! Give em the devil!"

"Save your ammo, men! Don't waste any shots, make each round count!" Harper instructed. The oncoming brig shot up its Spanish flag, demanding a response from the *Whale*.

"Hoist the colors!" Levi ordered. A black flag was rolled out and raised up the main mast. As it unfolded in the heavy wind, it showed crossed swords under an octopus, the symbol of the Curse. With blackened hands, Levi held onto the lines running down from the mast; and standing on the railing, leaned off and pointed his sword at his foe. His dirty blonde hair blew loosely in the wind, hardly restrained by his leather cap. He glared over at his opponent until they would pass broadside.

"*El Leviatán!*" The Spaniards looked in shock at their enemies' flag, signaling just who was about to attack.

"Fire!" Levi ordered, leaving the railing to get to his rifle.

"*Disparad!*" The foreign captain called out on his ship. The *Whale* shook as its cannons thundered back with each shot. Cook and Welham still on one of the guns.

Leatherneck Jack laughing as he manned a cannon by himself. Opposing strikes came in, bashing in the hull. Levi ducked as shrapnel shot out, splinters flying through the air. The storm moved the two ships, oscillating up and down over the uneven waves. As the two ships dipped near each other, they exchanged shots. Harper fired at their powder kegs. As his bullet sunk into the wooden barrel, it ignited, bursting into flames.

"Nice shot!" The pellets of rain didn't put out the flames spreading with the gunpowder.

"Sir, how do we board? The waves are getting too heavy for the ship! We'll crash if we try to hook her!" Crofton yelled over. He held onto the railing to keep himself upright, his wooden leg not providing good balance.

"Let me think," Levi said under the roar of the tempest sweeping over the ocean.

"Captain, they're heading ashore to land. Should we cut them off to keep em out?" Gail called.

"No, let them land, back off the sail!" Levi turned. "We'll take em on the beach! Gail, put us downwind from her on the shore!"

"Aye sir," Gail turned the wheel back, steering the rudder. The *Whale* was pushed ashore by the crashing waves, docking only a hundred meters from the Spanish.

"Fire a few rounds from the cannons as we run over, then join us as soon as we reach them!" Levi ordered Welham. He led the crew down the shroud onto the sand and ran with their swords toward the enemy ship. Crofton able to run surprisingly well on his prosthetic leg. Cannonballs flew over them, breaking the enemy's hull. The Spaniards docked perpendicular to the *Whale*, their ship pointing towards the caravel, leaving them with no way to fire back with their own guns. As the crew reached their opponents, Cook and Welham stopped the barrage and took up their swords to follow. Both men on the heavier side, took a bit longer to reach the assault. The Spanish shot down from their ship at the attackers. Levi's men returned fire as they began climbing up the ropes.

"The other side! They're coming up from both sides!" The Spaniards yelled. They panicked at the two teams pressing in, Levi's men reached the deck and began engaging their foes. Crofton threw a knife across the deck and struck a Spaniard in the back. Levi's men were fewer, taking some losses under the gunfire, but they were more heavily armed. Only a handful of the Spanish had guns, the rest fearfully fought with their fists. Levi slashed at his unarmed opponents. The swordsmen overtook the Spanish, striking them without mercy. Jack dwarfed his enemies. He worked across the deck with his cutlass, with slow but heavy swings. Gail also became proficient in swordsmanship. He dueled well with his rapier; patient as he defended, he waited for an opportunity to attack.

"*Misericordia!*" The surviving Spanish put up their arms. Their weapons falling to the deck with the rain. "Mercy!" When his crew saw Levi stop attacking, the fight was over.

"Tie them to the railing," Levi sheathed his sword. His men quickly worked to move the surrendering forces. The Spanish were put on their knees with their hands bound behind their backs, to the spokes of the taffrail.

"Gold!" Levi demanded of their captain. The finely dressed sailor stammered, not understanding. "*Oro!*" The captain nodded at this. With his hands up, he walked out of his office and down to the cargo hold. He showed Levi five large trunks sat with the shelves full of other various goods and equipment. "Someone get that crane, we'll need to lift these out," Levi shouted through the grate of the cargo bay hatches.

"You," Welham ordered at his prisoners, still working to tie them up. "Get that hatch open!" He employed the defeated sailors to lift the grate with their pully system. The chests were then lifted and lowered to the sand. Welham had them dragged by teams over to the *Whale*. Using their own crane, Levi's crew loaded their plunder into the belly of the *Whale*, where piles of gold were now accumulating. Levi had the captain tied as well, next to his crew. Only the Spaniards who were moving the chests were left untied. Levi and his men crossed the beach back to their ship, picking up their fallen comrades on the way.

"Join?" Some of the Spanish hesitantly went to Levi "Join your crew?" They looked back at their broken ship, where they would soon be abandoned.

"Fine. You'll replace the men you shot," Levi was used to the idea of picking up men from ships raided by the pirate captains he sailed with. They raised anchor and pushed their ship back to sea.

"Look who it is," Samuel met Henry as the *Bersheba* pulled into the ports of Nassau.

"Bellamy," Henry nodded as he was walking past.

"Henry, wait," Rolling his eyes, Henry turned back towards Samuel. "Benjamin knows."

"What?"

"Benjamin knows," Samuel said again. Jennings eyes raised, understanding what exactly the man was talking about. "He isn't going to do anything yet, but he might."

"Why are you telling me this?"

"Hornigold has changed since you've been absent. He's becoming less of a pirate and more of a governor. I sailed with him because we took from the rich. Now *he* is the man in the castle demanding his tax. He's the governors we wanted freedom from."

"Do the others feel the same?"

"We don't dare talk of it. So, forget I warned you," Samuel walked away, leaving Jennings at his ship.

"This could be our chance," Charles Vane came around the corner, hiding where crates were stacked.

"What do you mean?" Jennings turned.

"Some days I wonder about you," Vane chuckled. "This is our chance to rule here. We have a hefty crew now. You have the charisma to gain a following from those leaving Hornigold. You could be governor."

"Turn on him more than I already have?"

"You have no loyalty to him. You heard Sam; he's got it after you anyways. Are you going to wait for Benjamin to rally his armies against you or do you want to command those armies?" Jennings did not respond, he just stood thinking. "We're in a war, captain. You best prepare," Vane went back to the ship.

Jennings shook his mind clear and went into town. The tavern was starting to pick up a crowd in the early afternoon. Men inside sitting on barrels and stools, drinking out of their glasses. For most pirates in town, if they weren't out at sea, they were in the many taverns. They quickly spent what money they made, most not able to count or keep track of what they earned and spent. The gold circulated though, shopkeepers paid the captains for their stolen goods, which would go back into the pockets of the pirates.

"I thought I saw your hat when I got back to town," Levi came from behind and sat across from Henry on the porch of the Shark Bair Saloon.

"You look worse than I remember. Yer going to hurt yourself one day, kid." He chuckled. "How are you?"

"Well," Levi said. "Tried not to plunder all the gold in your absence."

"I appreciate the curtisy. You still sailing with that Benjamin?"

"He doesn't go out on the water much any more. I was working with Edward, but since he's been gone I've been running my own ship again. And I wouldn't dare go out with Samuel."

"I'd drink to that," Henry smirked. "Why don't we try Florida again? With yours and mine crew, we'd surely have enough men."

"I told Hornigold I would wait until Edward returned. Seems he had something for the two of us."

"Forget him," Jennings shook his head. "Forget Edward, forget Benjamin. This is about the gold, Levi. We want the gold," He took his hand out of his glove. "If we're dying, we might as well get rich while we're at it."

"You're right," Levi sighed. "It's the gold we're after. None of the rest matters. It's *that* gold that started me down this path. That's what we need to focus on."

"You're a smart kid. Two days, we sail. Don't bother to tell the *governor*. We don't need him."

"He won't like us crossing him."

"Oh, no. I don't imagine he will," Jennings smirked. Levi nodded and left.

The young man walked to the docks and followed the beach down to a house built up on the shore. A wooden structure jut out from the rocky hill and sat on pillars up from the sand, keeping out of the water. The shack was where Levi spent his nights while in town. It was well furnished; a bedroom, a kitchen, a study, and a basement that was a cave in the rock. Some of the locals suspected Levi had hundreds of thousands of gold pieces stowed away in his modest house, yet no one had ever seen the inside.

Legends of Levi spred quickly once John Howell started telling stories regularly in town. He took any rumor he heard and made it into a fantastic tale. Specifically, the story of Levi capturing a ship of the Treasure Fleet. The young man would deny it though, trying to ward off unwanted attention and to avoid people suspecting that he had the biggest stockpile in New Providence.

April 1716

I've been getting swept up in the rising tide of the other captains. The Republic has been taking down ships and bringing back prizes so often that I hadn't the time to stop and think what this is all about. I hadn't considered why I was doing this.

I was exiled from what was left of Shorehaven, they made that clear when Northrop and I went back. So I took up what exciting life I could but always felt there was something missing. Hunting treasure, running goods will never be enough. I have to finish what I started. That much is clear. I have to reclaim my gold and as much of it as I can. I've already earned fortune to last me into the next life. Yet that is only a fraction of what I saw on that island. Jennings is right. Forget the others. This is about the gold.

The Port of Gold

25.

The Surging Curse.

Bells rang through the fog as a ship pulled into port. Northrop tied the packet boat off and helped set up the gangplank. Torches lit the dense substance as its mist covered the earth. A few other ships were docked on the pier, but they were empty and only appeared as shadows in the clouds.

"Good day to you, Englishman," The navy sailor walked off the ship and greeted the old man.

"Same to you, sir. What can we do you for?"

"I am here to deliever a proclamation sent from his excellency, the Governnor. We've been going from port to port delievering his letters. All English territories have been getting the message."

"Must be of urgence, then?"

"Quite. If you would, call for your mayor."

"I can bring it to him," Northrop suggested.

"The contrary. I need to hand this straight to the officials of this port. Not some peasant."

"Very well," Northrop handed the sailor his lantern. "Head straight that way," The old man pointed off through the fog. The buildings of town were hardly visible.

"I beg your pardon?"

"Well a peasant like me certainly can't escort you. *Your highness*," He chuckled as he disappeared into the thick cloud. The sailor huffed and started walking through the ruins.

"Who's there?" He called as a shadow appeared in front of him. The towering shadow studied him. "In the name of the king, who goes there?"

"Hold fast," Segar became visible. "Who are you?"

"I am a messenger of his excellecy, the governor. Lord Hamilton. I am looking for the mayor of this port."

"Well you found him. What is it?"

"A letter, he sends out to all islands under the crown."

"And?" Segar asked bluntly.

"May we speak in your house? This is quite informal."

"Forgive me. We don't have visitors here," Segar led the man back to his mansion. His house was one of the few untouched by the attack. Candles burned from the walls and from the dinning room table, where they sat. Segar went to a cabinet and poured himself and the English official a drink. "This letter?" The old privateer asked as he handed off the square glass and sat down at the table. "What significance does it have?"

"It's a proclamation from the king. To be posted and distributed so that all of his subjects, loyal *or not*, get the message. Concerning these notorious pirates."

"What would the king say concerning these pirates?" The sailor slid over the tan envelope. Segar took a dagger from his belt and broke the red wax seal. "'By the King. A Proclamation. For the more effectual redusing and suppresing of pirates and privateers in America...'" He mumbled the words as he scanned the ink on the page. "You're pardoning them?" He set down the letter.

"I, as well as his excellency, stand by the king. Anyone pirate who turns himself in will be given full pardon."

"They must hang," Segars voice grew tense.

"Those who run, will."

"They've taken so much. How can you let *any* of them live?"

"This is the king's order."

260

"They burned my town, killed my people," Segar shook his head in denial.

"If you feel so strongly that they be brought to justice, you might be interested in his incentive. Rewards for any pirate brought in. Captains, first mates, even cabin boys. They've been the hunters for too long. Now it is Englands turn."

"And this is in effect?"

"You bring Hamilton a pirate tomorrow and you'll get your share," He assured.

Over at the poorly rebuilt Rogue Star, the townsfolk huddled inside to keep out of the cold. Several warmed themselves at the fireplace, others used liquor. Some of the houses had been pieced back together, using the islands palm trees as lumber for roofs or walls. Though living conditions were only worsening.

"The Island's getting angry," Smith said to Northrop, he was the only man at the counter.

"Just cause we haven't rebuilt doesn't mean our island's angry."

"Not Shorehaven…" Smith raised his brow.

"How do you know this?" The old man grunted as he took a swig from his pint. "No one's been on the water in months."

"The fog, the foul smell in the air. All of it be drifting towards us from that place."

"It's smelled bad once we turned our town into a planation. Chickens and pigs everywhere. People farming in their manuer."

"I feel it though. The Island lost her gold. It wants it back."

"The *Island* doesn't want anything but to punish," Northrop set down his drink with his rotting hand. "I'd say we got our share."

"I don't know, mate. I think the storms are just going to get worse," Smith shook his head.

"There's nothing that can be done."

"Do we know that? The Curse didn't come with a scroll, telling us its secrets. For all we know the cure is right in front of us."

"I'm done fighting the Curse."

"Well maybe you've given up, but it hasn't. It'll curse us all before it's through!" Smith threw his hands up.

"I've dreamt of a cure for so long," Northrop studied the veins in his hands. "I just don't know if it's possible."

Three ships set out from Nassau's bay. Hundreds of men sailed under the three captains. Jennings on the *Bersheba*, Levi on the *Whale*, and Charles Vane captaining his own sloop, the *Lark*. Thompkins now took the rank of first mate aboard the *Bersheba*. They sailed over the rolling waves, spraying refreshing mist into the hot air. Florida was in their sights. The men ran on the hopeful knowledge that most of the gold had yet to be found. After two days at sea, the fleet entered the keys that branched off from the mainland. Islands dotting the shallow water like stepping stones.

"Ship ho," Thompkins called and waved at the two ships behind them. A small spanish sloop emerged from the north side of an island and found itself flanked by three different pirate ships.

"It's turning back," Jennings said as he watched his prey quickly change course. "Give chase!" He called down to from the sterncastle. "Pin it down on the shore from whence it came!"

"Raise the colors!" Levi ordered after seeing Henry throw up his new black flag. Vane quick to do the same, both men flew the same skull and cross bones, The Jolly Roger. Henry, eager to see where the sloop was going, ran to the bow of his ship. As the *Bersheba* turned the corner, Jennings was the first then to see. Thunderous shots startled Jennings before he could even comprehend that he was looking at a small fortress. Next to the fleeing sloop sat a Spanish ship of the line, now firing on the pirates.

"Christ!" He ducked as cannons rained out from the warship. "Stations! Man your guns!" He hollered as he ran back to the stern to arm himself. Jenning's men split up in their teams and began firing retaliating shots.

Levi took the *Whale* around, passing Jennings, trying to stay out of aim of the docked ship. The *Lark* followed, all three ships firing on the big tank. As the fleet arched around the docked boat, the Spanish sailors quickly worked to loosen the lines and put out to sea to be more easily defensible. The ship of the line swung from the dock, the bow still secured. It sweeped and shot at the three spread out pirate ships. With its two decks of guns, the Spanish ship was able to fire at an incredible rate. Each team in rhythm, shooting down the line, one after the other. The fort had guns of its own, firing out if a ship crossed its fixed mounts. Cannonballs flew over the harbor and struck the stone walls. Bricks fell down onto the men working below. The pirate crews worked tirelessly to keep up their barrage. They jammed the powder and loaded the muzzles. Even with the experienced seamen, the machines were only able to fire once every few minutes.

The heavily armed warship could normally take down all of these three in the open water. But being utterly surrounded, nearly immoble, and caught by supprise, it stood no chance. The bombardment of steel tore the ship from all sides. Splinters shot out with each direct impact. Not willing to let his prize sink, the captain on deck raised a white flag. The fort raised on as well.

"Hold your fire!" The fort's captain yelled, continuing to wave his white flag.

"Avast, men," Henry ordered his crew to stop. "Bring us into the bay," What was left of the Spainsh ship was being resecured to the docks. All three ships dropped anchor and their captains rowed in with some men to meet on the docks.

"Henry Jennings, no?" The Spaniard inquired the captains.

"Aye. You best remember," He smirked.

"Ah, *El Leviatán* as well," He looked at Levi, who stood resting his hands on his weapons, holstered in his belt.

"You pirates have no end. You kill needlessly, taking innocent lives."

"You were wise to surrendor then," Vane stepped forward as he jeered. "Makes our jobs easier."

"That it does. Filthy bastards," He spat on the dock.

"What are you terms of surrendor?" Jennings asked.

"Spain will pay you twenty-five thousand."

"To what?"

"To leave us alone. No more bloodshed, no more usless fighting. Just take your money and leave us be."

"Is that all the gold you have here?" Levi asked. He could feel the ink pulsing through his bloodstream, he knew part of the original treasure was there.

"Every coin. It's everything we have at the fort. None of our men need die today," The Spaniard insisted, still enraged at his misfortune. Henry was smiling, about to agree.

"The guns," Levi interrupted. "Your ship's cannons. We'll take those too."

"Arr," Vane flashed his yellowing teeth. "We'll take those too."

"So be it," The Spaniard hissed and turned.

Jennings walked behind the Spaniard to the storehouse and collected his ransom. Levi sent Welham and Cook to help carry the heavy chests. Terek and his brothers oversaw the stripping of the ships guns. Cannons lowered onto the dock, where Jennings' fleet now moored. Barrels of powder and crates of ammunition were walked down to the harbor and loaded up, filing each ship.

"As far their surrendor goes?" Vane asked openly with the two other captains that night. "Are we done raiding Florida?"

"I've thought on it," Jennings answered, taking a sip of brandy that they all were drinking. "We have to go back, to sell off the extra cannons either way. We're too slow to overtake any vessel as loaded as we are. Let them think we'll honor their terms, the men are happy with the raid."

"But we'll be back?" Levi pressed.

"Of course," Henry nodded. Vane smirked as he got up to leave, though Levi stayed seated. The flotilla stayed anchored off the bay and would sail out come morning.

"You know I am grateful for everything you've done for me."

"What are you talking about, Levi?"

"I am. I just wonder what's in it for you. Why help me? A smaller crew, younger captain? Usually if two men are going for the same prize, they fued over it."

"I see no reason for us to fight over the endless plunder we pull from land. It does seem a bit odd that us pirate captains take men under our wings and mentor them. I've thought of it, too, you know. I think it has to do with who we *aren't*. We're building a republic from the ground. England, Spain, the French all have generations of heirs. But look at us. None of us have offspring. We die before we'd ever have a child, let alone raise em to take after us. That's why I take you in. Heck, that's why Hornigold takes people in. It isn't just to build a powerful navy, with fleets of well trained, dashing rogues like yerself. It's to invest in the future of all we have here," Jennings stopped for a moment. "I had a family, but I left them for this life. My own lady couldn't produce a son. How I always wanted to take a son sailing. You are like a son to me, Levi. A bit old to be *my* son, but nonetheless. You remind me of myself, ambitious, daring. I don't get a chance to raise a boy, but I have a chance to mentor a great man."

"Well thank you," Levi smirked. "I don't remember my family. So, I'm glad I found one here."

Levi didn't unload the *Whale* when they docked in Nassau. He kept the ship as is, but unloaded his crew. Only the Mutiny Crew and himself remained.

"Heading out again?" Charles Vane called up as Levi was working on casting off the lines.

"Have places to be. I have use of these guns elsewhere. Don't fret, I'll be back."

"Wasn't worried," He chuckled and walked away.

"Gail," Levi called over as soon as Vane was away. "Get the barrels from-" He stopped, not wanting anyone to hear. "Just get the barrels," He patted Gail on the back, knowing he knew where and what Levi was speaking of.

"Need a guard, captain?" Crofton went up to Levi.

"Yes, like last time," Levi handed him a few coins from his pocket. "I'll have the rest of your cut when I return."

"Understood," He nodded and left the ship.

Gail Wickman returned with a cart full of barrels. He, Harper, and Welham rolled them up the gangplank and secured them below in the cargo hold. At dusk they pushed off from port and headed out to sea. The *Whale* was slow, weighed by its plentiful cargo, but Levi and the others were cautious not to be followed.

"Have you seen Levi?" Sam went up to Vane in town, both drinking under the light of lanterns and the moon.

"He left port as soon as he got back," Vane replied. Samuel not bothering to sit down with him, intending to keep his words brief.

"Very interesting. He's never around much."

"Young kid doesn't want to get warpped up with you I imagine," Charles smirked.

"Funny. Some think he's paranoid, afraid if he leaves his gold unattended, it'll be stolen."

"Living in this town, I would not blame him. All theives here."

"Maybe so," Samuel sighed as he walked away. Vane grunted at the moment, then drank to whisk it away.

"Is he there?" A shadow asked in the alley.

"No. He's at sea," Samuel replied.

"Then we must go quickly."

"I don't like this," Sam replied, following the shadow out of town. "We're just taking a look. Understand?"

"Of course. But if the rumors are true, and Levi is hoarding all that gold, then he is worse than Benjamin. And we both know how you feel about the rich."

"The boy's done me no harm."

"People starve here, Bellamy. If he has enough to feed the masses and doesn't, then you know what we must do."

"Are not the other captains in league with Levi? I'm telling you, this is a bad idea."

The cloaked man did not reply. Across the beach, perched on a rock was Levi's house. No lights were lit, it looked entierly abandoned. As the two men walked in the blackness of night to it, they saw a figure move within. They ducked behind a boulder, trying to remain invisible if possible.

"Shoot," Sam muttered. "Someone's guarding."

"Undoubtably guarding a treause hoard."

"We can't go in. Word gets out we broke into Levi's house, we're done. He's too well liked. On all sides."

"Maybe *we* don't need to go in."

A knock came on the wooden door. Crofton peered out the window, trying to remain unseen.

"Please? Is anyone there?" A soft female voice came from outside. "It's so cold and I haven't anywhere to stay."

"Don't do it," He said to himself and shook his head.

"Please if there is a gentleman home, can you let me in? Just to warm myself for the night?"

He grunted and opened the door. A short lady, long hair and thin composure shivered and looked up at Crofton with teary eyes. Her dress was thin and airy in the night breeze. "Come in," He said and looked around before closing the door. Crofton limped into the living space and pointed into the bedroom. "You can sleep in there," He said as he sat down on an armchair.

"You don't want to keep me warm?" She brushed her hand through her hair.

"No, ma'am," Crofton shook his head. "I wouldn't dare touch you."

At dawn, the *Whale* came through a wall of fog and appeared off the coast of Isla Maldito. The greenery was lush compared to the sickly plants in town at Nassau. They sailed into the southern bay, the ring of trees hiding yet another secret. Across from where the *Puerto Oro's* masts were revealing themselves from the water was anchored another ship. *El Dorado*, the ship Levi and Northrop sailed out of the hurrican. It was anchored on the sands, with wooden scaffolding built around it and a ramp leading up to the deck. Levi took the Mutiny Crew here several times, none of them phased by the things the island did to them.

They unloaded the cannons on shore, lowering them to the sand. They brought up the barrels and took off the lids. They tipped the barrels over onto a screen and sifted out the sand. Clinking of metal soon rattled as all that was left were golden pieces. Then, the men brought the barrels of gold over to *El Dorado* and went down into its cargo hold. Barrels filled parameter and stacked on top of each other. Dozens of unassuming wooden barrels filled the ship. Out of this stockpile, Levi paid each of his men, giving them their share.

"Anything?" Samuel asked a hooded girl the next morning in the alleyway. Rats crept along the walls, looking for spilled food from the night before.

"The house was empty. I checked everywhere," She replied. "Once the man inside fell asleep, I swept the whole house. There was nothing."

"Knew he had nothing to hide," Bellamy sighed. "Appreciate your business, lassie."

"My pay, then? We charge per the hour."

"Right, uh," Samuel took out a bag of coins and counted out several pieces for the wench.

26.

The Turning Tide.

Rockets lit the air, exploding with light and color, leaving a ghost of smoke. Under the red fireworks flew a black flag, waving a skeleton in the wind.

"Fire starboard cannons!" Edward commanded. The *Ranger* blasted at the enemy frigate. Each gun firing in succession, one after the next. The second gun deck fired as the first reloaded. Men in the masts fired rockets above their prey, sulfur raining down on them. The English ship fired back, though hesitant between each shot. Steel rammed through, bursting the wooden ship. With the constant battery against the hull, the Englishmen flinched as they worked, not knowing when they would be taken. Cannon fire was known for taking out legs from under men or heads off of shoulders.

As the *Ranger* prepared to board, Edward took out his dark tricorn hat. Coming from the brim, sticking out among his hair, were cannon wicks. He lit the ends and let them burn against his heavy beard and wild black hair. Across his chest were six pistols, all loaded and ready to be fired. The Englishmen that were fighting valiantly against the pirates stood frozen in fear when they saw the great man step onto the deck of their ship.

"God save us," One muttered. "It's Blackbeard!"

"God ain't here!" Edward barked and took out his sword. "Only the devil," He chopped down at the cowering foe, slicing into his neck. Taking his saber out of him, Edward swung across at those attempting to blindside him. His sword sweeped across the deck and warded off his attackers. They jabbed with their rapiers, Edward fought the two sigle handedly as the rest of his crew were occupied in their own battles.

"Crazy man, he is," Benjamin took a sip of bourbon, still seated in the cabin of the *Ranger*.

"Indeed," John Howell peaked out the glass window, trying to stay out of sight of stray bullets. "There was once a time you would have fought like that."

"I much prefer to let Edward do the brute fighting. I'm comfortable where I am," Hornigold said, closing his eyes, taking in the sounds of battle from his cushioned chair.

Edward stabbed one man in the gut and kicked at the other. Taking his sword out, he sliced the second foe across the face. Seeing the battle nearly over, Edward sheathed his sword and pulled two pistols from his custom vest. With one in each hand, he fired rounds into two defenders. Holstering those two, he took out two more guns and again fired at two different men respectively. He took out his last two and shot down two more men.

Edward looked around to see the battle was won. All the Englishmen were either killed or dying on the deck. He howled at the victory, his men screaming as well. The fuses that were still lit on his hat were running out, sparks now burning close to his ears.

"Rip it apart," He ordered. "Every coin must be taken!"

"You'll hang for this," One sailor coughed on the ground, blood pooling in his mouth. Edward marched over to the man and stepped on his chest with his heavy boot.

"I'll what?" He demanded. The dying sailor couldn't respond. "String up a noose! Let em dance the hempen jig," Edward turned to his crew. They threw a line over the lowest yardarm and tied a noose. Edward grabbed the mans shirt and pulled him to his feet. He wrapped the rope around the man's neck. Only with the upward pull on the line was the man able to stand on his own. Edward's crew found the short gangplank and stuck it out the side of the ship. With his sword, Edward pushed the man out onto the plank.

"What was it you said to me, boy?" Edward asked again, his yellow teeth

"You pirate! You'll-" Edward kicked the legs out from the man. He fell back, breaking his neck. His body swinging out from the plank like a pendulum.

"Leave em up. Makes a fine decoration," Edward ordered as his men were about to untie the other end of the line. "Rest of you! On your feet. We still a ship to plunder!" Hornigold was standing on the sterncastle, watching the other captain continue his work.

"Curse the King!" One pirate toasted at dinner. He stood on the bench, raising his bottle of rum. The galley was dimly lit that night, the moon wasn't out to reflect into the port holes of the lower deck. Yet the men roared as they chomped their food, celebrating their victory. They sang as they lifted their glasses:

Curse the King! Doom ol' George!
We drink to Hell, that golden shore!
We plunder long, what vile chore!
We drink to Hell, that golden shore!

The pirates laughed as they knocked glasses and stiens together, liquor spilling out onto the food that littered the tables. Victories were easy for the large crews, pillaging ships of maybe one dozen men. Yet they celebrated all the same, overjoyed with riches and the excitement of battle. They talked loudly as they tore their food apart. Chicken legs and apples, loaves of bread and anything they stole from their prey. As their dinner winded down, men slowly returned to their posts or relaxed on deck.

"Bellamy would," Some of Edward's crew still sat in the galley, around a lone lantern that night. "He's known Hornigold's changed. As much as us."

"And we know Thatch would be for it?"

"I can't imagine Edward likes being Hornigold's puppet. He'd go for it. He's hungry enough."

"What of Nassau? Who rules there?"

"Well, Thatch. He succeeds Hornigold."

"Edward hates politicing. What of Jennings?"

"Jennings is too docile on his own to be governor. He'd want it but he'd be worse than Benjamin."

"And Vane? That man's brutal enough."

"Aye, but he's loyal to Jennings. Most likely he'll try to have Henry take the position."

"Edward and Bellamy against Vane and Jennings?"

"Edward could kill Henry six times over. We know it!"

"Aye, but Jennings has more men. He has another captain, that boy Levi. That's a war I don't want to see."

"Jennings can be pushed around. We can nagotiate with him. He takes care of port, but he doesn't tax our spoils. He has more men, so he makes more gold. Enough to keep town well on his own. No war. Just overthrow."

"Aye, so we make Thatch captain and we have Jennings governor. No taxes. No more Hornigold."

"But we can't just mutiny, Thatch would fight us if we took up arms. We need to be smart about this," They schemed in the night.

"Benjamin Hornigold," A crewman hollered to the captain the next morning. The finely dressed man was drinking coffee from the sterncastle, where he had a chair fixed.

"What is it, boy?"

"What kind of government is our crew?"

"A sophisticated question. Tis democracy."

"Aye. Then we shall have a vote," He called back. Hornigold coughed on his hot drink.

"What?"

"Just observing your government, sir," He snickered.

"Fine," Hornigold barked. "Who are your canidates?"

"You," He paused. "And Thatch."

"My own second in command? This is absurd."

"Hold a vote, Hornigold," Others gathered behind him. Edward raised his brow at the scene. Smirking slightly under his bushy beard. Benjamin scowled as he went down to the weather deck. He had several crates brought to him and a board to make a table. Hornigold got parchment and ink from his cabin and wrote at the top, *Benjamin Hornigold* and *Edward Thatch*.

Men came and marked with the pen who they were voting for. A few sailors put an X under Benjamin's name, but the large majority put their marks under Edward's. Not without having to ask whose name was who, since they couldn't read.

"This is mutiny," Hornigold grumbled. He stood and adjusted his long coat. "This is rebellion! I'll see you all whipped for this!"

"Forget it, Benjamin. Your system says Thatch is our captain now," The sailor provoked. Hornigold turned to get his whip.

"Enough," Edward stepped forward. "The men have spoken."

"Very well," Hornigold sat back down. "You are a man after my own heart at least. Not all bad."

"I am my own man. Not yours," Thatch walked away. The crew quick to disperse back to their duties.

"Levi," Bellamy came to the young man as he returned to Nassau. "Gather Jennings and Vane and meet me in the Shark Bait," He said quietly and quickly.

"What is it?"

"Do as I say," Samuel put his hand on the young man's shoulder before walking away. Levi finished securing his ship to the docks and went to the *Bersheba*.

"Jennings, where is Vane?" The young man called as he boarded the ship.

"Right here, Benson," Charles came from below deck. "What's the matter?"

"We're being summoned," Levi said as he got close to the two captains. "I don't know what for."

"Get your guns ready," Charles said, pointing to the flintlock on Levi's belt. "We don't know what be waiting."

Levi led them down the plank and across the pier to the Shark Bait Saloon. The tavern was closed off for the private meeting. The sun shone through the boarded windows. Sounds of the town were muffled by the walls. As Levi opened the door, he saw the other captains sitting around the large table.

"Enter," Edward said plainly. The three walked into the dark room and closed the wooden door behind them.

"There's a shifting in power," Bellamy started as the three sat down with the others. "We need to be sure we're all on the same side when this goes off."

"What is it you want?" Jennings ask.

"We are asking you to be governor," Samuel said plainly.

"The crews already demoted Hornigold. He's no longer a captain," Thatch coughed. "They'll be rioting soon if he's still in office. He must go."

"So I to take his place?" Henry said quietly in the dark hall.

"Aye. We have terms if we're going to appease the crews. No taxes from spoils. Money spent here will go towards the town, not into your pocket," Edward listed.

"So I keep pirating, but I am also in charge of taking care of the town's upkeep?"

"The men didn't like Benjamin sitting in his mansion, taking their money and stuffing his own trousers," Samuel added. "That's why they made Thatch their only captain."

"So we all continue our raids as normal," Levi started. "But Jenning's spoils go towards the town?"

"Who ever wants to pay to keep up the place can do so," Thatch added. "We all live here."

"If you are made governor, you cannot turn to be the aristicrat Hornigold became. That is why you pirate for yourself," Samuel continued. "We want him gone. So do not repeat his mistakes."

"Fine," Jennings agreed. "Are we all in accordance?"

"Aye," The four other men each said.

"Then we must act hastely," Samuel got up.

The five captains walked up the streets to the governors mansion. The streets were littered. Mud covered the cobblestone paths. The town reeked from sewage running down into the bay. Each man had a hand ready on their pistol. When they got there, Edward knocked on the heavy door. No reply. He knocked again, his fists thundering. No reply.

"What?" Samuel looked through the windows into the empty house. Thatch used his shoulder and broke the door in.

"Hornigold!" Edward yelled. His voiced echoed through the hallways. No response came.

"Benjamin, we're here to talk!" Jennings celled. Only their echoes replied. The five wandered slowly through the corridors, looking for the governor. Each splitting up and carefully walking from room to room. They each had their gun drawn, all prepared to end the life of Benjamin Hornigold. The servants rooms were empty. The kitchen was empty along with every hall and chamber they checked.

"Edward!" John Howell ran into the mansion, huffing to catch his breath.

"John?" Thatch turned to the familiar face.

"Hornigold took the *Ranger*. He's sailing out," John Howell pointed behind him toward the bay.

"What?" Bellamy rushed to the doorway, looking out to the water. "Who's sailing with him?"

"His supporters, I think. His servants," John shook his head. "Those too dumb to know otherwise."

In the other room, Levi hadn't heard what the noise was about. He rummaged through Benjamin's desk and found on his desk a single letter. A knife was stuck through it, pinning the parchment to the table. Levi took out the blade and lifted the paper, with the red wax seal.

"He's betrayed us," Levi found the other men in the entryway.

"What is that?" Edward asked in a heavy tone.

"A king's pardon for all pirates who turn themselves," Levi started. "And commission to hunt those who don't."

"The apostacy," Edward threw down his arms. "Benjamin turned to hunt the bloody thing he built."

"Slimely bastard turned before we ever overthrew him," Samuel took and skimmed over the note. "This was the letter from the governor I delivered."

"It's settled then," Edward began before storming out. "Jennings, you're the governor now. If Hornigold intends to hunt us, then it's war."

The Port of Gold

27

Beginning of the End.

Segar opened the tavern door. In his hand was a rifle and the letter he had received from the governor. Those who were in the Rogue Star turned to listen, accustomed to Segar's announcements.

"Hearken me, you men," He started. "We have abstained from going out on the water since our town was destroyed. We have not fished nor gone out to sea and yet we have still suffered long for the evil inflicted on us," Segar had everyone's attention. His eyes were fierce and his muscles were tense. "I say that time is done."

"What do you propose?"

"Our king is offering reward for every pirate brought in. Dead or alive. I have thought on it. They do not deserve to live. We will rebuild Shorehaven on the bounties we collect. We will rebuild this town by putting their race into the ground! Arm yourselves, men. We are going out to sea," The men in the tavern hollered and cheered in reply. "Meet at my ship tonight. We'll load then and come morning, we sail."

Shorehaven burned that evening. Men took out their old guns and weapons and mustered in the tavern. The privateers put on their old navy coats and hats. Fishermen brought harpoons, the butcher brought knives and meat hooks. As the mob grew rowdier and moved with hatred in their eyes, Smith snuck out. The man looked over his shoulder as he left the back door and went around to the lighthouse.

"Northrop," He stepped into the house and quickly shut the door. The old man was smoking tabacco in his lonesome. "Northrop, the men in town are arming themselves," Smith peered out the window to make sure he was not seen.

"Arming themselves for what?" Northrop didn't seem amused.

"Battle," Smith let out.

"What?" Northrop turned and looked at his friend. "What do you mean 'battle'?"

"Segar is getting a crew ready to hunt pirates. The king is offering rewards. They want revenge."

"I see," He coughed.

"No, Northrop. I fear they will try to hunt down Levi," To this the old man stood up. "You know many blame him for this. We both know where he is. If they even find him, they will kill him."

"I cannot talk them down," Northrop sighed. "If they have it in their hearts to kill him, I cannot stop them."

"Not with words," Smith said.

"What do you suggest?"

"They blame Levi, but the root of this is the Curse."

"Smith," The old man grumbled.

"Listen to me. If we can lift the Curse, wouldn't that satisfy the town? The fog, the dead fish. It's here, we know it is. The men in the tavern are possessed, I've never seen anyone so vexed on killing before. Look at em! They've all gone mad! It cannot be anything else. The Curse set all of this in motion. I truly believe it can be stopped. There be no other way."

"I don't know," Northrop shook his head. "It's gripped me for decades. I have no idea how it could be cured."

"But if it could, it could bring back Levi. You told me how obsessed he was. We lift the Curse, maybe he'll snap out of the madness he's in. Maybe the town will, too."

"How can it be done?" Northrop asked sincerely.

"I've put it to thought. The Curse was born from the ship going down without her captain. The crew hunts and strikes from the dead, seeking their revenge. What if we give them their captain?"

"Return his bones to the ship?"

"Is it not worth a try? To rid us of this evil."

"Ridding the Curse does not rid all the evil in the world. If we do this, we need to know it may not fix it all," The old man put on his wool peacoat and hat.

"Where are you going?" Smith turned.

"Should at least try to talk Segar down," Northrop brushed passed his friend on his way out the door. He heard the noise from the tavern as men fueled each other's rage. They pounded their fists on the tables and served themselves drinks from the bar. He went down to Segar's ship, anticipating the mayor would be there. Northrop scanned the pier, but saw no one. From behind him, he saw a lantern approaching.

"You cannot kill the boy," Northrop hollered.

"I will do what I must. This town deserves justice," Segar walked up to the old man.

"It has received justice. The Spaniard is dead," Northrop urged. "What you want is revenge."

"The boy has had his chance! He is not without fault," The mayor snapped. "We will hunt down everyone like him if it rebuilds our town."

"Revenge does not satisfy."

"You cannot sway me," Segar said between his teeth, stepping toe to toe with the old man, looking Northrop in the eye.

"This is gone too far!" Northrop shouted. "I won't let you kill him," From town, the mob was going down to the pier, to load the ship. All the men now armed standing only a few paces off from the two.

"Then you best hope we don't find him," Segar turned towards his ship, knowing Northrop would not attack with the rioting crowd upon them.

The *Ranger* cut through the water, going with the wind to pursue its target. Hornigold raised the British flag, to which the frigate raised a black flag in response. The pirate ship turned back, aiming to take a pass at bombing their British enemy.

"Arm the cannons," Benjamin said to his officer.

"Arm the cannons!" Roger then turned to yell the order across the ship. "Stations, let's move!" Gun ports were pulled open and cannons extended out of the side of the ship. Hornigold had taken his light crew from Nassau and received a pardon from Hamilton. From there, he filled his crew again with men eager to hunt down the criminals.

"Oi, who is that?" The captain of the pirate ship peered through the spyglass. "Hold on, men. That's Captain Hornigold!"

"Must have forgotten about us, we've been at sea so long!" One of the pirates joked.

"He's just giving us a scare, he is," The pirate captain took off his hat and waved at Hornigold as the ships drifted past. "Stand down, men."

"Fire," Hornigold said, standing gloomly as he stared back at the pirate ship. Guns from under him roared and blasted into the unsuspecting pirates. Englishmen took their muskets and shot at the pirates, now cowering on their ship. Cannons continued to pelt them, whose captain was too in shock to return fire. They raised a white flag as

Benjamin gave the orders to hook and board their ship. "How unforunate that you did not get the news."

"What happened, Benjamin?" The pirate captain said, horrified. "What governor attacks his own crews?"

"I am no longer your ruler," Hornigold said plainly. He paused as he watched his men chain and tie down the pirate crew. "Consider me an enemy of the state."

Benjamin left the men bound on their own ship, towing it behind the *Ranger*. He set sail again, bringing them southward. His men guarded the prisoners to ensure they could not escape.

"What'll you do with us?" A pirate asked the guard. It was late in evening and the men left exposed on the weather deck shivered.

"We're turning you in," Roger said frankly.

"Will they hang us?" Another prisoner asked.

"Most likely. They were building a bigger gallows when we left port. I suspect they plan to hang a lot of pirates at Kingston in the coming months."

"Christ save us," The pirate muttered and shook his head. Roger scoffed at the remark.

When they arrived in the Jamaican town, Hornigold was taken up to Hamilton's office by a horse-drawn carriage. The ride was rougher than the motion of a ship, as the road was poorly built. Though, Hornigold liked the idea of being chauffeured rather than walking himself.

"A catch already?" Hamilton asked the esteemed man.

"Yes, your excellency," Benjamin bowed. "Fifty men waiting aboard their frigate."

"Good work, your knowledge of their ranks and movements will prove invaluable to the Crown."

"Quite indeed, your excellency."

"I'll see to it your ship is resupplied before you set out again."

"My reward, sir?"

"Patience," Hamilton was taken back. "When my secretary has counted the men you brought in and they have been surely tried and hanged, you will be given your dues," He took a drink of his tea and then waved the man away. Benjamin bowed his head and turned to leave the room. The heels of his boots clicked the stone floor as he went to exit the mansion. Leaving out the front door, his carriage was still waiting for him. As the door was opened for him, he saw there was someone he did not recognize waiting inside.

"What is this?" Hornigold demanded as he sat in the cabin.

"Relax," The old Spanaird said, annoyed at the man's temper. "I have gold for you if you are indeed in the pirate hunting busniness. I am told you know of a certain Jennings."

"Henry," Benjamin nodded.

"I know what English are paying you to turn in captains."

"Go on."

"I will pay more for Jennings to be brought to Havana."

"Who are you?"

"I am the Spanish Viceroy, Laureano. Jennings has been the barb in my side for too long. Bring him to me and I will see you will be duely rewarded."

"Double," Hornigold negotiated.

"A hundred and fifty percent."

"One-seventyfive."

"Very well, Mister Hornigold. A hundred and seventy five percent if the living body of Henry Jennings is brought to my house in Havana."

"Anyone else you want? His accomplices?"

"Just Jennings. You can dump anyone else into the ocean for all I care. But I want that man alive. Do we have a deal?" Laureano held out a bag of coins to Benjamin.

"Yes."

"Quickly now," Northrop crept along the beach.

"Who's ship are we taking?" Smith insisted, both in the cover of night. "Northrop."

"Clay won't protest if we borrow his."

"That's just disrespecting the dead."

"Let's get there before we're caught."

"What could they do if they saw us?"

"Try to stop us, I suppose," Northrop huffed as they reached the Clair house. Clay's fishing boat was pulled ashore. Smith pulled the cover off as the two pushed it back into the water. The boat slid in the sand and onto the waves. The men each grunted as they boarded, Northrop helping to pull Smith out of the water. Once on deck, they found long paddles and pushed themselves out from the shore. Working in the blackness of night, Northrop fixed the single mast and pulled up the sail. The dark triangle standing against the dotted starlit sky. Smith turned the rudder and had the small sailboat pushing north away from the town; flickering lights slowly fading. The wind was with the two men as they drove away from the island.

Soon dawn appeared in the east. One by one the stars they were navigating by disappeared and were replaced by the yellow light of the sun. As the sky dyed blue, a silhouette could be seen on the horizon. An island with a mountain, fog covering the foothills. The fishing boat sailed over the foam collecting around the bay as they neared Isla Maldito.

"There it is," Smith chuckled. "It's a beautiful island."

"That she is, but a deadly one."

The sail boat glided over the sunken ship, it's skeleton below water dwarfing the boat on the surface. The waves were crystal clear and as blue as aquamarine. Sea grass grew from the sand that built up towards the shore. Northrop lowered the sail and tied it to the boom after their ship rode up onto the beach. They jumped into the shallow water and pulled it all the way on shore.

"Here," Northrop handed Smith a sword he had taken.

"What for?" Smith grabbed it as he saw his old friend securing his own in his belt.

"We don't know what we will find or what will happen if we move his bones," Northrop started walking toward the trail. "These swords came in handy when we were banished here."

"Why don't you start telling more stories at the tavern?" Smith joked as he followed behind the old man. "I have a feeling there's a lot more to ye than you put on."

The jungle was dense with plants and ripe with fruit and flowers. Bugs gave off every sound they could as birds called to each other and soared above. Mist came down from the mountain and rolled off the river and across the trail. The smell of sea air met with the blooming plants still covered in the morning dew.

"I've never seen a jungle so green," Smith took in all the sights. The two were in no hurry. They took their time as they walked deeper into the rainforest. Low hanging vines and branches made an interwebbed canopy above them, shading them from the beating sun. One of these vines began to move.

"Hold up," Northrop caught the back of Smith's shirt. The vine, looping down from a branch started to slump down and slithered onto the ground. It was green and had diamond scales running along its spine. The snake stuck its piered red tongue out and hissed softly as it took in the atmosphere. Northrop pulled out his sword, careful to not take his eyes off the predator moving towards them. Smith slowly unsheathed his weapon, too. The scratching of steel mimiced the sound of the snake. Each man stepped to the other side of the trail, keeping their swords ready. The snake hissed again, louder this time. Smith took baby steps forward, Northrop right behind him. Turning towards them, the snake retracted its body and folded on top of itself. Shooting like a dart, the snake unhinged its jaws and bite Smith in the hand, its teeth sinking between the bones.

"Christ almighty!" He yelled. Northrop drove his boot into the snake's neck and chopped down with his sword. The snake let go, opening its mouth in pain. Yellow liquid dripped down from its fangs as the snake eventually stopped moving. Smith fell on the ground clenching his hand, which bleed from two distinct marks.

"Get up, We need to move," He warned.

"You go," Smith waved on. "Let me stay here and like my wounds."

"You'll surely die if I leave you. We cannot stay in the jungle," Northrop pulled Smith to his feet, the bitemarks already bruising. The two moved quickly to escape the forest, Smith holding his own hand as they ventured towards the end of the trail.

28.

The Dispersion.

Nassau was emptier than usual. There were less ships in port, less men drinking around town. Those who were around seemed a bit quieter than usual. No recent scores to celebrate. That night there were only a handful of men in the tavern.

"Hunters have taken several boats already," Vane spoke somberly at their usual round table. "Bet it's Hornigold, gunning down his old friends. Swine, he is."

"Don't we outnumber our hunters?" Thatch growled. "Do we not have more guns than they?"

"They have the backing of the English navy. Some think it could turn to a direct assault," Vane took a drink from his pint, trying to steady himself.

"We're losing men by the day," Jennings shook his head. "Not only with the crews being taken down."

"Deserters?" Thatch grumbled. "Well, God curse them all! Is this going to be the end of our kingdom? Our freedom? I will not believe that Benjamin held that much power to single handedly turn the tide. We are all more powerful than he ever was!"

"If we stay they will come for us," Samuel lowered his head. "Eventually they will attack Nassau."

"So, we give up, abandon post? Over war?! Mere *rumors* of war?!" Edward Thatch threw down his hands. "If none of ye have the brass to take on Hornigold, I will do it meself!"

"It's not just him," Vane said back. "It's the navy. They're growing as we're losing numbers. Who knows the size of the fleet he will have behind him?"

"So what?" Thatch turned to his fellow captains. "Can we not hold out? Are we not defensible?"

"Edward," Samuel started. "It is no longer safe to be established here. We are sitting ducks if we try to hold on."

"You're ending the republic?" Edward sat back in his chair.

"It *is* ending," Samuel sighed. "If we want to survive, we have to go back to how we were. Each man his own. No more routes, we're too predictable. That's how Hornigold is picking us off."

"Back to cloak and dagger? The dark ages when we had no money? No loyalty between men?" Thatch was appalled. No one replied, but stared blankly. "Is no one siding with me on this?"

"What loyalty?" Vane asked. "Men have been leaving. We were only strong if we had *all* of our numbers. Yes, back to cloak and dagger. Back to hiding if it means we survive."

"We kill and steal," Thatch began slowly. "Shed our own blood so that we don't have to *survive*. We do all that we do so we's can live like kings! At all costs! We've been risking it all, putting our necks on the line so that we could enjoy riches beyond measure. Is that no longer worth it to ye?" Edward pounded his fist on the table as he got up. "I'll kill the man myself! Good luck, ye cowards," With that, he left the room.

"God save us. Now we are doomed," Jennings said, all of them knowing Edward was their most powerful ally. "I suggest we stock up, gather our men, and put out to sea."

"Where do we go?" Vane asked the two remaining men.

"Anywhere," Samuel put on his hat as he was preparing to leave. "Sail from prize to prize if you must. Do anything to evade the hunters and keep yer crews fed," He sat for a moment before he walked away.

"We'll be seeing ya, Henry," Vane grabbed his pint and pushed out the door. Henry Jennings remained, sitting alone. The tavern now empty, most clearing out when they overheard the heated argument. He drank from his pint then went behind the counter to pour himself another. Thompkins found him sitting at the bar when he walked in.

"The crew's wondering…" Thompkins hobbled over and sat net to his captain.

"I know," Jennings said to his first mate. "What do they want?"

"I think this is a decision you have to make for yourself."

"I would like to honor my crew," Henry took a drink.

"Then either way they would not disgrace you."

"There is only one we get out of this."

"Aye…" Thompkins sighed and took a bottle for himself.

"But I *will not* turn to hunt my comrades."

"Understood."

Levi was on his way into town the next morning. He stopped only when he noticed Henry packing his ship. Looking around, the young man diverted his course and went up to the pier.

"Where are you going?" Levi asked worriedly.

"Kid," Henry sighed.

"No," Levi shook his head before allowing Henry to say another word. "You can't leave. You *can't* leave me."

"Levi... I urge you to follow me in this."

"The *gold*, Henry."

"I value our lives," Jennings put his hand on Levi's shoulder. "Come with me. This is the only way to escape this life of danger."

"What about the republic? What about all we've built here?" Levi stepped back.

"It is collapsing around us. Those who stay will not stand. I know I was the purveyor of this adventure. I know I encouraged you, but now I care to protect you. I'm looking out for us, come with me," Henry pleaded excitedly, looking into the young man's brown eyes.

"What am I to do?" Levi pulled away. "Nothing will ever be as exciting as this."

"It isn't about the excitement. This is life or death, Levi! You will not live long if you stay. Go find yer family. Go find your home, Levi. You're lost at sea... You forgot you were lost," Henry whispered.

"They would not accept a pirate," Levi chuckled in disbelief and started to tremble. "This was where I belong. This life, these men, *you*. You're my mentor, my comrade! Henry!"

"Please surrendor. You are a fine man, Levi. You can live a long life. You have enough saved up to still live in luxary for the rest of yer days."

"I am not a good man. None of us are!" He laughed. "There's no good men in this game. We won't be accepted in high society. Pardoned or not."

Henry sighed before beginning.

"You *are* a good man. I've seen bad men. Wicked, evil men. Men who are backed by empires. Men who are patriotic. There are no clear lines between good and evil among us. We just fight for our sides. Being on this side does not make you bad.

"Levi, I know it can seem we are too far gone. That we're too gone, reprobates destined for hell. That we've done too many horrific things to ever be redeemed, but that is not the case. You worry about being a bad man, here's your shot at redemption. They will pardon you no matter what. Take it, I am begging you," Jennings pleaded.

"I am afraid I won't stop wanting that treasure. I have gold, *storehouses* of gold. And yet I have slain men to get more. Ended who knows how many lives by my blade. Boys younger than me. Men too old to fight properly, it didn't matter. I've led men into battle to die so that I can take of the spoils," Levi looked away, hiding the tears swelling around his eyes.

"We are all guilty of that sin, Levi. No Curse needed. I promise you, there is a place for you. I have land you can settle on, live in hiding there. Live in peace. Mercy is being offered, you just have to accept it. I just need you to be safe because nothing but death will come of this town."

"Do not forsake me," Levi shook his head.

"This is the only way," Henry turned back to board his ship. "Thompkins, get us ready by the hour!" He swiftly ordered and went into his cabin. Levi nodded to himself as he stepped back and turned to go into town. Going into the abandoned Shark Bait Saloon, the young man found an abandoned bottle of rum. Sitting at the large round table, he poured himself a glass. Levi held it up as if to toast, but couldn't find it in him to say anything. He sniffed as tears fell from his nose, then tapped the glass on the table and knocked it back.

The *Bersheba* sailed out of port not long after. Its striped sails flew brightly in the clear afternoon. The weather was clam and not a cloud interrupted the sky. Henry Jennings stood on the stern castle wearing his bright coat and hat. He looked out over the city as they sailed away. Hardly any ships were left in the harbor. The camps on the beaches had been mainly dismembered or left fallen over. Thompkins had the helm behind him. He didn't say a word, knowing where his captain aimed to go. Just as New Providence Island became nearly out of sight, Jennings turned from his view.

"Listen here. All of you,," Henry addressed his men. They stopped their worked and gathered on deck. "You have been a good crew, but this will be our last voyage. Upon recent events, I have had to consider what the best move would be. I will be turning myself in to receive this full pardon. I wish it very much to see all of you alive so I suggest you request the pardon as well. I will honor your descision, whatever it be. I know, uh, I know it can be hard leaving a life on the sea. Leaving the freedom we had. So, I will respect your choice. If you do not wish to accept the pardon, I'm offering up the lifeboats. You may row back to Nassau or anywhere you wish. You have my leave."

Men turned to one another. Some mumbled, all looking for a clear direction. Jennings went down and receded into his cabin to leave the men to their decision. He knew it was best to gain some distance from Nassau before proclaiming his intentions, not wanting to face the other captains.

"Brother, what are we going to do?" Keon asked Terek as the three brothers scrubbed the deck.

"I'm thinking," Terek did not stop grinding with the sandstone.

"They will enslave us for sure," Akia said. "They will ask us, 'were you slaves or free?' If tell them we're slaves, they will put us to a camp. If we say free, then they would hang us for piratry."

"Would we not get pardoned?" Keon asked.

"I would not think so," Terek grumbled.

"Then we must get to a boat, right?" Akia stood, but he saw Terek was not moving. "Brother, we have to flee."

"Would they not find us when the English come to reclaim Nassau?" Terek stopped to look at his brother. "We're doomed either way."

"No. If we go, we have a chance to be free. Join Captain Vane's crew. You've worked for him, we could be free aboard his ship," Akia stood beside his brother.

"You are right. We must try," Terek stood. The three went over to one of the lifeboats, not having anything in their possession to take with them.

"Where are you going?" A man went over to them as they were lowering themselves.

"We have to leave," Terek did not stop the pully.

"Are you not loyal to Jennings?" The sailor called down from over the railing, seeing the rowboat in the water.

"You do not understand," Terek said bluntly as he fed the last of the line through and began to drift away from the *Bersheba*. The ship sailed south for Kingston as the brothers began to row back to Nassau. The Island of New Providence was still in sight. Their journey back didn't take more than a few hours. The wind was in their favor, and the waves were calmed. They rowed around the south of the island to the east bay. None of the three spoke much, only keeping their heads down as they worked. With the help of the tide, they were pushed to shore. Terek and his brothers left the boat and walked through the sand to the cobble ground.

"Captain," Terek bowed his head as he addressed Charles on deck of the *Lark*. "We wish to join your crew."

"Didn't you just leave?" Vane questioned. "Where's Henry?" The three didn't respond. "Where is he?"

"He is going to Kingston," Terek answered.

Vane swore and turned away.

"They would have hanged us if we stayed with Jennings."

"Yes, find a spot to stow your things," Vane shook his head as he walked down the gangplank to the pier. Storming up to the patio by the tavern, he found Samuel.

"Afternoon," Bellamy greeted, raising his pint.

"Get your men and leave."

"What?" Samuel set down his drink.

"Jennings has left us," Vane said sternly. "We no longer have enough men to be safe here."

Samuel rubbed his face in frustration. "Okay, I'll muster my men. It was good while we had it."

The two walked down from town towards the docks, where most of their crew hung around. Levi was on his way up to meet them, but they paid him no attention.

"Now where are *you* going?" Levi asked.

"Away, into hiding," Samuel brushed passed him.

"Will you not stay here?"

"Congrats, you're governor now," Vane rolled his eyes as he also walked by the young man.

"Men," Levi pleaded, but they did not stop. Levi went back to his ship, his men lounging on the wooden barrels and stairs.

"Seen a ghost?" Gail called over. "What's the matter?"

"Pack your things. We're leaving."

"What?" Welham stood up.

"The rest of the captains are gone," Levi went over. "We're not safe here anymore. Get your belongings and get ready to set out."

"Back to drifters, I see," Crofton sighed as he got up. "Aye, sir. We'll have the ship ready to part."

29

Waiting Judgement.

The *Ranger* stalked the waters of the Bahamas like a lion waiting in the grass. White sand rose from the sea, dotting the ocean with clumps of green land, perfect for an ambush. Between the islands and the coastlands the ship lurked, looking for the right villainous sailors to come along. Benjamin knew to hunt a pirate where pirates themselves hunted: in the shipping lanes. Hornigold knew these waters, between New Providence Island and the keys leading to Florida. They were the territory of his enemy. As the *Ranger* sat off the coast of one of these islands, a sail came into view. It was white and flew from the bowsprit of the passing frigate. As the ship's body drifted by, the masts could be seen. More white sails blowing in the wind, flying overhead was an English flag. Hornigold slumped his shoulders, eager to catch Henry in the act. Benjamin had turned around from where he stood on deck to go back to the helm when he heard a cannon fire. Spinning around, the leaned against the rail on the bow of his ship. From behind this English frigate another shot came, blowing a hole in the stern.

"Full sail!" Benjamin shouted. "Bring up the lines!" His men dropped the sails all the way and brought up the ropes they had been dragging to slow themselves. As the *Ranger* started propelling forward, the attacker came into view. Captain Levi was on deck of the *Whale* as he ordered his men to fire another round at their prey. "Cut em off," Benjamin went back to the coxswain.

"Levi, starboard side!" Gail called from the helm. Levi turned to see the *Ranger* charging straight at them.

"Stir us away!" Levi called as Gail turned the wheel, giving up the chase they were on. The *Ranger* had just glanced off the hull, the two ships now running parallel. "Benjamin you traitor!" Levi hollered up at Hornigold.

"Hold your fire!" Benjamin called to his men. "Hello Benson. What a pleasant surprise," The older man jeered as he walked down towards his weather deck to meet Levi face to face. "Have you by any chance seen Henry? I miss the fellow, would love to catch up."

"Drown in the abyss," Levi said as he slowly pulled out his sword. "You'll be destroyed!"

"You can't possibly win. I more than double your crew! In men as well as guns," Hornigold lifted his arms and looked around him.

"I'll take *you* then. Man to man," Levi pointed his blade at Benjamin.

"You are remarkable. You truly have no restraint," Benjamin laughed. "I double your age. Triple you in experience! I've killed more men than you've seen in your life. You think because you have somehow lived this long that you could beat me?"

"Love to try," The young man said between his teeth.

"If you do not surrendor, I will blow your ship in," He warned. Roger stepped up to the railing and looked down on Levi. Even from the distance, Levi recognized his old crew member by his awkward hieght.

"You bastard!" Levi yelled up at his former crewman. "Is killing pirates righteous enough for you?!"

"Levi," Gail grabbed his shoulder. "We're done," Before Levi could turn back to say any more, Hornigold's men started to board the *Whale*. They began to bind the men up in shackles.

"Is that it then?" Jack looked around, waiting in case his captain gave the word to retaliate.

"Aye," Levi glared up at Horigold as he was chained to the mast with his crew. "We are done for."

"I'm sorry," Gail rested his head on the wooden beam as he was shackled to the mast.

"All things have to end," Levi spoke quietly.

"We could not have ran forever," Welham spoke up. "They'll hang us for sure. A just end to a pirate's life."

"Aye," Cook nodded.

"You know we always said it was worth the risk," Harper said, chained to the other mast. "I believed that until now. But now that we're awaiting judgement," He shook his head and didn't continue.

"God," Smith looked down at his hand as the two reached the north bay. The bruising was turning black and blue, and spreading over the face of his arm. Smith sat down against a tree trunk and groaned in pain. Nausea taking over.

"Drink water," Northrop ordered. Smith reached out to grab the old man as he was walking away. "I have to get the captain," He said sternly. Smith nodded and leaned back, groaning in pain. Northrop took a torch from his bag and went for the beach. The old man walked along the shoal as more of the cave came out of the water. Wind softly blew from the depths as Northrop stepped into the dark cavern.

Deep below the earth, the old man descended, to retrieve what he had buried. To dig up his past, once and for all, hopefully, put the Curse to rest. He followed the path he knew, he needed no guide or signs. It was him who first walked this cave and buried his comrades at the bottom. On the dark rock, bones laid where his drowned crew fell. The body of one of Amaro's pirates littered the ground as well. It stank the corridor, the rotting skin looking like the undead that killed him. Northrop put his shirt over his mouth as he walked around the poor corpse. At the open mausoleum, the pedestal had been toppled over from the crews of sailors and slaves taking gold from the pile. Northrop saw his inscription still untarnished above the door:

What beneath the earth was whelved,
Fools and thieves now only delve
To seek the treasure cold
Behold the Port of Gold

Water from the ceiling now dripping onto the rubble. Northrop didn't pay any mind as he walked over the stones and into the dark hall. He held his hand along the wall, using it for support. Down the steps, he descended until he reach the lowest point on the island. The deepest point in the earth any of these men ever knew. He passed the three occupied tombs and an empty one, then went straight for Captain Hector's.

Putting his hand on the stone lid, he remembered the men who carved it, men who used to live on the island. Men who would not be the last to suffer from the gold's Curse. Northrop set down the torch and took off his bag. Kneeling down next to the tomb, he put is palms on the lid and pushed. Nothing moved. Adjusting his feet, he pushed against the ground as he heaved the heavy stone. He grunted as the rock began to slide. Standing slightly, he pushed more, until the lid tipped off the coffin and broke in half. Dust flying into the damp air. Northrop breathed heavy as he went for his bag and light. Shining the torch into the tomb, he saw a white skeleton with a single gold coin resting on its sternum. He sighed and then began taking the bones and putting it into his pack.

"You caused quite some trouble, captain," Northrop said to the skull as he put the last of the bones away. Looking up, and holding out the torch, he saw the empty cavern behind Hector's tomb where all of the gold had been. Northrop walked back, admiring the stone that had been covered by gold for decades. He peered around the curving rock, curious if anything had been left behind. He stopped to see another skull, hiding in a nook hollowed out on the cavern wall. Bringing his torch through the cobwebs, Northrop went to get a closer look. Circling the skull was a necklace of sharp teeth. He scoffed at the remains before turning back around.

In Kingston, many gathered around the public square to see the hangings about to take place. The gallows were built in front of the brick fort that overlooked the bay by the harbor. Hamilton came down from his mansion, as one of many duties of the governor to oversee executions. The *Whale* was anchored off the pier, released from the *Ranger* who tugged it all the way back. Benjamin had only just brought the men in, but the locals were eager to see more action. These were not the first hangings to take place over recent weeks. Levi's crew was being held in the forts jail, which looked down on the gallows. Each man still in iron cuffs at the wrists and feet. Guards stood numerous, patroling the fort and town square.

"Quite some ending, huh?" Gail asked, but the young man in the other corner did not answer. Wickman turned his head to look down onto the row of nooses being tied by the hangman. "Don't suppose all the gold on the Cursed Island could brib them to let us go," He sighed, remorsefully.

"Knew that island was nothing but trouble," Crofton shook his head. "We should have never set sail with you."

"Don't blame Levi for this," Harper said through the bars in the other cell. "We kept sailing. It's our own dam fault."

"Leave me," Levi spoke up. "Or stand by my side. That does not matter now. If you revoke me as your last living wish, so be it. For whether you are loyal or not, we are all on death's row. Casting blame will not save us."

"I'm sorry, captain," Crofton sat back, leaning his head on the stone wall.

The crowd was growing loud below. Kids were playing in the streets and shop owners were watching out of their windows. Kingston was in a buzz. It didn't matter to them if these men were once privateers who brought them gold, all they cared about was a good hanging.

"Who is being hanged today?" A man in a wide hat and leather cloves asked one of the locals in the crowd.

"Some captain named Benson. Hornigold just caught them," The townsman pipped back. "Small crew, but still a hanging. Should be an exciting show."

"Aye. Should be," The man in the hat walked off and went down to the pier. Going against the flow of people gathering for the impending execution.

"What is it cap'n?" A voice came from behind some barrels.

"It's Levi," The man looked around to ensure no one was overhearing him. "They're going to hang him."

"What's the move?"

"Are the men still in the ship?"

"Aye sir," The hidden voice replied.

"Tell them to get it ready to launch. Then tell them to sneak onto the *Whale* and get that ready as well."

"Aye, cap. Then what?"

"Do we still have some powder kegs?"

"Why, yes sir."

"Get those ready as well," The covered man quickly spun back and towards the crowd. Behind him on the pier, was a docking ship that had just arrived.

"Are you sure about this? We don't know where he'll be," A sailor asked as he tied off their boat.

"Which is why we start looking here," Segar stepped off the ship and holstered his pistol. "If pirates are being tried here, some will surely be in the shadows."

Benjamin stood in the crowd. With his arms folded, he leaned back against a shop's wall. Roger and others in Hornigold's crew were gathering as well. Young ambitious patriots that liked seeing their enemies hanged. Most of town was happy to see that the oceans were getting cleaned up. With no more pirates, trade could flourish again. The congregation cheered as guards brought out the first of the prisoners. They were hooded as they were escorted down from the fort and towards the platform. The crowd started to taunt and shove the pirates, walking blindly to their doom. From across the commotion, Benjamin spotted someone familiar. A man in a big hat, wearing leather gloves. He stepped forward and started to make his way through the mass of people. Hornigold was cautious to remain unseen as he crept up on his target.

"Henry, my boy!" Governor Hamilton called down to the man in the hat. "What on earth on you doing down there? Come sit up by me," The Governor was seated on a raised platform, built onto the gallows. Henry Jennings walked up the steps to sit next to his high ranking acquaintance.

"Thank you, your excellency," Henry said, looking forward at the hangman. Benjamin walked back, receding into the crowd to remain hidden.

"I am very pleased you have accepted the king's pardon. It is men like you, men of class, that we seek to redeem."

"I told you, Jamaica is my home. I am honored to have been given the opportunity to return."

"As you should be. Pirates like this rogue are the reason we have bounties on those who do not surrendor," Hamilton pointed at the first pirate to be escorted to the noose. Levi was unmasked by the hangman. The crowded booed him as he was walked to the front of the platform, the noose being tightened around his neck. Crofton was next to be escorted on, limping on his wooden leg. Then came Gail, Welham, and Cook. The five stood still as the rope was being pulled around each neck. The crowd roared and threw cabbage and tomatoes at the men.

"You better watch it!" Welham struggled.

"Aye! Screw off, you landlubbers!" Crofton yelling back at the crowd as well. Gail was flinching as he was being pelted by the vegtables. Cook sighed and shook his head at the amusement. Levi, though, stood in pride. Not giving the rioting townsmen any satisfaction. The barrage stopped when drums began to beat and roll.

"Here today!" A guard called. "We witness the death of the notorious captain. Levi Benson, otherwise known as the Leviathan."

"Hardly call him notorious," Henry bantered to Hamilton. "Never heard of this kid," They snickered.

"For sedition and rebellion against England, murder of countless lives, and piracy!" The snare drums rolled as the executioner walked over to the lever. "Any last remarks, filth?" The guard turned to Levi who held his chin up, refusing to speak. "Fine."

Henry slowly moved his hands to his hips as he sat, resting his thumbs on his belt. As the hangman grabbed the lever, Henry unsheathed his dagger and stabbed Hamilton in the thigh.

"Jesus Christ!" Hamilton screamed, wrenching his leg. The Hangman turned to see what had happened. Standing, Henry took aim with his pistol and shot the executioner. Screams came from the crowd as they dispersed. Guards raised their muskets, but hesitated when they saw Hamilton still squirming in his seat next to Jennings. Hornigold pulled out his pistol and fired, the bullet chipping some of Henry's seat.

"Now!" Thompkins called from the pier. Edric Shore took a torch and set it to a barrel of gun powder He ran away as it caught fire. The explosion blew out the stone brick, breaking open the fort's prison. Harper, Jack, and the rest of Levi's crew ran out. Thompkins then threw Henry his sword. Henry jumped over to the platform and slashed the line of nooses. "To the docks!" Thompkins yelled. The men in chains hopped off the platform and shimmied quickly to leave the square. Harper stole keys off a dead guard and unlocked himself, passing them to others as they ran.

The rest of Henry's crew fired at the soldiers, trying to take the heat off of the escaping prisoners. Some of Hornigold's men also armed themselves and shot into the fleeing bunch. As Levi rounded the corner, he was met with a fist between the eyes. Segar grabbed his collar and brought down another punch. With his hands bound, Levi hit Segar in the gut and standing on his feet, swung to hit the mayor again.

Henry and Benjamin exchanged shots with their pistols, hiding behind carts or barrels as they reloaded.

With the docks in sight, Henry observed that Levi was not among those running to the *Bersheba*. Running off the platform, Henry tackled Segar who was still wailing on the young man. Then he slashed at Segar's chest, the tip of Henry's sword only cutting into the skin. As the man bent over and yelled in pain, Henry unlocked Levi's hands and quickly left him the keys. As Levi unlocked his feet and stood, he was met with another punch from the side.

"Bastard," Levi stumbled back as he readied his fists.

"Pirate," Roger sneered. Levi yelled as he charged. Bringing Roger to the gound, Levi pounded on him, breaking his nose. With each strike, spreading blood across his face until Roger was beaten unconscious. Levi spat on his eyes.

"Get to your ship!" Henry pulled Levi to his feet and pushed him toward the docks. Soldiers were marching in from the square as Henry's crew was retreating back to their ship. Levi ran to the *Whale*, only tied with on line. He waved forward as he sprinted, signalling them to cast off. His crew dropped sail and threw over the mooring line. Bullets whizzed passed the fugitive, but missed. Levi dove off the edge of the dock into the water. He swam and caught the shroud hanging off the sides and climbed up as his ship sailed off. Looking behind him, He saw the *Bersheba* was following with Henry aboard firing back at the English.

"Isla Maldito," Levi said as he climbed over the taffrail. "That's the only place I know to go."

"Aye," Gail hurried up to the helm and stirred them east to clear the island before heading north. Levi wiped the blood from his face and hands with the bucket of water on deck.

"Get up!" Hornigold yelled to his men. "Get my ship ready!" Benjamin paced on deck of the *Ranger* as his men scrambled to loose the sails and untie the moorings.

"Blast!" He flipped over a barrel and stormed into his cabin, slamming the thin door shut. Segar went down to his ship with the rest of his crew.

"Follow them," Segar pointed to the *Ranger* as he unloaded an armful of muskets.

"Where did you get those?" A townsman asked.

"The dead can't shoot," He set them in their weapons crate and hurried back to the pier to find more dropped guns. He took the pistol off of Roger and left him there, assuming the young man dead.

30.
Sea of the Lost.

When Northrop reached the surface again, he found Smith exactly where he left him, except he was worse off than before. His hand was decaying, the tissue eroding from the inside out, blood swelling the void of muscle. Smith had leaned over to vomit several times, while Northrop was absent. All the water he had was gone and Smith was continuing to sweat profusely.

"Did you get him?" Smith groaned, trying to raise to his feet.

"Aye," Northrop steadied his friend. "Let's hope this works."

The two started down the trail again, Smith stumbling and swaying from side to side with each step. Vertigo blurred his sense of up and down. The host of trees around him became the ground and the trail was the sky, clouds circled from his feet to far above his head. Smith stopped and threw up, getting sick from both the venom and the motion.

"Oi, this island's looking worse by the minute," Smith said.

"Come on, you sick bastard," Northrop patted him on the back and looked around, scanning the forest surrounding them. "We have to keep moving."

Sailing through the night, the *Bersheba* caught up to the *Whale*. The crews tried the two ships together at the railings, hanging barrels over the side to keep the hulls from scratching. The men were still sailing, pushing north through the darkness, hoping to gain as much distance from the English as possible.

"You gave up your pardon," Levi entered the cabin aboard the *Bersheba*. "Why did you give that up for me?"

"I was not going to foresake my friend," Henry sat exhausted in his chair. "At heart even us pirates are not all bad. You would have come to rescue me, I'm certain."

"Thank you. I was sure to die and couldn't see a way out. I think me and my crew simply accepted our fates."

"I think our lives are nearing its end," Levi wasn't shocked by the statement. "Without the republic, without our brethern, our actions be a lot more costly."

"Aye. The stakes are high."

"What is your plan?"

"I'm sailing us to an island I know. The bay is well defensible, narrow entrance, surrounded on all sides. I have another ship docked there, more cannons already in position along the beach. We hunker down in the bay and draw them in, obliterate them from all sides."

"What are you guarding at this island that you've already built a fortress?" Henry squinted at him.

"Just a stash of money I was saving for a rainy day," Levi smirked. "We'll still be a short on men. We've no stone forts, we'll be open targets along the beach."

"Maybe we won't need stone. Do you have a map of the island we can look at?" Henry thought. Levi went into his blue jacket, almost surprised it was still there, and pulled out his first sketch of Isla Maldito.

"Sir," Thompkins entered the cabin. "Should we send word to Nassau? See if any would rally?"

"There's no one left in Nassau. Vane, Bellamy, they're all gone," Levi shook his head.

"Isn't it worth a try to send word?" Thompkins asked.

"They're a days journey apart by ship," Henry Said. "Who knows how long it would take to row? By the time word reaches New Providence, the battle've been over. I'm afraid we're on our own, Mirster Tompkins."

The next morning, the two ships were still pressing north, never ceasing in their course. Once Levi boarded the *Whale* again, the two were untied and continued on independently, staying a stone's throw away from each other. Men who stayed up to sail during the night shifts now rested in their hammocks, while the new crew was taking over. The men were quiet, they knew they had become refugees, criminals on the run. Once living in luxury, now having no home. There was hardly any one speaking, only men sailing onward. Working out of habit.

"We haven't any food aboard," Cook went to Levi.

"I know," Levi nodded. "We'll eat when we get to the island."

"They can't fight if they're starving."

"We can't fight at all if we stop to fish. Making it to the island is our best bet. It's only a day."

"Aye, sir. Guess I'm just bored in the galley," Cook went back below deck.

"Cook," Levi called after him.

"Aye, sir?" He looked up the steps.

"See what food we have to get the wounded or sick back to health. Feed them first. We need as many men when we get there. I'll signal over to Jennings, see what they have."

"Aye, sir."

Levi took the semaphore flags and called over for assistance. When the *Bersheba* responded, Levi spelled out *food*.

"Gail bring us closer to Jennings," Levi went up to the helm. The two ships angled towards each other, sailing side by side.

"We haven't much," Jennings went over towards the rail "But this is what we can spare."

"We appreciate it," Levi caught the box that was being lowered on the ships crane. "Have you any wounded?"

"Not severely. All of my men are stable."

"Good, we'll need every hand when the time comes," Levi called back. He climbed up onto the railing and stood above those on the wheather deck. "Muster your crew. All hands present!"

"You heard the man, get up here!" Jennings called from his ship. Men who were sleeping shambled out of their hammocks and gathered to listen.

"Hear me," Levi called out, holding onto the shroud for balance, strung off the mast. "Our empire has fallen. Our brethern have turned to hunt us. Some have died, the rest have gone into hiding. We are all that's left of our republic, yet we will not go out quietly!" The men on deck looked up, listening intently. "We may be theives, marauders, killers. Aye, *pirates*! But with each battle, we fought for something. We fought for our lives, our livelihoods. We waged war so that we would not have to live as peasants under arogant kings. We fought so that we each could be a king! That is why we are to go down fighting, that is why we are to live from battle to battle. Die on our own terms! So that unto death we uphold our ideals; we take what we want and give nothing back! So, come hell or high water, that is a pirates end!" Levi unsheathed his sword and held it high.

"And this may be our end," Levi continued. "I cannot promise you we will live through this. I do not know the strength of the enemy who pursues us. But I know our strength and that is not measured by our cannons or fleet.

Our strength is in us! I can promise this though, there is glory in dying for a cause you believe in! So rally, all you men of faith. Faithful to our cause. Fight this last time with me even if we are the last boat in the ocean. Would you fight, no matter the wreckage?!"

"Aye!" Henry hollered.

"Aye!" Gail called. More of the assemblage yelled and lifted their swords in response. They called from their guts, roaring their battle cry that echoed over the ocean as if the high seas themselves called out. The men went down into their respective gallies and ate what food they had. They burned with adrenaline, toasting and singing. After their meal, they gathered their weapons.

"Bring them on deck!" Harper ordered. On top of crates, they lined their muskets and piled their pistols and swords. Teams cleaned the barrels and polished the weaponry. Others sharpened the collection of swords, cutlasses, rapiers, blades acquired over many parts of the known world.

"Sir, *Ranger* is still in sight," The watchman called down to Levi. "No closer than it was yesterday!"

"Very well!" Levi shouted back up. "Let's hope we lose them in the fog," The two ships were only able to see each other from the crow's nest with a telescoping spyglass. Levi would not have a lot of time to prepare for the defenses.

Aboard the *Ranger*, Hornigold sat in his office. He took out from his desk a large book, known as a *waggoner*. Pages of miscellaneous sea charts filled the heavy tome. Though they were in no order. There were plenty of islands in the direction they were heading. The trick, Hornigold knew, was to place themselves on the right map. Levi could be heading for any number of them or none of them. For all Benjamin knew, Levi could simply be sailing for as long as he could. Back to England if he must.

"They cannot keep up their speed forever, they'll starve if they don't slow down to fish," Hornigold spoke aloud. He shut the heavy book and got up from his seat. "We'll all starve," Benjamin looked back down at the book. "Is that your plan, boy? See who caves first. You have to be going somewhere, but where?" He walked away and huffed in frustration. Pouring himself a glass of brandy, Hornigold went out to the deck. The sea spayed refreshing mist into the evening wind. Behind him were two other ships that launched from Kingston. Segar and the townsfolk of Shorehaven in one, and a deployment of English soldiers in the other. Hornigold leaned against the rail and drank, looking out to the sunset.

"Captain," The watchman called down.

"What is it?" Hornigold looked up.

"They've disappeared into the fog. There's a thick cloud of it on the horizon."

"Stay your heading," Benjamin turned back to the coxswain.

"Aye, sir."

"Watchman, keep your eye out. Let me know as soon as you've spotted them again."

"Aye, sir."

"Navigator," Hornigold barked. "My office," The man next to the helmsman ran down the steps and followed Benjamin into his cabin. "If he stays his bearing, where will Henry end up?" The navigator opened the tome and found the region they were sailing through. He took out his compass and ruler and traced a line from their suspected position in the angle Henry was sailing.

"He'll miss the last the islands here, he'll be in open water. There's a small chain, but he'll be north of it if he doesn't stir soon. It's unlikely he's going for them, though. He would have adjusted his course already if he were trying to land."

"Very well. Then we will pursue him as long as he runs."

"Segar," A townsman went to his mayor and captain aboard their ship, the *Storm*. "They're sailing to The Island."

"I know," The man didn't take his eyes off the sea in front of them. Fog clouding the horizon.

"Do we dare?"

"If they survived the Cursed Island twice. Surely we as well can live through it's perils."

"But the Curse…"

"Forget the Curse!" Segar turned back. "I say we sail to the island. Does my word no longer have merit?"

"Does, sir," The man stepped back.

"Then stop being a coward and get the men ready. I don't care about the Curse. I care about Benson. Is that understood?"

"Aye, sir," He nodded quickly and went away.

In the dark of the night, Henry and Levi first saw the island. His men knew the plan and knew to get to work as soon as they reached the shores. The ships slowed at the two peninsulas that curved to make the south bay. Each going to a separate point, they lowered two cannons each and a team of men. Pushing off again, they entered the bay. Levi and his crew went towards the beached *El Dorado*. The *Bersheba* circled by *El Puerto Oro* and dropped off more cannons. Men in the forests cut down palms and dug trenches in the sand. Levi excused several of the men to fish for food so the crew could have something to eat that night.

"Captain," Crofton ran up the beach to Levi with a net.

"What is it?" Levi sat near *El Dorado*.

"It's an omen. The first catch, sir, tis an octopus," Against the torch light, Levi saw shadows of tentacles reaching down and worming from the net enshrouding it. The octopus reached for Levi's hand. Ink dripping from the creatures wretched arm matched the blood pulsing from the man's body.

"Only omen is that mallusk dying," Levi assured him.

"It is your sign, sir," Crofton. "That's a bad omen for yer own ensign to be the first kill."

"The octopus is a sign of the Curse," Levi showed his right hand, with it the tattoo on his forearm. "Don't say you have no faith in me, Crofton. I need you on my side."

"Nay, sir. I believe in ye," He sighed as he brought the net back to the water, keeping it far enough away so the octopus couldn't grab his one good leg. Levi walked the length of the bay. Starting from where he was at the point, he passed wood cutters, men building their walls and digging their bunkers.

"All in place?" Levi walked by the anchored *Bersheba*, directly in the center of the moon-shaped bay.

"Everything as you wanted, captain," Henry saluted. Levi carried on to where the Spanish had camped.

"Divers find anything?" He asked the men on shore as he walked by the shipwreck of *El Puerto Oro*.

"The cranes were able to bring up what was on deck," Gail assured. He had sailed the *Whale* over to that side of the bay to use its cargo cranes to retrieve old cannons that might still be on the ancient ship. "No issues with the, uh, locals though, sir."

"Good work, Wickman," Levi nodded. "You know what to do with the ship when you're done?"

"Aye, cap," Gail said. Levi walked over then to the other point, only a hundred meters or so from the first point by water.

"Harper, those guns set?"

"Yes, sir. All of them."

"Then it looks like we're ready."

"Will it work?" Harper asked his captain.

"I'd give my soul to God if it does," Levi laughed briefly. "But I'm confident that it will," Levi stood, overlooking the bay.

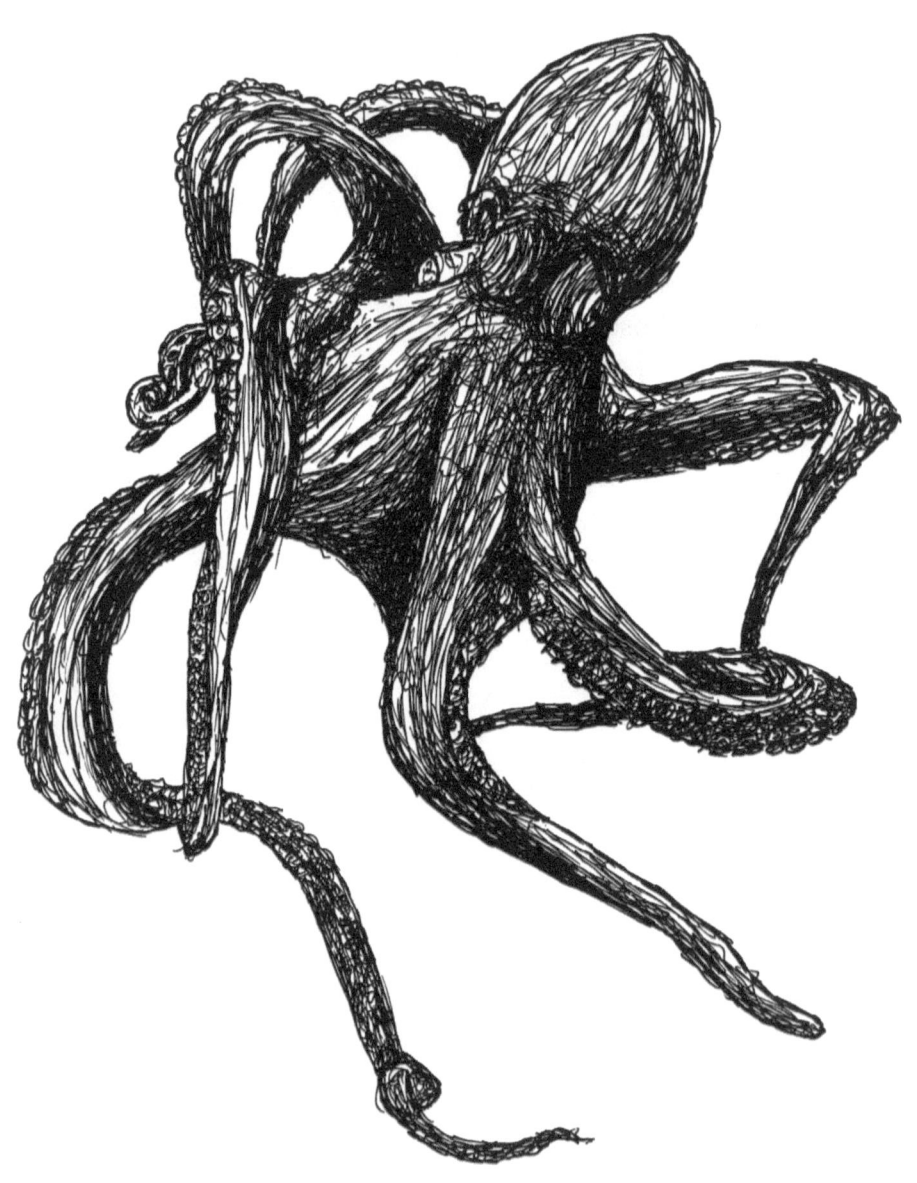

31.

War.

At first light, Hornigold stepped out of his cabin. The fog was still around them, the navigator was still working beside the coxswain, keeping their steady course. Benjamin went up the stern castle and looked at the ships behind them, still following faithfully.

"A coffee," Benjamin got his servant's attention as he sat on his chair, bolted down next to the helm. The captain took in the fresh morning breeze as his servant ran below deck. Soon though, he came back from the galley with a tea cup trembling in his hand. The small, delicate cup was steaming in the cold of morning. The sailor was careful not to spill as he delivered this drink from across the rolling ship. Captain Hornigold took the cup of coffee and sipped carefully before setting it down on the ceramic saucer, which he held in his lap.

"Land, ho!" The watchman leaned over the crow's nest. "I see a mountain out of the fog, dead ahead!"

"Any sign of him?" Hornigold called back. There was a pause as the watchman went back to his search.

"I can't see the water," He finally replied. "Only the mountain top. We're getting close!" As Benjamin was about to give the order to slow, the cloud they were in began to thin. They drifted out of the fog to see an island covered in trees, with a natural harbor in front of them, and right in their sights was the *Bersheba*. It sat anchored in the bay, no men to be seen.

"There it is!" Benjamin jumped out of his chair. "Get ready, men! Full sail, let's get that bastard!" The English guards on the ship behind them looked in amazment as well at this forgotten piece of land. It was perfectly preserved and seemingly untouched by civilization.

"Isla Maldito," Segar muttered at the sight of the island.

"God save us," One man gulped and made the sign of the cross over his chest. Other sailors quick to do the same.

The *Ranger* passed through the cannel, the points of the bay practically reaching for the ship. As if going through an opened gate, Benjamin sailed straight through. He stared dead ahead at his target, not seeing the island around him. A whizzing sound went up in the air. Hornigold watched the firework rise above them until it cracked into a red explosion. Moments later their ship rocked.

"We're taking fire!" One man yelled.

"From where?" Benjamin frantically looked around the bay to notice hundreds of cannons all pointed inward. Another firework went off and exploded as more cannons were fired. Steel bombs borrowed into both side of the ship. "Take us out of range! To the center of the bay!"

English men on their ships looked to each other as they passed through the pinch point. Again, fireworks followed by cannon fire.

"They're in the trees!" An English sailor yelled. "Fire both side cannons!" Before they could open their gunports and have rounds loaded, more steel bombarded their ship. Bombs blowing up on the sailors trying to load their own guns.

Harper sat in the brush, giving the signal to men as soon as the rockets bursted in air. The teams on both points hid in their forts. Built with palm trees and covers in sand and brush, these bunkers were near invisible to the invaders.

"Fire on those moving bushes!" The English captain ordered as he saw palms shaking with each fire. Men with muskets rushed to the rails and fired into the jungle. Bullets pelted the wooden fort, some found their mark and went into the hidden gun ports. Harper saw one more firework rising. With its explosion, he waved to the team in his bunker to light the fuses. The heavy guns dug themselves deeper into the sand with each blast. The cannons were aimed to hit low on the ship. After the last battery, the keel was blown in and started to fill with water.

"We're sunk! Abandon ship!" The soldiers yelled while diving off their frigate.

"Good work, let's move," Harper led his fighters out of the bunker as Englishmen swam to shore with their swords in hand.

"What was that?" Smith looked up in a daze. "Is the mountain erupting?" They had to camp in the jungle overnight, Smith greatly slowing them down.

"No, the mountain is not erupting," Northrop looked through the canopy of trees.

"I can feel it, though," Smith was wide-eyed as his hand trembled. The old man sighed, having to deal with his friends delusions. "The Island," Smith crawled over to Northrop from their dead bonfire. "It wants its captain back."

"Would you look?" Northrop pointed up to see the rockets burst. "There is battle going on! Cannons firing everywhere."

"Who?"

Levi signaled to his men behind his trench on the beach. Around the bay, cannons were fired. They were random and seemed to come from all directions. Hornigold was still on what was left of his ship, looking for each gun after it went off.

"They're not all firing," Benjamin said to himself. "Sneaky bastards. They don't as many guns as they led on to have," He then turned to his men. "Bring us to *Bersheba*! They're trying to confuse us! Do not waver!" Rows of logs had been angled over the wooden walls to look like cannons. In reality, the teams of gunners were few and far between.

In the forest, Englishmen high stepped over bushes and ferns to try and flush out the pirates in hiding. They cut down the thick vines with their swords and slashed at leaves hanging in their path. From the outside shore, a charge of men came in to flank the English. They yelled as they raised their swords to clash with the enemy. The soldiers quickly turned and took on their foes. Harper delivering a flurry of attacks with his saber.

On the other peninsula, Welham led the same attack. Once the English had turned over the empty bunker, they were flanked from the outer beach as well. Welham fought with heavier swings than his young crewmate across the way. He kicked at their legs and threw punches, preferring to brawl over swordsmanship. Some of the English brought over their muskets to use their bayonets, the gun powder rendering useless in the water they swam.

"Fire on that ship!" Hornigold ordered to turn the *Ranger* and open the gun ports. As the frigate was still swinging from the rudder, a line of cannons blasted the *Bersheba*, wrecking holes into the notorious pirate ship. Shrapnel flew from the wooden craft and littered the waves. The brown and white striped sails shook as the masts fell to the water. When the gunsmoke cleared, Benjamin saw only wooden boards and line in the waves. No bodies.

"Row ashore, we fight on the beach!" Hornigold hollered. His men responded and loaded the longboats. They lowered themselves to the waves and began to row to land. Levi peered over the wall to see the landing party, as well as a third ship coming into the bay. He went over to the rockets and launched three in succession. Seeing the explosions in the sky, his men that were stationed on cannons receded back into the forest and rallied toward the center of the bay. The English were closing in after them from both arms of the bay.

"Wait," Cook stopped Crofton as he was getting up to leave from their post. "We can take them."

Hornigold and his men stormed the shores towards the *Whale*. It sat crooked as it was anchored in the sand. The gun ports flared up as the row boats neared. Cook and Crofton fired the first cannon onto the incoming assault. Two more of Levi's men fired a second gun, spacing out shots to fire evenly. One shot landed in the water next to a rowboat. The explosion tipping over the vessel. One of the hunters watched a bomb grow closer before it blew up in his lap. When the boats landed, men fired their guns into the wooden structure. Bullets taking off bits of the outer hull.

"Now we run," Crofton got up, the others followed with him. The amputee skipped with his good leg, the wooden peg sinking into the sand otherwise.

Segar landed the *Storm* at *El Dorado*, on the other side of the bay. His men drove their whole ship onto the sand before running on the beach towards the abandoned ship. With no on firing from within, the men dismissed it and kept running. As Segar passed, something blinding caught his eye from inside. He slowed to peer into the craft. The glisten grew the closer he approached. He stared at the golden light, mesmerized by what could be within.

Gunshots overhead snapped Segar's attention. He quickly ran to catch up to his men who were firing on the retreating pirates who shot back as they ran for the forest.

"They're closing in on us," Henry said to Levi as they met in the jungle. "Is the bomb set?" Levi nodded in reply. "Who are these men in the small boat?" Henry caught his breath as other pirates rallied with them in the jungle.

"That's Shorehaven," Levi shook his head.

"That *was* the mayor in Kingston," Henry realized.

"Yeah, they hate me more than pirates," Levi looked through the trees to see the enemies rushing in from either direction. "We ready?" He asked as he drew his sword and pistol. As Hornigold's men were meeting Segar's, Levi and Henry aimed toward the beach. They fired not at their opponents, but at a mass of barrels covered in sand. Earth and fire shot up from the ground. The explosion taking down several men, stunning those surrounding the blast. The ground was scorched and set ablaze.

Out from the trees Levi then led the charge. Behind him were his loyal crewmates, beside him were Gail and Henry. All running with their swords drawn and yelling rage out of their lungs. Those who were still standing after the blast readied themselves. Hornigold took aim with his pistol and fired at Henry. He missed, but struck another man behind him. Segar picked up speed and ran to collide with Levi. Both men clashing swords and quickly began parrying each other attacks. Segar yelled and flashed his teeth as he used two hands to swing his weapon at Levi. Thompkins hobbled into the battle behind the first line. The short man swung at an English soldier. The soldier blocked with his musket, then turned to slash with the bayonet. Thompkins brushed off the attack, but the bladed ended up driving into his good leg.

"Not me leg!" He grunted. As Thompkins fell, the soldier knocked him down with the end of his gun before engaging another pirate. English soldiers and hunter surrounding the pirates who fought viciously.

"They're all dying," Northrop looked on from a vantage point leading up the mountain. "Poor men throwing their lives away."

"It's the Curse," Smith held onto him. "Curse brings death. It won't end until the Curse does," Northrop looked back to his friend. "The bones, Northrop. Return the bones."

"You wait here," The old man grabbed his pack and put in over his shoulders as he went down the trail to finish what they had set out to do. He hustled down the trail until he could see the beach. Bullets flew between palm trees as men ran to fight one another. He saw uniformed English soldiers dueling with rough looking pirates. They fought from the water and up into the jungle. Men trashing in the waves, struggling in the sands, and weaving through the trees. All of them, fighting to survive. As Northrop crept around to the shipwreck, he noticed something else.

"I could use a hand!" Gail called out as he was defending himself from two soldiers. A knife soared and stuck into the back of an Englishman. He fell dead in the foliage. Crofton hobbled over with his sword as Gail fought the last one off. Northrop nearly fell backwards trying to stay out of sight. He looked through the bushes and saw Segar cutting at Levi as they matched on the beach. Levi's sword was forced into the sand, then Segar cut upwards and slashed the young man's forearm. The young man staggering backwards.

"No!" Northrop gasped. He leaned forward to charge in, but felt the weight on his back press against him. "It won't end until the Curse does," He recalled then took off running. Each man too occupied in their own fight to notice. Leatherneck Jack laughed hardily as he swung at his opponents. Grinning with the thrill of battle, he threw men to the ground and cut with his sword.

"At one point I had moved on from you," Segar stood over the young man, who had fallen backwards. He chopped down with his weapon. Levi rolled, the sword driving into the sand. "But when I heard you were like to be the pirate who destroyed *my* town," Segar slashed down again. "I knew all the scurge like you must die if there is to be any justice in the world!" Levi waited until Segar swung down again. This time, slicing at Segar's shin as he evaded yet again. The man bent down in pain.

"Killing me won't bring anyone back," Levi dashed to his feet and turned around, readying his sword.

"No, it won't," Segar stood, ignoring his bleeding wound. "But we both know it's what you deserve," He said as he lunged forward and began attacking again.

Northrop made it to the shipwreck. Taking the bag of bones off his shoulder, he stepped into the shallow water. The old man saw dead sailors emerge onto the deck of the sunken ship, but he did not stop. He kept walking, waist deep now in the waves. He sighed and then inhaled a gulp of air before diving into the water. Swimming down to the ship, his vision blurred but he could see more drowned sailors were appearing.

"Take him," Northrop grunted between his teeth. "And your whole Curse back to the abyss!" He yelled as he threw open the bag. Bubbles of oxygen rose from his mouth. The white bones sank to the dark depths on the bay, the undead crew clawing at their captain's remains. When the sailors took in the bones, their movements slowed. The dead began to drift, lifeless and still. The skin and flesh dissolving into the salt water. Nothing but their own bones remained, settling on the sandy seafloor. Watching his old crew fade, Northrop tred water for a moment.

Below him, Northrop did not notice the sand beginning to stir. Nor could the old man see the surface above him. It rippled with movement. All reflections on the bay were distorted by the waters quickening pace. Northrop pushed upwards to swim to the surface when his legs were pulled by a riptide. He violently thrashed but the current held its grip. *El Puerto Oro* beneath him started to tip towards the center of the bay, shaken by the water's movements. He fought, but was pulled deeper , spiraling into the bay.

Benjamin yelled as he slashed down at Henry. Jennings was quick to brush off the attack and deliver some of his own.

"You traitor," Henry sneered. "Who kills their own brothers? Who betrays like that?"

"I told you I only hire criminals. I have no remorse for killing them," They bantered as they clashed swords. "Besides, you all were done with me. How else to repay you?" The captains swung quickly at each other, both skilled in the sword. A roar shook the island, staggering everyone. Henry and Benjamin quick to look at each other before continuing their duel. The fog surrounding the island began to creep up the horizon, covering the clear sky.

"What's happening?" Thompkins looked about, who lay injured on the ground, no one stopping the brutal match. The earth quaked and rippled out into the water. The *Ranger* began to drift along with the sinking English frigate. Slowly they started moving in the bay. The tide pulled on the *Storm* and that too drifted into the water. Wind rushed around them like a hurricane, circling the entire bay with the motion of the water. The clouds darkening the sky began to thunder and howl. Sand shifted around the beaches, and trees bent with the forming vortex.

Levi continued to defend himself from Segar, his sword glancing off the constant attacks. Between the ships, now picking up momentum, Levi saw a man in the water. His head bobbed in and out as he was trying to escape the current.

"No," Levi muttered as he saw it was Northrop. Levi pushed Segar away with his sword and ran toward the water. The man yelled as he chased after him, but his mind was set. Levi crashed into the waves, now growing higher.

Northrop being pulled with the spiralling water passed the remains of the *Bersheba*. The old man reached out and grabbed for anything he could, eventually finding a line. The rope trailed behind him, Levi swimming to get it. Segar didn't enter the water, but took this time to load his musket again and fire at his defenseless enemy. Levi reached the other end of the line and tied it around his waist. The vortex in the bay was dipping down in the center, starting to pull everything into itself. The tempests broke down trees and threw them into the water. Levi tugged on the line, bringing Northrop in as he kicked his feet to swim back to shore. Northrop held on as he too swam to outdo the current. They reached the shore, only a few meters of line left between them.

Henry and Benjamin brawled in the beach, both loosing their swords. Hornigold stuffed Henry's head in the sand, but Jennings threw back his elbow and knocked him off. Henry punched the man in the face, but Hornigold got to his knees and threw a hook. As the two men were beating each other, the fight on the beach was dying down. Between the cannons and the last charge out of the forest, the pirates had taken out their initially larger enemy. Those who were left of Honrigold's crew started to run at the sight of the treacherous storm eating away at the island.

"Get to the ship before it breaks!" One of the hunters ordered. They ran for their row boats with a handful of English soldiers, some of the pirates still chasing after them and shooting them from behind.

"Looks like we're both dying here," Henry wiped the dark blood running from his nose. Some of his crew standing around and caught their breaths.

"No," Hornigold pulled his pistol. "Neither of us are dying here," He aimed at Thompkins, who was still in the sand. Henry's men drew their swords again. Benjamin grabbed Thompkins' collar and dragged him over, keeping the man on his knee with the gun to his head. Thompkins covering his head with his hands.

"Why do you want me alive?" Henry held out his sword, himself intending not to spare his foe.

"The same reason we've done anything our entire lives. *Gold*. My men are retreating, your battle's won. But I can still take one more life," He pushed the barrel against Thompkins' head. "What's one more?"

"Alright, Benjamin," Henry started. His men looked at each other. "You let him walk, I will go with you," Hornigold pushed Thompkins over with his gun. The cripple now flat in the sand.

"See? That wasn't so-" A shot tore through Benjamin's side. Harper lowered his gun as the captain staggered backwards. Blood filling his black coat. Henry only stood and stared down at the man. Frightened, Benjamin turned to run to his defeated crew.

"Let him go," Henry said cooly.

"What are you doing here?" The old man coughed as he dragged himself further onto the sand.

"I had no where else to run," Levi shook his head to wick the water off his face. "What's going on?"

"I believe this may be the Curse ending itself," He looked around him. They had landed on the western peninsula near *El Dorado*, away from the action. The fog that clouded the sky also spun with the wind and continued to crack with lightning. Levi stood when he saw *El Dorado* rock and dip toward the water. The sand below the vessel spilling into the bay. On deck, one of the barrels filled with gold flew into the water.

"No!" Levi ran over to his ship.

"Boy!" Northrop warned as he pushed himself to his feet. Boarding his ship, he saw his crates and barrels filled with treasure were pushed up against the hull closest to the water. The wind of the vortex was taking all the belonged to the Curse. Levi knew his gold was in jeopardy. As he stepped down the stairs to enter the cargo hold, he heard a hammer clicking behind him.

"It's over," Segar held out a pistol. He kept his aim on Levi's head as the young man slowly turned back toward him. The boat shook as the gold inside was continuing to be pulled on. Levi drew his sword as they circled around the deck. "That won't save you."

"Not man enough to take me in a square fight?" Levi glared. Segar didn't reply, only continuing to hold out his gun. "You miss and it's over for you, you have no sword," Levi said noticing Segar had left his weapon across the beach.

"I hit and it's over for you," Segar extended his arm further. The blustering wind howled across the deck. Below, a barrel rattled loose and smashed against the far wall. The crash jolted the ship, knocking the two off balance. Segar fired as Levi charged him. Swinging up with his sword, he disarmed the gun and then pointed his blade at Segar's neck. Levi winced in pain as put weight on his left leg. Looking down, he saw he had been shot in the foot.

"Kill me, you pirate!" Segar antagonized, seeing Northop standing behind Levi and knowing the old man would witness Levi killing. "Take another life!" He jeered. "The man who's never lost at sea, the *Leviathan*! How many men did you kill to get that name?" Levi only held his sword out as he glared at Segar.

Wooden containers below them began to break, spilling open their treasure. Gold beams shone up through the grates at the mens' feet. Segar looked down in amazement to see the entire ship flowing with golden doubloons and coins. The ship rumbled as the wood began to strain and break. The deck caved in as the hull burst open. The two men fell onto the pile of gold, now flooding out of the ship. Segar was hit by a barrel, but he held onto the frame with each hand. The treasure was beginning to pile up at the man's feet, all trying to escape out of the hole that was made. He grunted and swore beneath his breath as his grip began to give out. Segar's hand slipped and the gold that was being taken by the vortex drove him into the water and down the vortex.

Levi reached out to catch a bag of gold, one of the last still on the ship. The tension pulled on it, but Levi kept it gripped in his hand. The storm of the island raged, clawing to get its treasure back. Dragging the Curse back to itself. Levi, who was exhausted from battle, began to strain and shake trying to hold on. He heard Northrop descend the stairs behind him.

"Let it go, son," The old man said. Tears fell from Levi's eyes. He gasped as he tried to stop himself from crying. The blood from his cut forearm was running out of him with the wind that was taking the gold. The dark ink dribbled towards his hand and flew off in drops to the sea. Levi slowed down his breathing when he saw the ink running off his arm turn red. He relaxed his hand slightly to let the last of his treasure slip into the ocean. After the island had swallowed up all that had been cursed, the vortex calmed and the wind ceased. Nothing remaining in the bottom of the bay, all of it vanished.

As Northrop walked Levi back to the rest of the men, they saw Hornigold and his crew rowing back to the *Ranger*. Climbing over each other, they scambled to board their ship. The two men didn't say a word as they went to meet the others. Only the crunch of white sand beneath their water logged boots was heard. They met Cook and Haper, both sitting from exhaustion. Welham and Gail were laughing, comparing their cuts. Crofton was sitting next to Thompkins, each man sharing the story of how he lost his leg. Jack was already asleep on the sand. Northrop looked up to see Smith walking out of the jungle, holding his blackened arm.

"My God," Northop ran to him. His friend collapsed into the sand and begun to shake. His eyes rolled back and closed. His head moved compulsively. Smith shook terribly until he eventually fell limp. "No, stay with me, Smithy!" Northrop grabbed the man's shoulders but he was unresponsive. He sat back on his heels. The old man covered his bearded mouth as he began to cry, knowing his friend to be dead. His hand trembled as he dug through his pockets to try and find his pipe. When he pulled it out, he realized the tobacco was drenched and beyond lighting. He threw it into the sand out of frustration.

Levi walked up to Henry, who stood looking out over the bay. They watched the ship sailing off in the horizon, fog no longer surrounding the island. The sun was near dusk already and the clear sky was warm and turning red.

"I'm sorry you lost your pardon," Levi said.

"Don't worry about it. I have nice mansion I could hide in," Jennings smirked. "Retire. I think I'm finally ready to settle down."

"Any chance you could get forgiven again?"

"After stabbing the governor? Not likely, but I think I'll manage. I'm more worried about my own lady than the Brits at this point," Henry chuckled and shook his head. "And what'll you do?"

"I don't know," He admittted.

"You won't be taking down any more ships? Hunting any more treausres?" Henry asked.

"No, I don't think so. I've had enough of treasure."

"Aye. This island doesn't look half bad. Ye could set up camp here. Heck, all of these convicts would join you. New Nassau, they would call it."

"No thank you," Levi allowed himself to laugh, still holding in the pain of his wounds. "I'm done with the pirate's life. Besides, I don't want to live with these swabs any more than I already have."

"So, you'll settle down then? I promised your old friend there, I would give you an estate if you helped me with the Florida job," Levi turned as Henry pointed back to Northrop. "My word is still honorable."

"No," Levi looked back to the bay. "Not ready for that yet. I don't know how I could rejoin society. I can't help but think us as reprobates… Too far gone to deserve any forgiveness. Maybe I should go home. Hope they never find out who I've become in my absence."

"Don't tear yourself down, Levi. No one is ever too far away from redemption."

"Maybe not."

"But that's it then?" Henry was trying to figure out where Levi stood. "No more sailing on the high seas?"

"I wouldn't say that. I may still have some adventure in me."

Sailors and their Ships

Levi Benson...*The Gail Wickman, El Dorado, Sundew, Whale*
Harvey Northrop.................*The Gail Wickman, El Dorado*
Gail Wickman.........................*The Gail Wickman, Whale*
Cook..................................*The Gail Wickman, Whale*
Welham...............................*The Gail Wickman, Whale*
Crofton................................*The Gail Wickman, Whale*
"Leather neck" Jack...................*The Gail Wickman, Whale*
Harper.................................*The Gail Wickman, Whale*
Clay Clair..............................*The Gail Wickman*
Flint....................................*The Gail Wickman*
Lea.....................................*The Gail Wickman*
Torie...................................*The Gail Wickman*
Tanner.................................*The Gail Wickman*
Admiral Juan Esteban.........................*Nuestra Señora*
Amaro "Pargo".....................*Nuestra Señora, Ave María*
Henry Jennings..*Bersheba*
Thompkins...*Bersheba*
Rory ....*Bersheba*
Edric Shore..*Bersheba*
Charles Vane...*Bersheba, Lark*
Keon..*Bersheba, Lark*
Akia...*Bersheba, Lark*
Terek...*Bersheba, Lark*
Benjamin Hornigld.......................*Marianne, Ranger*
Edward Thatch.............................*Marianne, Ranger*
Samuel Bellamy..................................*Marianne*
John Wills..*Eagle*
Roger.......................................*Sundew, Ranger*
Segar..*Storm*

La Florida
Atlantic Ocean
Nassau
Isla Maldito
Shorehaven
Havana
Cuba
Tortuga
Hispaniola
Jamaica
Kingston

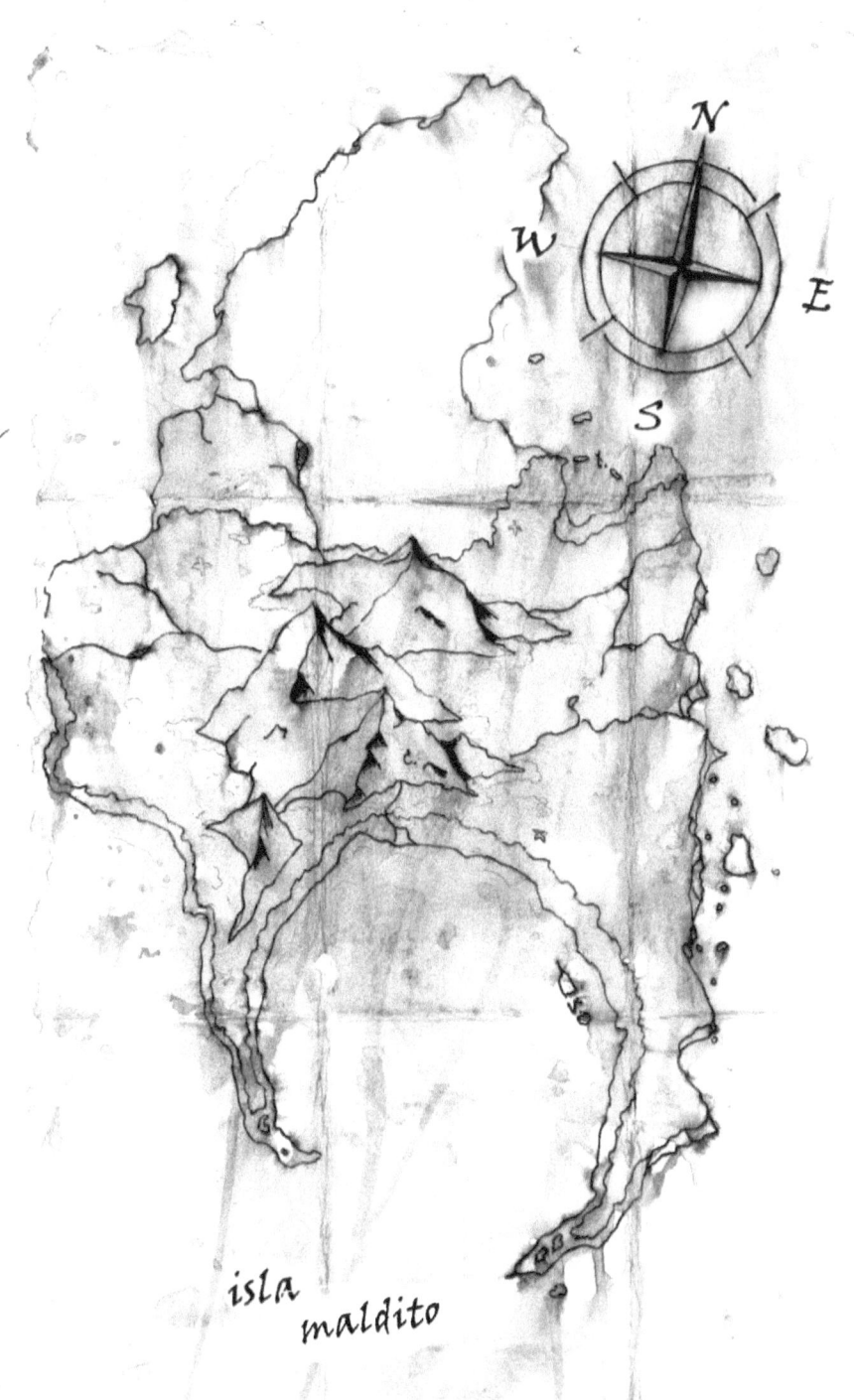

isla maldito

www.ingramcontent.com/pod-product-compliance
Lightning Source LLC
Chambersburg PA
CBHW031332020726
47499CB00005B/1227